You can't fight love..

There's only one thing MMA fighter Gunnar Wells is more devoted to than his career, and that's his mother, "Queen" Elizabeth. An elegant African American woman who adopted Gunnar and his two white brothers, Elizabeth was there when they needed her, and they'll do anything for her. For Gunnar, that means running her hair salon when she suddenly falls ill. And if that's not awkward enough for the champion fighter, he'll have to work alongside Eboni Danielson, the other love of his life. The one he left behind to pursue his dream. The one he's never forgotten...

Between the salon and her volunteer work, Eboni keeps busy to keep her mind off the man who broke her heart. So when Gunnar shows up again, she does her best to stay cool—on the outside. But the more she watches Gunnar step up and help out, the less she can deny her feelings. Soon Gunnar is doing everything he can to convince Eboni to give him a fighting chance. Can she trust him again—even when old secrets and new dangers come between them once more?

Visit us at www.kensingtonbooks.com

Books by Crystal B. Bright

Mama's Boys
The Look Of Love

Published by Kensington Publishing Corporation

The Look of Love

Mama's Boys

Crystal B. Bright

LYRICAL PRESS
Kensington Publishing Corp.
www.kensingtonbooks.com

This book is dedicated to my family and friends who all encouraged me to write again. Thank you for believing in me and encouraging me. Thank you to the love of my life, Jimmy. Your love and support means everything to me. I love you.

Acknowledgements

Thank you to the professors at Old Dominion University and Seton Hill University who taught me a lot about crafting a great story. Thank you to Lyrical Press for taking a chance on an unusual series. Thank you to every author I have read. I learn from each and every one of you.

Author's Foreword

I have always had a soft spot for rough and tough men who are put into awkward situations. I think it brings out a vulnerable side to men...plus it can be a bit comical. Movies like "The Nanny", "The Tooth Fairy", and "The Game Plan" are examples of men put in strange situations but also make them endearing.

Because of that fish-out-of-water type of genre, I got the idea of having three brothers, all stars in their sports, put into a situation where they would have to run their mother's very feminine businesses. I also wanted to write a series about brothers. What's hotter than three sexy brothers?

I hope you all enjoy my story about the Wells brothers and the way they run a hair salon, a flower shop and a clothing boutique.

Enjoy!
Crystal

Chapter 1

The adrenaline coursing through Gunnar Wells's body needed some release. The muscles in his arms and thighs tightened, ready for activity, for combat. A good workout would ease his tensions. Tonight, his mixed martial arts match would have to do.

He paced the cramped dressing room that smelled like rose petals and bleach, too dainty and too clean for what he had to do. The delicate aroma and the rough sport he would be engaging in soon reminded him of his mother, always a lady in demeanor and look, but a tough taskmaster.

A smile tugged at the corner of his mouth before he could arrest it and pull it back down to a scowl. He needed to keep his mind on his match. Staying away from his childhood home helped keep him on track.

A mural of the famous Welcome to Las Vegas sign painted on the locker-room wall snagged his attention for a brief moment. The blue, red, and white neon sign full of diverse geometric shapes attracted tourists every day. Gunnar saw the city as a place to start another part of his life. He didn't need a reminder of the location he'd made his home for the past ten years.

The Silver Streak Hotel and Casino spared no expense in keeping both the crowds and the performers entertained. Gunnar had heard that hosting these mixed martial arts matches had afforded the hotel enough funds to add a new wing to the hotel with another two hundred hotel rooms. He guessed beating a man to a bloody pulp meant good business.

Gunnar tilted his head from one side to the other to stretch his neck and help clear his head. Even with the door closed to his dressing room, the sounds from the audience in the main arena area filtered through the walls.

With each chant of "Guns" from the crowd, Gunnar's heart pounded harder and harder until both the chant and his heartbeat became one.

"Guns! Guns!"

Thump! Thump!

He swiped the back of his hand over his sweaty forehead. The tape on his hand scraped across his skin, leaving a tingling sensation in its wake. Gunnar glanced at the tape to make sure he hadn't ruined its integrity. After doing this sport for so many years, he found that every little thing mattered. A loose binding on his fist would distract him. Like a hunter, he needed to keep his focus.

For his match against a fairly established mixed martial artist like himself, he didn't feel unnerved. In his ten-year professional career, he'd battled absolute monsters. Being six-foot-three and two hundred forty pounds, he fit in the behemoth category. Like his mama always taught him, it's not the dog in the fight; it's the fight in the dog.

Gunnar attempted to push thoughts of his mother from his mind. He couldn't help but think about her and his brothers before each match. One brutal fight could leave him broken, destroyed, or dead. After all his family had done to support him, he couldn't let them down. He fought for them as much as he fought for himself and his career.

Truly the only woman who had ever understood him, thinking of her would only turn him into mush. For what he had to do in a few minutes, he needed to be on his game, an animal. He needed to be Gunnar "Guns" Wells, the heavyweight International Ultimate Fighting champion that the spectators loved to hate. Or maybe they hated to love him since he hadn't lost a match since starting the sport.

As he marched in his bare feet, he closed his eyes and envisioned the entire match, a calming technique he'd employed for years thanks to his yoga-loving mother. He stomped on the thin carpet that covered the concrete flooring. The hardness reminded him that nothing came easy to him, and it shouldn't. Only hard work would get him the rewards he wanted. Fighting afforded him the lifestyle he'd only dreamed of as a youth. If only he could have shared the success with someone.

"No negative thoughts. No negative thoughts." Gunnar talked to himself a lot to get into the headspace needed for his match.

As usual, he'd made sure to clear out his locker room before his match. No one disturbed him or retrieved him until he got called to the ring. After each winning match, he did the same ritual. He called his mother and then his two brothers, Gideon and Thane. All three of them understood the mentality it took for him to psych himself up to perform.

His brothers, as professional athletes themselves, had their own pregame rituals. Their mother proved to be a bit harder to train. She would call to wish Gunnar luck every now and then, probably when she thought his opponent looked too gruesome or menacing. She'd gotten better lately about letting him have his space.

After this match, he really had think about going to visit her. It'd been far too long since he'd been down to Virginia Beach and seen his mama. As soon as the thought entered his mind, his gut wrenched like he'd already been kicked in it by his opponent. The usual cold sweat he would get anytime he ventured close to the East Coast covered the back of his neck and back.

Although his mother would welcome him back home, not everyone would. Time and distance hadn't cleared Gunnar's mind of his past mistakes. He had a feeling some other people he'd left wouldn't be as open to his appearance.

Gunnar squeezed his eyes shut and stopped moving, stopped marching. He allowed the moment to be real for him, this fight, his job. He squeezed his taped hands, allowing the tightness of the adhesive to stretch over his achy knuckles.

He gazed down when a sharp pain struck a nerve in his wrist. He shook his hands to relieve the ache. The discomfort would be temporary. Security would last forever.

A two-rap knock sounded on the door before his trainer, Chuck Wilhelm, poked his shaved head into the locker room. Gunnar's insides twitched as soon as he saw the man. He knew what the next step would be. Showtime.

On instinct, Gunnar raised his hands, readying them to have them outfitted with his trademark black gloves with an eye embroidered on the backs of each. He already had his hair pulled back into a ponytail, something Chuck hated.

"Shave it all off," his trainer would tell Gunnar.

"What? And look like you? No way." Gunnar never thought his shoulder-length hair caused him a problem, especially since he never lost a fight because of it.

As Chuck approached him, Gunnar noticed his trainer carrying a cell phone.

"Call." Chuck held up the phone.

Gunnar shook his head. "You know the rule. No calls. No interviews. Just fighting." He picked up a plain black T-shirt and slipped it over his head.

"It's Mama." Chuck smirked.

"What?" Gunnar stopped moving.

"Queen Elizabeth." Chuck snorted. "Still don't understand how a big, blond dude has a black mother who calls herself Queen Elizabeth."

Gunnar didn't answer Chuck's standard question. He'd heard that comment about his relationship with his adoptive mother since she'd taken him and his brothers into her home.

Gunnar snatched the phone from Chuck's hand and turned his back to him. "Mama, how are you?"

To anyone else, Gunnar would have bitten their heads off and yelled about calling him before his fight. For the woman who had given him more chances than he deserved and a better life, she'd more than earned his respect.

"Darling," his mother said her standard opening that she gave to everyone. "How are you?"

As much as he didn't want to, Gunnar couldn't help but smile. She'd done it. With her smooth delivery and tone, she turned his insides to pudding. "Kind of a strange time to call to ask me how I'm doing, don't you think? I have my match starting in a few minutes. Chuck is getting me ready." He turned back to Chuck and held up one hand so that his trainer could slip on at least one glove.

"Oh, you have that thing tonight, don't you?" Her enunciation of each word further solidified her Queen Elizabeth nickname.

This time Gunnar did laugh out loud. "You can call it work, Ma."

"Good luck at *work* tonight." Elizabeth coughed.

The way she coughed raised the hairs on the back of his head. A standard Queen Elizabeth cough consisted of something that sounded like a slight puff of air through her always richly painted lips. She would usually follow what she considered an impolite expression with an apology. This time, she said nothing.

"Ma, what's wrong?" Gunnar squeezed his now-gloved hand into a fist.

"Why do you always assume the worst? You, out of all of my boys, are the most pessimistic, and I don't--"

"Don't start with me on that. You know--"

"Did you just interrupt me?"

His mother's stern tone came through clear on the small cell phone.

"I apologize." Gunnar had violated rule number one from his mother. Always hear a person's complete thought without interrupting. He certainly wouldn't want someone to cut him off midsentence.

"That's better. I think you hanging around those, um, those--"

"Coworkers," he added.

Elizabeth released an exasperated sigh. "You've done this fisticuffs thing long enough. I think it's time for you to come home."

Gunnar blinked. In all the years he'd done MMA, his mother had never asked him to quit and come home. Goose bumps sprang over his arms and crept up to his neck to the top of his head. He swallowed hard as he digested every word in her request. Then he heard a high-pitched beeping noise in succession…like in a hospital. A stone dropped in his gut.

"What's that sound?" Gunnar grounded himself to one spot. "Where are you? Are you in a hospital?"

"Guns, you've got to go." Chuck grabbed Gunnar's other hand.

The hold forced Gunnar to brace the phone against his ear using his shoulder. "One second." Gunnar didn't care about the match or Chuck. He needed to know what Elizabeth had neglected to share at the start of the call. "Ma, what's going on with you?"

"I know you have to go. We can talk later." Her voice cracked a little.

Gunnar's heart snapped. "Ma, don't hang up."

"You will be disqualified if you don't get out to the ring now." Chuck pulled on Gunnar's arm.

Gunnar snatched his limb out of his trainer's grip. "One damn minute!" he snapped at Chuck.

"We will talk later. Go do your fighting thing."

Her light voice made Gunnar imagine his gorgeous mother smiling. He couldn't smile. At the moment, his chest felt like every opponent he'd fought in his lifetime sat on it and constricted his air. He couldn't get out from under the weight. Right now, with his mother across the country, an arena full of people waiting for him, a ravenous opponent in the ring, and his impatient trainer, Gunnar found obstacles everywhere he turned.

Gunnar heard another woman's voice in the background.

"Queen, you cannot be on the phone."

"Who is that? Is that a nurse?" Gunnar scratched his head.

His mother cleared her throat. "No, it's not."

Gunnar heard some shuffling on the other end of the line.

"You need to get your rest. You can make your calls tomorrow before your tests."

Gunnar strained to hear this stranger's voice through the phone. It sounded a little familiar, but he couldn't place it.

"I love you." Elizabeth made a kissing sound through the phone before it disconnected.

Not content with ending the conversation that way, Gunnar tried redialing his mother. As he'd suspected, the number went to the reception

desk at Virginia Beach General Hospital. After demanding to get
transferred to Elizabeth Sommerville's room, he waited through several
rings before disconnecting the call. Then he tried calling her cell phone.
The call went straight to her voice mail.

He tried calling the hospital again. Once he got the main desk
representative again, he asked about his mother. At the word cardiology,
he nearly dropped to his knees. How could a woman who opened her
home to three strangers have anything wrong with her heart?

After being transferred to the nurses' station, Gunnar unleashed a
verbal assault. "I need to speak with a patient on your floor." Before she
could ask for a name, he spouted, "Elizabeth Sommerville. Get her."

"Okay, please hold, sir."

Listening to the easy-listening jazz that played when the nurse placed
him on hold didn't help to calm his nerves. Gunnar marched back and
forth this time.

"Guns, you *have* to go." Chuck held the doorknob. He must have
thought better of his decision to touch Gunnar again.

"One second." Gunnar held up his finger.

The music stopped. "Sir, Ms. Sommerville's daughter has requested no
more calls for this evening. You can call again in the morning after eight."

Gunnar felt like flames engulfed his body. "Daughter? My mother
doesn't have a daughter. She has three sons, and I'm one of them."

"Sir, I'm sorry. Your mother concurred with the young woman in the
room with her, and we did just give her medication to help her sleep.
Please give her a call in the morning when she wakes up." The nurse kept
her voice even and authoritative, and before Gunnar could keep up his
argument, she disconnected the call.

"Keep trying to call her." Gunnar shoved the phone at his trainer before
cursing.

He hadn't even found out why his mother had to go to the hospital.
Had she had a heart attack or a stroke? Every scenario he thought about
had him grinding his teeth in anger.

"You have got to go." Chuck opened the door to usher him through.

A wave of chants flooded the room. The support should have been like
a warm blanket around his body. Instead, Gunnar likened the shouts to
spectators in a coliseum waiting to watch a hapless gladiator get mauled
by a lion. Little did they know, he had enough fire in his belly to crush a
lion, a tiger, and a whole damn safari.

"Something is going on with my mother. I'm fine just walking away right now. Just hop on a plane and go all the way back to Virginia." Gunnar put his fists to his hips and glared at Chuck to get across his intent.

The idea of going back to Virginia brought a layer of cold sweat that dripped from his head. He chewed the inside of his cheek, a habit he hadn't done since childhood when he'd prayed in his head that the foster father he'd had before getting with Queen Elizabeth wouldn't come home drunk with his own need to fight...anyone. Gunnar had left Virginia for a reason. Returning to it would stir up more questions and problems than what he faced in the ring.

Chuck held his hand up as a way to calm Gunnar, but Gunnar couldn't be reasoned with, calmed, or reassured until he either spoke to his mother or, better yet, saw her.

"Tell you what. I'll keep trying her. After your fight, you can talk to her again." Chuck placed Gunnar's heavyweight championship belt on Gunnar's shoulder.

Gunnar nodded. "Get her on the phone after the fight." He adjusted the heavy metal belt on the thick black leather backing.

Without another word, Gunnar stormed out of the door and headed to the octagon. The cheers from the audience roared in the large auditorium. He kept his stare directed on the lit ring. Fans grabbed at Gunnar's shirt and his arms as he stormed to the middle. He paid no attention to them.

The closer he got to the ring, the more his surroundings got smaller until his competitor became the only thing he saw at the end of his tunnel vision. He stepped into the ring and didn't bother stomping around like Tony "The Shark" Palombo. With it being a championship match, Gunnar handed his belt to the referee.

He didn't like the entertaining part of doing MMA. He just wanted to fight. Right now, he had a lot of aggression to get out of his system.

Gunnar broke his attention away from Tony for a moment to check Chuck. From the side of the ring, Chuck held up his phone to Gunnar and shook his head.

Gunnar wanted to race to the side and scream at his trainer to keep trying to get his mother. Why the hell was she in the hospital? Why wasn't that the first thing she'd said to him? Whatever afflicted her, it scared her enough to want him to come home. That fact consumed his thoughts more than anything else. He attempted to look at Chuck again when Tony got in his view.

"You're going down!" Tony screamed and stood an inch from Gunnar's nose.

Gunnar gritted his teeth. Right now, this hefty man sporting a Mohawk and tattoos covering the vast real estate of his enormous, chestnut-colored body stood in between him talking to his mother.

Gunnar removed his T-shirt and tossed it to Chuck. The screams heightened, especially from the women. He didn't pay attention to them. He had a job to do. He kept women out of his personal life so as not to get diverted from his goals, a decision that haunted him since jumping on a Greyhound bus ten years ago.

The referee spouted the rules and regulations that Gunnar ignored. The sounds in the arena blurred into one muted hum. His laser focus remained on Tony, directly on his eyes. He called this feeling right before he threw his first punch the glaze.

Chuck had once told Gunnar at the beginning of his career that every time he would start to fight, he got this glazed-over look in his eyes like he couldn't see anything else but the opponent in the ring with him.

A single sweat droplet rolled down between his shoulder blades. He planted his feet on the hard mat as he shoved his black mouth guard over his teeth. He tasted nothing but the bitter plastic. The palms of his hands itched in anticipation of what would happen. He had a job to do.

As soon as the match started, Tony surprised Gunnar by landing a solid punch to his left eye. A whole fireworks display lit up in Gunnar's head with the contact. He didn't even notice the pain. The man did carry some power behind his punch. Gunnar had something on him that even Tony didn't have--a purpose.

As soon as Gunnar filled his head with images of his mother in a hospital bed with tubes coming from her nose and wires attached to her fingers and hand, a volcano erupted inside of him that he couldn't contain or control.

Gunnar gave Tony a roundhouse kick to his head. The contact of the hit against his foot stung. That first strike sent an adrenaline rush through his body that gave him the needed boost for the next move.

When the big man hit the mat, Gunnar leapt on top of him and pounded his fists in his opponents face and head repeatedly. He heard nothing. Crimson shaded his gaze. He felt Tony's tree-trunk thighs attempt to hook him under his arms to bring him down. Instead, Gunnar moved down to the mat, cradled Tony's head in the crook of his elbow and framed the top of his head with his other arm.

Gunnar squeezed and clamped his legs around Tony's waist to keep the man still. Whenever Tony moved, Gunnar tightened his arms and legs around Tony's neck and body.

For every match, Gunnar kept his mind focused on winning, on his next move. Now, his mind clouded over with thoughts of his mother. What would he and his brothers do if something happened to her?

Until he felt the referee tapping his shoulder, Gunnar didn't realize that he had rendered Tony unconscious. He blinked and peered down at the person in his arms. Tony's blood dripped from his forehead and nose and onto Gunnar's arm.

"He tapped out, son. Release him." The referee grabbed Gunnar's arm and attempted to uncoil his hold on the limp body. "Stop fighting."

Gunnar blinked and unraveled himself from Tony. He sprang to his feet and gazed down at his handiwork. Tony's body lay motionless, curled in an unnatural position like a discarded marionette, as his trainers and handlers attempted to revive him.

Gunnar wanted to run from the ring, leave his belt, and get on a plane. He had to wait until Tony's trainers revived him. In that time, he paced in the ring, waiting for his moment.

Once Tony rose to his feet, the referee raised Gunnar's hand as the winner. A bit of relief washed over him. He'd finished work, and in record time. Now he had to go.

"Did you get her?" Gunnar asked as he climbed out of the ring and headed back to the dressing room.

He ignored the interviewers who shoved microphones into his face right after the match. From their grunts and groans, he knew they hated his silence.

"Are you kidding? You just did that match in about seven minutes. I barely had time to breathe let alone make calls for you." Chuck ran alongside of Gunnar.

"Guns! Guns! Just a quick question." An interviewer tried stopping Gunnar's trek by stepping into his path. "That match seemed too easy for you. Are you ready for Seamus Flannery, the second-ranked contender?"

Gunnar didn't answer. He stepped around the suited man and continued to his dressing room. If he didn't have another man's blood on him, he would have just thrown on some shoes and caught the next red-eye flight.

"You can't just blow off journalists." Chuck slammed the dressing-room door behind the two of them. "They can make or break your career."

"They haven't so far." Gunnar stripped. "You talk for me. I'm going to Virginia."

"Virginia? You can't go right now. You need to start training for your match with Seamus." Chuck started pacing.

Gunnar couldn't think about how Chuck felt. As much as he loved his career, Gunnar loved his family even more. With the threat of losing his mother, he would brave going back home to be with her.

Until he saw his mother and could see that he'd overreacted to whatever he'd heard on the phone, he wouldn't be able to rest. Then he would find out what woman had posed as his sister.

"What am I supposed to say as far as booking your next match?" Chuck asked.

Naked, Gunnar stood in the doorway leading to the bathroom to take a quick shower. "Tell them I'm going home."

* * * *

Eboni Danielson stirred awake with a throbbing pain in her neck thanks to sleeping in a steel and barely padded hospital chair. She should have slept on the couch, but she'd wanted to be as close to her friend as possible. She blinked to get a sleeping Queen Elizabeth into focus.

Yesterday morning, when Elizabeth had fainted in Press 'N Curl, the hair salon Elizabeth owned where Eboni worked, Eboni had wasted no time getting her friend and mentor to the hospital. Ever the diva, Elizabeth had refused to go until her hair had been styled and her nails had received a fresh coat of deep red polish.

Elizabeth looked like she'd redone her makeup sometime during the night. Her light brown skin glowed, especially with the morning sunlight streaming through the hospital-room window. Bright red lipstick covered her lips. Even her fake eyelashes looked like they had been curled.

As a child, Eboni and her girlfriends had all wanted to grow up to be just like Miss Queen Elizabeth. Not only did the woman always look amazing and have the best clothes and cool shoes, she owned not one, not even two, but three businesses.

The hair salon, more than her flower shop and the clothing boutique, had the most customers in Eboni's eyes, and the most buzz. Although she didn't plan to work in a hair salon for the rest of her life, Eboni definitely wanted to be close to the woman who could guide her into being a success in business.

The morning Queen fainted, Eboni had planned on talking to her about doing a fund-raiser to help renovate the community center. Kids with nothing to do had a tendency of finding dangerous activities to pick up from other wayward souls. Eboni didn't know how, but she knew she had to break the cycle.

A nurse walked into the room. "Ms. Sommerville, time to get your vitals." She opened the blinds and allowed the February sun to stream through them. The morning rays reflected off the gleaming-white snow that covered the ground.

Eboni wrapped her camel-colored dress coat around her body. The businesslike apparel didn't give her a cozy feeling like the poncho her grandmother had made for her. Appearances meant everything for Eboni.

Eboni remembered being a child and watching her grandmother knit the whole thing. She couldn't wait until she got to a size to wear it. Of course, her grandmother made the garment large anticipating that Eboni would never lose that baby weight that plagued her for most of her youth.

She'd changed. Times had changed. Eboni had to give up childhood fantasies, including finding that one true love. Seeing Elizabeth in a hospital bed made everything real.

"Do you have to wake her now?" Eboni rubbed her eyes. "She just got to sleep."

The nurse glanced down at Elizabeth's face and chuckled. "Is she going to an opera later? When did she put on all this makeup?"

"*She* can hear everything you're saying." Elizabeth opened her eyes and glared at the nurse before cutting her gaze over to Eboni.

"Darling, you didn't have to sleep in that awful chair." She shook her head.

"I didn't want to leave you alone." Eboni stretched her arms over her head attempting to relieve some of the ache in her neck. "Besides, I would have slept on the floor if I had to."

Elizabeth smiled, showing off an impressive set of straight, white teeth. "You're silly. The staff here would have taken care of me just fine." She finally turned her smile to the nurse who had already placed a black cuff around her arm and pumped away to get her blood pressure.

As the nurse allowed the blood pressure cuff to hiss out the air she'd pumped into it, she said, "A very loud and angry man called the desk for you last night." She removed the stethoscope from her ears. "He claimed that this woman is not your daughter." She glanced at Eboni.

Eboni swallowed but continued returning the nurse's stare, hoping to convince her of the lie Queen had told. Eboni hadn't corrected her. In a lot of ways, she did feel like she belonged in Queen's family.

"That's ridiculous," Queen said when she no longer had a thermometer in her mouth. "This beautiful young woman is as much as my child as my sons are."

Eboni smiled. She stood from her chair and held her friend's hand. The warmth of it as well as Elizabeth's words hugged her heart.

"Did you already pick your breakfast items today?" The nurse held up a menu.

"Yes. The lovely woman from food services got my order about an hour ago."

The nurse nodded and exited the room, partially closing the door behind herself.

Eboni felt her eyebrows draw together. "I don't remember hearing anyone coming into the room."

"Because you were out cold." Elizabeth placed her soft palm against Eboni's cheek and then brought it down to cover Eboni's hand. "You will need to go home at some point today to shower and get some real sleep."

Eboni shook her head. "Until the doctors tell me what's going on, I'm not leaving."

"Oh, honey, I know what it is. Back in my day, we called it having the vapors. I just got a little overwhelmed with work and had a little fainting spell. That's it." Queen removed her hand from Eboni's and turned her face away like she wanted to watch something on TV.

Eboni knew better. "I know Virginia is the South, but we're not that far south. I don't believe in this vapors nonsense. Something's going on with you, and I'm not leaving until I know what it is."

Elizabeth shook her head. "Stubborn. You're just like Gunnar."

At the mention of his name, Eboni became quiet. Like when he'd walked away from her ten years ago to pursue his fighting dream, Eboni's heart stilled again.

She'd thought she and Gunnar would have a future together. Her being African American hadn't stopped him from pursuing her, not that Eboni thought it would. If he didn't have a problem with his adoptive mother being black, she knew he would date outside of his race.

Eboni had been surprised the day he'd given her the critical ultimatum--go with him while he trained as an ultimate fighter, or break up with him and stay home. It had broken her heart to turn down his offer, but she couldn't leave. Not just yet.

"You talked to Gunnar?" Eboni backed up to her chair.

"I called him last night before his thing." Queen huffed. "I told him he should stop that stuff and come on home."

Eboni collapsed in the chair. "You told him to come home? Why?" Would the man who'd had no problems running from her ten years ago come home because his mother asked him to?

"Darling, while I'm a touch incapacitated, I'm going to need someone to run the businesses."

At that bit of news, Eboni's spine crumpled enough for her to melt her back into the chair. "I thought you would let me run Press 'N Curl."

"You are running Press 'N Curl. Gunnar will do what I do there." Elizabeth waved her hand as though this aspect meant very little to her.

"So he'll have his nails and hair done?" She winked at Elizabeth. The little bit of levity helped her not think of Gunnar.

Elizabeth gasped. "I do more than just have my hair and nails done."

"I know."

"Don't forget eyebrow waxing." Elizabeth winked.

Eboni laughed. Queen Elizabeth wouldn't be a success if she'd been an absentee owner. The woman defined hands-on. When a stylist didn't show, she had no problem taking their clients.

"What in the world am I going to do without you at the shop?"

"You'll be fine, and Gunnar will be fine in my spot." Elizabeth nodded. "I'll eventually have to bring my sons in to the businesses. I was just hoping it would happen later than sooner." She sighed. "Besides, all three have signed power-of-attorney forms for the businesses in case something happens to me."

It made sense to have Elizabeth's sons to acquire the three businesses when something happened to her. Eboni just hoped Gunnar would stay away from her while she worked.

"Speaking of bad timing." Eboni made sure to make eye contact with Elizabeth. "Before you, um, caught the vapors, I was going to propose that we do a fund-raiser for the Oceanfront Community Center. You know that in my free time I volunteer there."

"I know. That's why you haven't dated in forever and a day." Queen wagged her finger at Eboni.

Eboni sighed and ignored Elizabeth's comment about her sad personal life. "Anyway, besides volunteering, I've donated all of my tips to the center too. But it's not enough. You know business at the salon has dropped lately."

Elizabeth's expression changed to a forlorn one. "I know. I've tried drumming up more customers."

Eboni held up her hand. "We all appreciate your efforts. That's probably what landed you here." She patted Elizabeth's shoulder. "If the center doesn't get more money just for operating costs, they're going to have to close, and at-risk kids will take a wrong turn."

Queen Elizabeth regarded her for a moment before a broad smile lit up her face. "That's what I love about you." She sat up higher in her hospital bed. "Other people would have asked me for money. Hell, my own family has asked me for money just to go to Vegas. Not you. Not my girl. You want to *raise* the money."

Eboni's heart beat stronger. "I learned from the best. Working with you, I know that only hard work will get me what I want."

"You're right. You know I'm in for anything to help out that center. I know that after your mother passed, that place--"

"And your shop," Eboni interjected.

"Helped you growing up." She patted the mattress beside her. "Right now, I'm a little stuck. This is something that needs to happen soon, right?"

Eboni nodded. When a distressed expression crossed Elizabeth's face, Eboni had a change of heart. "Look, don't worry about it. I'll figure something out. I shouldn't have said anything." She waved her hands and backed up.

"If I wasn't out of action, I would love to help you." Elizabeth's eyes lit up. "I'm hoping Gunnar comes to town. If he does, he can help. Wouldn't it be great for you to see him again?"

Eboni swallowed hard. Did she want to see the man who'd been her first love? She wanted to hate him. He'd had a goal like she had when they'd severed their relationship. She and Gunnar had stubborn streaks as long as the universe.

Before she could answer, the hospital room door burst open. Encompassing the entire frame stood Gunnar. He had his dirty-blond hair pulled back into a ponytail. His crystal-blue eyes drew her attention to his strong face. His jaw looked like it had been chiseled from stone. He looked beautiful and scary all at once, especially with the addition of a black eye.

Eboni couldn't look in his face. She refused to watch any of his matches, but she imagined that his current hard expression matched what he would look like before each of his fights.

Her gaze volleyed between his full, very kissable lips and his barrel-sized chest. The more she stared at him, the more her heart accelerated. This man had given her the deepest heartache she'd ever had. Within a millisecond, she found herself still wanting him. She could kick herself for being so stupid now.

Eboni didn't remember Gunnar being that immense. Seeing him again made her want to stand up to him like one of his opponents. He'd caused her to cry more than she cared to admit. The hell she would allow him to make her feel less than her best. If confronted, she would let him know that.

"Ma, what's going on with you, and who's this daughter you said you have now?" Gunnar's voice boomed throughout the room, and probably all down the hall as well.

Guess the man came for a fight. She wouldn't back down.

Chapter 2

Gunnar threw his bag on the floor and marched over to his mother. As he suspected, his Queen Elizabeth had her regal face painted. Not a blemish or a wrinkle could be found. As usual, she wore a ring on almost every finger and had silver and gold bracelets dangling from her wrists. She lifted her arms to accept him into a hug and he remembered her telltale jingling that he'd loved listening to as a kid.

Seeing his strong mother in a hospital bed crushed his heart. He could only imagine what she felt inside beneath her tough exterior. The closer he got to her, the softer his steps became until he reached her. He kissed her cheek as she cupped his face.

The feeling of home came flooding back to him in that one touch. All at once, his breathing slowed. His heartbeat decreased in its speed. He'd gotten what he'd wanted since talking to her last night.

"What are you doing here?" He held her hand. Before his mother could answer, he peered across the room and spotted a woman sitting in a chair. "Who are you?"

The woman with an almond-butter skin tone blinked at his inquiry. Her hazel eyes seemed so familiar to him. It had been a long time since he'd been home. She reminded him of Eboni Danielson. No way could she be his old love.

When they'd dated back in high school, Eboni had carried a voluptuous frame that he'd enjoyed touching and holding. In her structured wool coat, this woman looked to be about fifty to seventy-five pounds lighter than his high school girlfriend.

Back in high school, Eboni had light brown hair that she'd kept in loose, natural curls. Once Gunnar had gotten his act together as far as his attitude, Eboni had allowed him to experiment with her hair. He created different concoctions in his mother's kitchen. Besides his mother and his brothers, no one had trusted him that much.

The woman here had jet-black hair that she kept in waves that cascaded down her shoulders and back. He'd been involved in the hair business with his mother long enough to spot relaxed hair with generous amounts of hair extensions.

Gunnar never understood a woman's desire to show a false front. If it made this woman feel good, he would respect that. He had to bring his attention back to his mother when the woman licked her lips.

"Darling, you remember Eboni? Good Lord, the two of you were inseparable in school." Elizabeth pointed to Eboni.

This time, Gunnar had to blink. Now that he stared at her, he saw a glimmer of that woman who had turned him down flat when he'd asked her to join him for his dream.

Eboni stood. He got to assess her from head to toe, especially when she removed her coat. Without the outerwear, he saw how fit she'd become, although her breasts had stayed large, firm, and amazing. Wearing a long-sleeved black turtleneck and charcoal-colored slacks, she resembled a copy of his mother with less jewelry...and fake hair.

Eboni walked closer to Elizabeth's bed, and Gunnar couldn't tear his stare from her. He tried to swallow but his throat had become dry. He'd fought absolute beasts in the ring and his nerves never got to him. Yet a woman he hadn't seen in years managed to make him feel powerless.

"Eboni, I barely recognized you." Standing on the opposite side of the bed from her, he presented his hand across his mother's body to shake her hand.

"Boy, you had better walk around that bed and give your friend a hug." Elizabeth swatted Gunnar on his backside, propelling him to move around the bed.

Keeping his face hard, he stepped up to her. At the last moment, she turned to him and held out her arms, a loud, long, audible sigh punctuating her move.

Great, she wanted this even less than him. A small part of him felt a little disheartened at her attitude. What did he expect? They hadn't parted on amicable terms. She'd called him a coward.

He embraced her. At once, her honey scent wafted up to his nose. The sweet aroma had him thinking of licking her from her head to her toes.

Her body had still retained some of its softness, although he found her back to be hard as well as her arms. He rested his hand on her waist, dangerously close to her ass that he wanted to touch, to squeeze.

At that moment, he felt a subtle throbbing below his belt. It had been quite a long time since he'd held a woman. At this rate, if he continued holding her, she would know just how long it had been.

Gunnar released his embrace and resumed his spot on the other side of the bed. He hoped he didn't look like he'd run, but in his mind he'd probably sprinted.

"Good to see you again." He didn't smile, still trying to wrap his mind around the surreal events.

"Nice to see you visiting your *mother*, Gunny." Eboni did smile, showing all her teeth.

The expression that he'd likened to a hungry shark along with the childhood nickname disarmed him. "Haven't heard that name in years." A smile threatened to peek through, but he kept it suppressed.

A tickle ran over his belly as soon as she smiled. A woman scorned shouldn't be this friendly to the man who'd burned her.

He couldn't think of that. He would be spending time with his mother, not Eboni, a decision his body detested him for making.

He gazed down at his mother. "Why are you here?"

"Caught the vapors." Elizabeth waved her hand with its manicured fingernails in front of her face.

"Don't give me that. What happened?"

When his mother slowed to answer, Eboni quickly piped in.

"She fainted at Press 'N Curl." Eboni glanced down at Elizabeth. "I brought her here. They've been running tests but haven't said what they've found yet."

Gunnar nodded at her. "When was the last time you went to a doctor's appointment?"

His mother huffed. "Doctors are for sick people. I'm not sick. I probably didn't eat enough that morning. I'm trying to lose these stubborn five pounds to fit into a gorgeous gold sequin dress I made."

Gunnar ran his hand over his face. "Ma, *you* made the dress for yourself. Why didn't you make it the right size?"

Her eyes widened as she glared at him. "I did make it the right size. I can't help it if the materials shrank when I sewed it."

He bit the inside of his cheek to keep from laughing. "Right. The materials shrank."

"You know nothing about making clothes, not like your brother, Thane. He had a gift."

"A gift? Yeah, like dodging me. I've been trying to call him since yesterday and he's not answering." Gunnar wanted to call his baby brother a brat, but that was rule number two with his mother. No name-calling.

"Leave him alone. He's busy. He'll be starting spring training soon." Elizabeth turned to Eboni. "Baseball. America's favorite pastime."

Eboni nodded. "I've seen him play. He's very talented."

Gunnar glared at Eboni. A pang of jealousy punched him in the gut. It shouldn't have. Gunnar had no plans of getting back together with Eboni. Two stubborn people together never worked.

"Gideon has time to answer his phone, and he's about to play in the Super Bowl." Gunnar smiled at his brother's accomplishment.

"I'm glad you're here." Elizabeth nodded.

"I'm happy to be with you, too, Ma. Now you have one of your sons and your *daughter* here." He nodded toward Eboni. "Did I miss a reunion somewhere?"

"You and your brothers weren't here. Eboni has been like a daughter to me. She could have been a real daughter-*in-law* had someone done the right thing."

Gunnar groaned and leaned his head back. "Not now." Arguing about past mistakes topped his list of things to avoid after he hopped a red-eye flight from Vegas to Virginia.

"I've taken great care of Queen Elizabeth since you, um, left." Eboni kept her stare on Gunnar almost in a challenging way, like she wanted him to defend his actions. "I've worked side by side with her at the salon."

"Thank you. I appreciate it." Gunnar meant that. With him, Gideon, and Thane being gone, it comforted him to know someone trustworthy watched out for his mother.

"I don't need anyone watching out for me. I'm fine." Elizabeth patted Gunnar and Eboni's hands.

As she said that, her hospital room door opened and a petite Indian woman in a white doctor's coat walked into the room.

"How are you feeling today, Ms. Sommerville?" she asked as she looked through a file.

"I feel as good as I look, Dr. Patel." Gunnar's mother pursed her lips. "Hand me my clothes and shoes and let me go home to my family." She sat up taller.

"You'll go home eventually, but not right now." The doctor's face became somber. "You have a ninety-percent blockage in your left artery. Because of it, you weren't getting enough oxygen, which is why you fainted."

Gunnar felt blood rush from his head. He kept his legs locked to keep standing. "What's going to happen now? Medication?"

"We're going to install a stent in the artery to open it up and see if that corrects the problem. She has a second artery that has a fifty-percent blockage, but that's not as bad as the other, so we're not going to do anything with that one yet. We'll watch it and see how it goes. One thing that should make you happy is you have a very strong heart."

Gunnar glanced at his mother, who now remained quiet. The joy dropped from her face. She chewed her lower lip, ruining her lipstick and staining her teeth. For the first time in his life, Queen Elizabeth Sommerville looked scared. Seeing her fear both worried him and pissed him off.

He held his mother's hand and kept his grip tight. "When will you do the procedure?"

"Tomorrow morning. After we install the stent, she'll stay in the hospital for a few days so that we can watch her, and then we'll let her go home." The doctor walked closer to Elizabeth. "No working at all. You rest and relax, understand?"

Elizabeth nodded.

Her silence worried Gunnar, who had never known his mother to be at a loss for words.

"For now, I would say get comfortable. Have your family bring you books or magazines, pajamas, and a change of clothing for when you go home. The nurses and care partners will check up on you all day today. I understand your family and friends all call you Queen Elizabeth."

That brought a smile to Elizabeth's face.

Dr. Patel continued. "We'll treat you like royalty. We promise. Any questions?"

"No." Elizabeth's voice broke. "No, I understand. Thank you for everything."

The doctor walked out of the room and closed the door.

Eboni broke the tension. "I'll tell everyone at the salon what's going on and that you'll be out for a while."

Elizabeth nodded and held Eboni's hand.

"I'm here, Ma. Whatever you need, I'll do it for you." Gunnar curved his mother's hand up to his mouth and kissed the back of it.

"Good, because there is something I need you to do." She cleared her throat.

"Anything. Name it." His mother had given him the kind of life that other disadvantaged kids could only wish for on a million stars in the sky.

"I need you to watch over the businesses. Right now, it's only the salon and the flower shop since I have the boutique closed for the winter. If I'm still incapacitated by March or April, you'll have to reopen the boutique in time for the spring school dances."

Gunnar glanced at Eboni, who now had a hard time looking at either one of them. "You got it."

"Eboni will continue to manage the salon. She can show you how things run. The keys to the shop and my car are in my purse. Take my purse home with you. These people are nice, but I don't know them." Elizabeth's smile broadened. "I'll be fine, son."

Gunnar chuckled. "I'm supposed to be reassuring *you*."

"By being here, you've shown me that I did a great job raising you." She pulled at his hand to bring his face down to her. She kissed his cheek.

"I'll call Gid and Thane, unless you want to do that?" He gazed at his mother. For the first time, he saw her looking weak, almost defeated.

"No, you call them. You'll keep a level head when relaying the news."

Gunnar nodded. "Yes, ma'am."

"Now, take my things, except for my makeup bag." Elizabeth smiled and it made Gunnar and Eboni laugh. "Bring back my black-and-white Chanel suit, the black Yves Saint Laurent pumps, and the pearls."

"All I understood in that request was the pearls." Gunnar constantly had to remind his mother he had no fashion sense.

"I'll get them." Eboni kissed Elizabeth's forehead.

In this situation, Gunnar appreciated Eboni's help. Otherwise, he would keep his distance from her.

"I'll stay with you, Ma." Gunnar looked at the chair Eboni had previously occupied and the small couch under the window that overlooked the hospital's helipad.

"I love you, but you need a shower and a shave and probably some good sleep."

Gunnar ran his hand over his chin and felt the scruff his mother must have noticed. "Ma, I--"

"Don't argue." Elizabeth brought her blanket up to her chin.

"Did you just interrupt me?" Gunnar put his hands to his hips and cocked his head.

His mother laughed. "You're cute. Go. Call your brothers. Get a shower. Get some sleep. I'll be fine."

Gunnar squeezed his mother's hand. "I'll go and make myself presentable for you. But I will be back earlier than tomorrow morning. I didn't come all this way not to see you."

She released his hand. "Love you both."

Gunnar glanced at Eboni. At one time, she'd had his heart. Then she'd refused to take a leap with him. His mother seemed to rely on her a lot. For that, he appreciated her loyalty.

After giving his mother a kiss on her forehead, Gunnar grabbed his bag. He held the door open for Eboni and then headed to the elevator. He pressed the down button and waited in silence until the elevator doors opened. He'd hoped there would be a crowd of other people in the elevator. No such luck.

Silence enveloped them on the ride down. He kept his gaze on the lit numbers over the sliding doors.

"Your mom is strong," Eboni began.

Gunnar brought his attention to her.

"She'll be fine." She brought her hand up as though she wanted to pat his shoulder but stopped herself.

"I know." No one had to tell him about the strength in Queen Elizabeth Sommerville.

The woman stared down monsters and didn't blink. He'd seen that firsthand. Surviving a marriage with that dick after she'd adopted him and his brothers had confirmed his mother's might.

The longer the elevator ride continued, the more Gunnar realized he missed a lifetime with her in the last ten years. Did she get married? Did she have children? Was she even involved in a relationship now?

When the elevator opened at the lobby, Gunnar held the door open as Eboni strolled by him. He headed to the front of the building but stopped when he realized she continued to the parking garage.

"Do you have a car here?" Eboni waited by the entryway to the parking garage.

Gunnar winced. "Took a cab." He took a step toward her. "I suppose you're not going by my mother's house, are you?"

He watched her shoulders bunch around her ears as though the sound of his voice irritated her. At that moment, his stomach lurched and he hated to even see her adverse reaction.

"Do you need a ride?" Eboni asked.

"I don't have a vehicle until I get my mom's car." Gunnar hoisted the strap of his bag onto his shoulder.

"I suppose if I don't take you, you'll tell your mother on me." She fished through her cavernous purse.

"If it's a big deal, just forget it. Just thought--"

Eboni expelled a deep sigh. "I'll take you to your mother's house. I have to go there anyway." She held up her car keys and jingled them in front of her face.

Gunnar thought about the ramifications of being in a confined space with Eboni, truly the one that had gotten away. Since starting his sport, a lot of fans, female celebrities, and starlets had thrown themselves at him. Every time, he'd refused their advances, telling them that he had to keep his focus. That didn't stop the women from still offering him favors. He turned those down as well. One thing for sure, Eboni wouldn't be offering him anything other than this car ride.

"Are you going to come with me?" She crossed her arms over her chest.

After he'd hugged her earlier, Gunnar couldn't stop imagining her body.

He took a deep breath before answering. "Sure. Let's go."

He'd been strong for ten years. A twenty-minute drive shouldn't kill him...he hoped.

* * * *

Eboni still couldn't believe she'd allowed Gunnar Wells to get in her car. Of course, in her compact Smart Car, he looked like she'd stuffed a silverback gorilla into a tin can.

"You can push the seat back, well, a little." Eboni glanced over at him, careful not to stare at him too long.

"It is pushed back as far as it can go." His knees looked shoved under his chin.

"I would tell you to lean the seat back, but, well, you can't." She shrugged.

"We're not too far from the house."

Eboni nodded and kept her stare on the road until she heard Gunnar laughing. She turned to him.

"You have a thing about small cars, don't you?"

She blinked, not knowing what he meant.

"Remember in high school, you drove that little Plymouth Horizon?"

Wow. She hadn't thought about that car in years. It shocked her that Gunnar had even remembered it, which made her smile. "You remember ol' Bee Bee?" She'd called her car Bee Bee for its distinctive yellow paint job with black accents.

As she recalled the memories of the car, she immediately remembered what she and Gunnar used to do in it. Although back in high school his size hadn't matched his appearance now, Gunnar had still carried a tall and slightly muscular frame.

After Gunnar had worked all day at Press 'N Curl, Eboni would pick him up from the salon, go park on a dead-end road, and they'd kiss until her lips went numb.

Eboni distinctly remembered how well he'd used his hands, those large, skilled hands that had massaged her into fits of ecstasy more than she cared to admit. Thinking about it now tightened her nipples. She turned the heat down in the car when her flesh became overheated.

"Can we talk about the elephant in the car?" Gunnar shifted his body to direct his full attention to her.

His sudden inquiry almost had her driving through a red light. Eboni slammed on her brake and took a deep breath before turning to Gunnar. Could he read her thoughts and know that she'd been thinking about them, about their hot, sordid past?

"The business," he said before she could ask him how he could walk away from their solid relationship. "I got the impression at the hospital that you weren't completely happy to have me run the salon."

The light changed to green. Eboni slammed her foot down on the accelerator, snapping both of their heads back in the sudden motion.

"You're not running the salon. I am. You're doing what Queen Elizabeth normally does." She gritted her teeth and tried to maintain her composure.

"Which is?"

"She oversees the supplies. She hires. She fires. She promotes the place so that we can get more clients. She's an owner." She glared at him. "I'm the manager. I'm there. I know everything about the salon. You would just be a distraction."

Gunnar paused before answering. "Are we still talking about the salon?"

Eboni pulled into the driveway of Elizabeth's home. "What's past is past, right? Can't change it. You've moved on just like I have." She put her car in park and turned it off. "You have moved on, haven't you?"

When Gunnar didn't answer, she turned to him. She found an expression she hadn't expected to see in the big man. Remorse. Had he found someone else?

No. Elizabeth would have said something if that had happened.

Gunnar cast his gaze downward. "I work. That's all I do." He exited the car and grabbed his bag.

A strange wave of relief consumed her as she got out of her car. As Eboni headed up the steps of Elizabeth's two-story brown-and-white gingerbread-like house, she didn't expect Gunnar to follow her. She thought he would have taken Queen's car in the garage and gone off to whatever hotel room he chose to occupy.

"What are you doing?" she asked at the front door before unlocking it.

"Going into my mother's home. Why? What are you doing?"

"Packing a bag for her and getting some sleep." She held the front doorknob behind her back as she faced him. "You aren't staying here, right?"

He furrowed his eyebrows and that expression intensified his hypnotic blue eyes. "Of course I am. Why would *you* want to stay here? Don't you have a place of your own?"

Eboni cocked her head. "Your mother asked me to stay here."

"Before she knew I would be coming home. Now that I'm here, you don't have to stay."

She shook her head. "No. I'm a woman of my word." Eboni turned her back on Gunnar to unlock the door. "You might be more comfortable in a hotel." She put her back to the door again like a guard protecting Queen's palace.

"I would be more comfortable in my childhood home." Gunnar reached behind her and grabbed the knob. The position put him right against Eboni's body.

She felt the rise and fall of his chest as he breathed heavily. His stare bored down on her until she felt like she would crumble.

"I'll open the door for you."

The rumble that emanated from his chest vibrated her body. The tremor hardened her nipples even more. She took in a deep breath and caught his masculine scent, a woodsy aroma with an undertone of sandalwood.

Eboni put her hand to his chest in an effort to push him back. Instead, she closed her eyes and flashed back to an image of the last time they'd made love. So vivid the recollection, she could feel his muscled thighs pressing against her legs. She remembered how good he'd felt inside her, moving in and out of her like they existed as one person, one entity. Her fingers itched to move over to his nipple to circle it, tease it, get him to moan again.

Without warning, the support of the door behind her vanished. She opened her eyes and stumbled backward, nearly hitting the floor until Gunnar wrapped his arm around her waist to save her.

"Sorry." He stared into her eyes. "Should have told you I was opening the door." Gunnar helped right her before backing away.

Eboni ran her hand over her hair. "You have a tendency of doing that, don't you? I get a little comfortable and then you pull the rug from under me."

She should be angry for letting Gunnar get physically close to her. She'd forgotten that Queen Elizabeth raised gentlemen. Now that she thought about it, since Gunnar had gotten back, he'd opened all doors for her, even her car door. It shouldn't have surprised her that he would have gotten this door too. She had to appreciate a man with manners.

"Now you're definitely talking about the past. Let's talk about this." Gunnar tried approaching her.

Eboni moved away from him. He'd already gotten too close to her.

She'd been inside Elizabeth's house more than her own home. Being in it now with Gunnar, the mood felt different. The delicate touches of the lace doilies on the arms of the sofa and chairs seemed in conflict with the over six-foot man wearing a black sweatshirt, jeans, and motorcycle boots. The powder-pink walls contrasted with the muscular being that took up most of the landscape in the dwelling.

"We talked about our plans. I wanted you to come with me to Vegas when I trained. You didn't want to go."

Gunnar summing up their relationship in three sentences angered her. So much more had happened than her being offered to go with him and then turning him down.

"Wow. So that's all that happened between us?" She waved her hand in between their bodies. "What were my dreams? You talked about your career. What was my goal?"

Gunnar remained quiet.

"Was I taking care of anyone here at the time you wanted to go?" She crossed her arms over her chest.

"You never told me you were caring for anyone. Were you?" He furrowed his eyebrows.

"When I was going to tell you, you were too consumed talking about your career. When I was going to tell you, you dropped the bomb on me."

"Who was it?"

Eboni shook her head. "Oh no. We are not in that place anymore." She huffed. "You never asked me to marry you. You expected me to uproot my whole life to be with you without a promise of marriage."

She watched Gunnar's jaw flex like he gritted his teeth.

"I'm going up to my room." Gunnar put his hand on the banister and started to go up to one of the four bedrooms.

The fact that he didn't address the most important aspect of her argument, the marriage that had never happened, drained her. At least she'd let her feelings be known.

"Your bedroom is not there anymore." Eboni stood behind him. "Your mother changed your room to a sewing room." She knew that firsthand since she'd helped cart up the heavy sewing machine. "Your brothers' rooms are now her gym and shoe room."

"You're kidding."

Instead of waiting for her to confirm, he took the stairs by twos. From the bottom step, she heard Gunnar cursing. She shouldn't laugh, but she couldn't help it. She covered her mouth with her hand when she heard his heavy-booted footfalls stomping back down the stairs.

"It has been a long time since you've been home." Eboni shook her head.

"The only room she didn't touch was her bedroom." He ran his hand over his head.

"And that's where I'm sleeping." From the way he stared at her, she almost wanted to offer him a spot in Queen's queen-size bed next to her. "Are you sure you don't want to just go to a hotel?"

He cocked his head. "She didn't touch the apartment over the garage, did she?"

When Eboni didn't respond, he must have gotten his answer.

"I'll take that as a no." He headed toward the kitchen. "If you need me, you know where to find me."

"Actually, I do need you." Eboni cleared her throat.

He raised his eyebrows at her proclamation.

Now that she had his attention, she had to ask to make a deal with the man who'd haunted her dreams for years.

Chapter 3

Gunnar watched Eboni take a deep breath before pacing in front of him. Didn't she know that after their encounter on the porch he needed to put some space between them to keep from getting distracted? He held his bag in front of his body in case a lower part of his anatomy decided to pop up to make a greeting.

Talking to family about his mom would help keep his mind off Eboni and her incredible curves. He had to call his brothers once he heard what Eboni had to say.

"Okay." She looked down to the floor before bringing her attention back to him. "Do you remember the Oceanfront Community Center?"

Gunnar froze. He clenched his teeth hard enough to bring on a piercing headache. He widened his stance to ground himself.

From Eboni's confused expression, her memories of the center vastly differed from his.

"You know what? I get it. I hurt you so you want to hurt me." He secured the strap of his bag on his shoulder.

"What are you talking about?" She took cautious steps toward him.

"Do I remember Oceanfront Community Center? You mean the place where I was arrested for fighting that guy for talking about me and family? Yeah, I remember it. Thanks for the great trip down memory lane." He turned to the back door.

"Wait! I wasn't referring to that."

Gunnar didn't wait for her to continue. He found the remote on the counter that went to the garage door. Thankfully, his mother hadn't changed everything about the house. He pressed the button and heard the familiar whirring outside of the door raising.

He started out the back door, stopped, and turned back to Eboni. "Nice talking to you. If you'll excuse me, I'm going to the garage to shower."

Gunnar hadn't forgotten his manners and remembered the third rule of excusing yourself whenever leaving a room. Even though Eboni had brought up a painful experience, it didn't mean he had to be rude.

As Gunnar stomped toward the two-story detached garage, he recalled the one time he'd gotten arrested. Disrespectful words said about his mother from the biggest bully in his neighborhood had triggered Gunnar's already short fuse. One minute he'd been hanging out with his friends at a special event, the next minute he'd had the boy on the ground and had been on the winning end of the fight.

The police had arrested him at seventeen years old for assault. Thanks to his mother's influence and smart attorneys, he'd received community service and six months of probation.

That taste of fighting and winning had propelled him to go into his sport. In a way, he should thank that bully and the center for his career. He couldn't figure out why Eboni would bring up the place now.

Gunnar stood outside of the opened garage door with his mouth agape. "You've got to be kidding me."

He stared at the hot-pink Mini Cooper that had the word *Queen* on the license plate. What the hell had happened to his mother's big Cadillac? He didn't mind driving a pink Cadillac. He couldn't squeeze himself into another tin can on wheels. After calling his brothers, he would have to get a rental car.

Gunnar punched the controller on the wall next to garage door. The metal door creaked as it lowered to the ground with the gentle hum of the motor buzzing behind it.

He climbed the stairs to the apartment he'd used when his brothers had gotten on his nerves. His mother had used it for guests. Gunnar never thought he would be a guest in his family home.

A cold chill met him as soon as he opened the door. He wondered if his mother used the place as a meat locker. He exhaled and saw a cloud of his breath in the air. He went to the thermostat and turned the heat on, hoping it would warm up the place in short order.

Sheets covered the furniture. As he removed each sheet, a cloud of dust swirled in the air. He piled the sheets on the floor by the door. He would throw them in the washer after completing his tasks.

Gunnar didn't remember the small kitchen having all stainless-steel appliances. Apparently, his mother had upgraded this tiny apartment. Dark hardwood flooring squeaked under his feet. She'd had each wall painted with all pastel and light colors.

Before making his bed, he called Gideon first. As the middle child, Gid had become the mediator whenever a fight had occurred.

"Calling me so early on a Monday morning." Gideon laughed. "Shouldn't you be on top of some supermodel or something right now after your big win?"

"You would think so." Gunnar opened a closet door and found a stack of clean sheets and blankets.

"Don't tell Mom I said that." Gideon laughed.

Gunnar knew his younger brother realized his crass statement about women wouldn't go over well with their mother. At least Gideon recognized that and chalked up the suggestion as a joke.

"Our little secret." Gunnar smiled. As he thought about what he needed to tell his younger brother, he sobered. "Look, need to tell you something. It's about Mom." He threw the set of sheets on the bare mattress and then sat.

"She's in the hospital." The levity left his brother's tone.

Gunnar scratched his head. "How did you know? Is it on that gossip site already?"

His brother laughed. "Mom called me."

Gunnar shook his head. "After she asked me to call you and Thane. I should have known she would have done it herself. When has Mom ever needed anyone to do anything for her?"

"She said she's going to be fine," Gideon said finally.

"They're going to install a stent tomorrow morning. Until she gets better, we're going to have to run her businesses."

"Without question. I'll leave--"

"No," Gunnar exclaimed. "Sorry for cutting you off. I'm sure Mom told you to play your game. She would be so disappointed if you didn't live out your dream."

Gideon sighed. "How the hell am I not supposed to worry?"

"I'm here. I'll watch out for the three businesses." Gunnar tried to make his voice as calming as possible. "I mean the two of them. Thank God, it's winter and everything is closed down at the Oceanfront."

"Got to love being in a resort town." Gideon coughed. "Right after the game, I'll come home to run the flower shop."

Gunnar smiled. "You do have a knack with the flowers."

"And it's what Mom wanted. Remember, she had us sign the power-of-attorney agreements a year or so ago?"

Gunnar had forgotten about that until Gideon mentioned it.

"Have you talked to Thane yet?" Gideon asked.

Gunnar cleared his throat. "I'm going to call him after this. But I've only been able to get his voice mail lately."

"You know him. He's busy with the team and his endorsements."

Good old Gideon. Still playing peacemaker.

Gunnar assured Gideon that after her surgery, he would call both of them with the results.

"Wish I could be there in person to root you on." Gunnar had the tickets his brother had sent him in his bag. "I can't leave Ma. Not now."

"You'd better not." The lightness returned to Gideon's voice. "Win or lose, I'll come straight home."

Gunnar smiled. "You and your team will win. You're the best quarterback in the league."

"Thanks, man. Keep me updated with what's going with Mom."

"Of course." Gunnar disconnected the call and then immediately called Thane.

After the fourth ring, Thane's voice mail kicked on to Gunnar's disappointment.

"Thane, it's Gunnar, again." He tried to keep the growl out of his voice, but his baby brother's attitude wore down on his last nerve. "Calling to let you know about Mom if she hasn't called you already." He thought about leaving a message about her condition and that Thane would need to take care of the clothing shop, but he decided that if Thane wanted to know, he would have to call Gunnar. "Call me back and I'll tell you what's going on." He paused and took a deep breath. "She needs us, man."

Gunnar disconnected the call. Before he did anything else, he fixed the queen-size bed, including covering the four pillows with pillowcases. He walked toward the bathroom that came complete with a full-size bathtub and shower.

Before stepping inside, he braced his hands on the doorframe and thought about everything, about his mother, his brothers, and especially about Eboni.

He dove into his bag and pulled out a roll of tape. He taped up his knuckles on both hands. Despite the slight bit of pain, he needed to work out some aggression.

Gunnar stomped back downstairs to the garage area. He had to thank his mother for getting the smaller car since it now gave him additional room to work on the heavy bag that hung next to it.

The black bag suspended on chains didn't move until Gunnar put his hand on it. The familiar training device felt stiff under his touch. The cold air had hardened the leather. Good. The harder the obstacle, the more it would punish him.

He started punching the sack. The thudding sound echoed off the walls. His heavy panting accompanied the sound of his fists connecting to the bag. His heart pounded, but with the thoughts of Eboni on his mind, he wondered if the workout or Eboni had a hand in his excited state.

"I need to be here for Mom," he said in between punches. "Have to keep my head on straight for her and not think of anything else."

Gunnar curved his body and landed an uppercut shot on the heavy bag. Like when he'd trained on the bag as a teenager, he attempted to get out all his pent-up feelings. Then he would take his shower, change, and go to the salon. With it being Monday, it wouldn't be open.

"Got to get things together. Have to keep the family together." Gunnar huffed between each word.

He fought through the pain of his tightening back. He got on the balls of his feet, as much as he could in his heavy boots, and he hopped around the bag, throwing jabs as he kept moving. He felt the burn in his butt and thighs, and he liked the sensation. The feeling meant that he pushed his body.

When he thought of his body, Eboni's form came to mind, or rather her new figure. He wished he hadn't seen her again, not here, not now. Too many memories came flooding back.

"Can't. Think. Of. Eboni." His punches became harder, like he wanted to put his fist through the bag. "Can't. Think. Of. Her. Body." His body trembled. "Work. Then. Go." Sweat rolled in his eyes. If he kept up this intense pace, he would have to go outside to cool himself off. "Stay strong. Don't think of touching her. Don't think of--"

Gunnar turned to the side door when he caught something in his peripheral vision. Eboni stood in the side doorway. She stared at him with her arms crossed over her chest. Her breathing matched his, heavy and ragged.

"Don't think of what?" She stepped into the garage and closed the door behind herself.

Gunnar kept himself on the other side of his punching bag. He wanted to claw off his sweatshirt to relieve the heat. He feared with his recent monologue that he'd exposed himself enough today.

"I want us to talk about the center." Eboni stalked him, never removing her stare from him.

Gunnar had almost forgotten about her stubborn streak. He knew she wouldn't give up without a fight.

She now stood close enough for him to catch that sweet scent again. His senses went into overload.

"I'm going to shower and change." He walked over to the stairs. "I'm a little sweaty right now." He climbed up the bottom two steps and turned to her. "I'm going to get a rental and then go over to the salon."

"It's closed."

"I know. Best time to look at it and get a lay of the land, so to speak." He stared into her eyes and felt hypnotized. "We can talk on the way and in the salon."

He waited for her to respond. Her simple nod satisfied him.

Gunnar excused himself and climbed the stairs to the apartment. If he planned on working with Eboni, he had to do two things--keep things businesslike and keep his distance. If he could do that, he might have a chance.

* * * *

Eboni glanced at Gunnar as he drove his big Hummer to his mother's hair salon. She thought she'd caught him smiling a couple of times in during the drive. Being in the large vehicle must make him happy.

"I'd forgotten about your arrest." Eboni had to bite the bullet and get Gunnar in a good mood before she relayed her plan.

He glanced at her but said nothing.

She kept talking until she could crack him. "I remember the good times there. Remember the dances?"

Gunnar shook his head. "I attended, but I didn't dance." He glanced at her.

"That's right. You did kind of have that white-boy dance thing going on." Eboni laughed. When he glared at her, she continued talking. "Have you improved since then?" She smiled.

He redirected his attention back to the road. "I do my dancing in the ring now."

"I don't watch your fights." She shook her head and settled back into her seat. "I can't. To see you like that." She pointed to his face. "How can Queen stand that?" Eboni remained quiet for a moment before she said, "Oh, because she doesn't watch your fights either, and you haven't been home."

He regarded her for a moment as he stopped at a traffic light. "I understand. To me, it's just work."

"Not to me. Seeing you fight one time up close was enough." She couldn't tell him why the entire fight bothered her.

Eboni balled her gloved hands into fists to ward off the cold. When she saw Gunnar driving down a side street, she turned to him.

"Why are you going this way?"

"It's the main road going to Press 'N Curl."

Eboni shook her head. "Not anymore." When she caught his confused expression, she explained. "There's been a ton of construction. They rerouted the main road. No one comes this way unless they live out here."

Gunnar gazed around the area and must have seen what Eboni had noticed for years. With traffic rerouted, businesses in the area had either collapsed or dwindled. Homes looked dilapidated with faded paint jobs, broken-down cars in driveways, and lots of for-sale signs all around.

Stray dogs and cats ran in front of the vehicle as it rolled through the neighborhood.

"Mom never told me about this." Gunnar kept scanning the area. "How's business?"

Eboni kept quiet. No use saying what he would soon find out in moments.

Gunnar pulled the massive vehicle behind the shop. He parked and turned off the truck. Gunnar got out of the driver's side, ran over to the passenger side, and opened her door as Eboni had put her hand on her door handle.

As much as Eboni hated to admit it, she liked gentlemanly side of Gunnar, a man who looked like he probably never used utensils. Her insides rattled when he held his hand up to assist her out of the tall ride.

When she got out and nearly buckled from his touch and the feel of his hard body against hers, she blamed the wobble on ice on the parking lot. Thankfully, he didn't peer down to verify her claim.

Gunnar used his mother's keys to unlock the back door. He opened it and allowed her to walk through first. She appreciated that, not because she liked the generous gesture, but because she wanted to view the salon before he could see it, not that she would have an opportunity to change anything.

Eboni skipped turning on the lights. With the blinds drawn, it cloaked the shop in darkness. Too bad Gunnar knew where the location of the light switch and had no problem flicking them.

"Wow." Gunnar walked by Eboni and scanned the modest salon.

"Still the same shop." She placed her purse on the reception station desk.

He turned to the wall of hair bonnet dryers. "The hair bonnets look the same from when I was here."

"Queen makes sure everything works." Eboni stared at Gunnar.

He walked over to the row of inky black sinks. He put his hand on one sink and ran his fingertips over the midnight-colored bowl. "Nothing has really changed. It all looks...good."

"You know your mother. She has high standards."

Gunnar strolled over to the styling chairs. One sat in the front window and six sat along the wall of mirrors. Gunnar ran his fingertips over the gold frame surrounding one of the mirrors.

He glanced down at the black-and-white checkered floor before bringing his attention back to her. "The place smells like her."

Eboni smiled. "This place is her in every sense."

She couldn't wait any longer to talk about her idea. No time like the present. She took a deep, cleansing breath and spoke before he could say anything.

"Since you left"--she noticed his glare but kept going--"I've been donating my time and my money to the Oceanfront Community Center. That place really does help a lot of kids. I was one of them. It's gone downhill a little." She stepped closer to Gunnar so that he can see the intensity in her eyes. "They're in dire need of some money."

Gunnar tilted his head. "You're asking me for money?"

Eboni blinked and took a couple of steps back. "Hell, no. I don't want your money or your time." She needed to corral her emotions otherwise she would end up arguing with the man, and she did not want her day to go that way. "I talked to your mom about doing a fund-raiser. She liked the idea but said in her current condition she can't really help." Eboni moved in closer. "She suggested I talk to you." She licked her lips. "I was thinking of maybe doing a hair-cut promotion where a portion of the proceeds will go to the center."

Gunnar put his fists to his hips. From his stance, Eboni knew he had some objections to her proposal. Whatever he said, she would have an argument to spin it around.

"Fund-raiser? My mom is in the hospital, business has slowed, and you want her to raise money to help the center?"

"I would only ask for the tips."

"From everyone?"

Eboni nodded. "Yes. I would even do hair for one of my shifts and give all proceeds to the center."

"You can't ask the other employees to give up their money for your endeavor." Gunnar moved away from her. "I don't approve of this."

It felt like flames engulfed her entire body. The throbbing that filled her head wouldn't be going away with just an aspirin. "You have no right to tell me what I can do here. I asked your mother and she gave me her approval, and she's the one who owns this place. Like I said before, you're simply a distraction."

"I can see now that the demands of this place put her in the hospital. My mother needs to rest. That's not going to happen with selfish people around her." He scanned the shop. "No, I'm going to do what my mother hasn't been able to do. I'm selling this place."

Chapter 4

Eboni glared at Gunnar for what felt like twenty years before she sprang into action. She pulled out her cell phone from her purse and activated the speed-dial number to Elizabeth. She paced in order to keep somewhat calm.

As soon as she heard a *click* on the other side of the line, Eboni launched into an attack. "Queen, I hope I didn't wake you."

Eboni heard heavy footfalls, turned around, and caught Gunnar charging toward her.

"Is everything okay at the house?" Queen Elizabeth sounded very wide awake considering. Her medical prognosis must be keeping her restless.

"The house is fine. But if you leave your business up to your son, he's going to try and sell it from under you."

A pause lingered before Elizabeth said, "Put him on the phone, please."

Eboni held up her phone to Gunnar. "Your mother would like a word with you."

Gunnar's jaw flexed before he accepted the phone. The brief graze of his fingers against hers ignited a small spark in her that quickly died down as soon as he turned his back on her.

"Hey, Ma."

Eboni tried to hear what his mother said. Queen Elizabeth couldn't be classified as a yeller. When she spoke, people couldn't help but to be wrapped up in her every word. From the stiffness of Gunnar's body, he must have fallen under that same spell.

"You don't understand." Gunnar paused. "But I made the decision because of you and your health." He waited again. "Yes, I know you're a grown woman."

Eboni snickered. When she did, Gunnar glared at her. He shook his head and paced back and forth in front of the styling chairs.

"Yes, ma'am." He cleared his throat. "I'll leave running the business to Eboni. I'll take a step back." His voice lowered. "I love you too." He handed the phone back to Eboni. "She'd like to talk to you."

Eboni took the phone from Gunnar. As soon as the device left his hand, he stomped to the back door and pushed his way through it on his head full of steam.

"Hey, Queen."

"Although I appreciate you keeping me in the loop about Gunnar's misguided plans, don't you ever undermine him by running to me like a child."

Elizabeth's harsh words forced Eboni to sit down in one of the chairs. The air deflated out of her lungs and her head weighed as much as a tank.

"I thought you would want to know what Gunnar had said. It's not right for him to try and sell the place that you worked so hard to build." Elizabeth had to see that Eboni came from a good place with her intentions.

"Gunnar and you are a lot alike. You're both passionate, you two want to see results, and you think you know what's best for everyone. I appreciate both of you. If you want to be a business leader, you're going to need to learn how to communicate with stubborn fools like Gunnar. It's easy to lead when you have folks who are rooting for you. It's a challenge to sway an adversary."

As usual, Elizabeth's wise words rang true.

Her friend continued. "Put on your big-girl panties. Apologize to my son for putting me in the middle of this and do what you two do best. In the short amount of time since you left the hospital, I doubt you two have had much sleep. Why don't you go home and get some rest. Calmer heads will prevail."

Eboni smiled. "Yes, ma'am. You rest your nerves."

"Oh, no. Now I'm wide awake thanks to all this drama. I'll see you two later. Love you."

"Love you too." Eboni disconnected the call and took a deep breath.

Damn Queen Elizabeth for being right. Eboni secured the shop. She locked the back door and then headed to Gunnar's rented monstrosity.

Like before, he jumped out of the vehicle in order to open the door for her. Damn his home training.

As soon as she sat down and closed the door, she took a deep breath to apologize to him as Queen Elizabeth had instructed. Before she could get a word out, Gunnar spoke.

"I apologize for trying to take over the decisions of the salon," he began. "As my mother so succinctly stated, this is her shop, not mine."

Eboni liked this kinder, gentler side of Gunnar. She knew that the man still had his fighter side inside of him that he didn't mind pulling out when needed.

"Thank you." Eboni nodded.

Gunnar put the SUV in gear, but didn't move. He turned to her and waited as though anticipating something.

Eboni shook her head. "Your mother told you she wanted me to apologize too, right?"

He nodded.

Busted. She didn't think she'd done anything wrong, but she wanted to be a woman of her word. "Fine. I'm sorry for calling your mother on you. We're both grown-ups. We should know how to resolve issues without a mediator."

He shrugged. "You're right." Then he backed out of the spot and headed to the road. "And you're not sorry."

She started to open her mouth to refute his claim.

"You've *apologized*. But there's absolutely nothing sorry about you." He scanned her with a slight smile before driving back on the road.

"Did you just flirt?" Eboni crossed her arms and pressed her back against the door as he drove.

"Nope. Just stating facts. Lord knows, I don't want to make your boyfriend jealous." He put his hand to his chest to express sincerity.

Eboni laughed. "You are so transparent. Just ask me if I'm seeing someone."

"I don't care about that. Why would I care if you're dating or married? It's not like we're going to date each other again." He accelerated down the road.

"You got that right." She glanced out the window. "Besides, I'm sure you have lots of little groupies throwing themselves at you. We love you, Guns." She puckered her lips and made a kissing sound.

He laughed. "Really? You think I would go for a woman like that?"

"I have no idea what you want anymore."

Gunnar glanced at her.

She finished off her statement. "And I don't care." In her mind, Gunnar had pushed her away so that he could go off and have a different life, one that didn't involve her. "Let's get through this for Elizabeth's sake. Any problems we have, we talk about it. Agreed?"

Gunnar regarded her for a moment at a traffic light. "Agreed." He continued on back toward his mother's house.

"Will you turn down this road?" Eboni pointed to the right.

"Why? What's down there?"

"The center. I want you to see what it's like now." She watched Gunnar shift in his seat as he kept his stare on the road. "I think if you saw the state it's in now, you'll feel differently about helping."

"Or I'll feel exactly the same." He glanced at her when they stopped at another light.

A stray hair escaped from Gunnar's messy ponytail. Eboni had to fight the urge to secure it back behind his ear. She shouldn't care what he looked like or about making him happy. He certainly hadn't thought about her when he'd left.

"But I'll go." Gunnar turned down the street and headed to the center. "I don't want you thinking I'm inflexible. A lot can be said for someone who recognizes his mistakes and wants to right the wrongs of the past."

Eboni stared at him. She couldn't get drawn into Gunnar's web and world again. She had no doubt in her mind that once Elizabeth got better and came home, he would be out of Virginia and back in Vegas fighting again.

Gunnar pulled into the sparsely filled parking lot of the Oceanfront Community Center. "So far looking exactly like it did when I was here." He turned off his rental and got out first.

He crossed the front of the SUV and opened Eboni's door. He'd been here less than a day and she'd already gotten used to him opening doors for her. That alone should make her feel uncomfortable. Eboni couldn't get used to him and his ways. Disappointment always followed her complacency.

As he'd done before, he helped her out and escorted her over the slick terrain to the building. The automatic doors did Gunnar's job. He allowed her to walk inside first and followed her.

The sounds of basketballs dribbling off hardwood floors echoed through the open floor plan. A circular ramp ran up the right side of the wall to the upstairs area.

"That used to be the game room up there." Gunnar pointed up.

"There are a couple of game rooms still up there. Mainly there are classrooms. They teach nutrition classes here, sewing, knitting."

Gunnar snickered. "That sounds great for a kid."

Eboni fought to keep from rolling her eyes. "Children aren't the only ones who use this center." After speaking to the man at the front desk, she led Gunnar to the upstairs area.

She showed him the classrooms first. Paint peeled from the walls in every room.

"Besides a basic sprucing up of the place, it also needs equipment." She touched a sewing machine. "I think your mother donated this machine from her boutique."

"So my mother has done a lot for the center."

Again, Eboni kept herself from commenting and rolling her eyes. "The games in this room may have been here when you and I used to come here as kids." She pointed out the stacks of game boxes in the next room. "Some pieces are missing." Eboni walked him over to a platform overlooking the empty swimming pool. "The pool has been broken for over a year. Not enough money in the budget to repair it."

Gunnar remained quiet throughout the sad tour until Eboni brought him to the basketball courts. The players' sneakers squeaked across the glossy hardwood floor as they played.

"The nets all need to be restrung. And the floor needs--"

"Okay, I get it. The place needs work." Gunnar turned around and headed to the front door.

Eboni had to step up her walk to a trot to keep up with him. "It's a school day, so you can't see all the kids that are normally here."

Gunnar burst through the door and stomped to his vehicle. He glanced to the side. "What about them?"

A group of teenage boys hung around the back of the center by the dumpster.

"Probably skipping school."

Gunnar shook his head. "Maybe the place should be leveled and made into a park or a parking lot." He unlocked and opened Eboni's door.

"That's your answer? Make something that could help people into a parking lot?" Without his assistance, she jumped into the passenger seat. When he got into the driver's side, she lit into him. "What happened to you? I mean really. You turned your life around when you were here. Then all of the sudden, you had to go. It was like you lost your heart."

Gunnar stared at her for a moment before pulling out of the spot and driving back to his mother's home without saying a word.

"I knew it." Eboni settled back into the seat. "You're a cruel, heartless man who doesn't give a damn about children or your community or anything else but yourself. I wish you hadn't come back home."

Eboni didn't care if he stopped in the middle of the road and put her out of his vehicle. She'd tried making the best out of the situation. He made it impossible by offering no explanation or showing any compassion.

After the grocery trip and a very long nap, Eboni decided to take a bath before making herself dinner. Eboni needed and deserved a break. She had hoped that she would be in Queen's home without intrusion.

Eboni had had no idea an apartment even existed in Queen's two-story detached garage. She hoped that Gunnar had his own kitchen within that apartment. He must since he'd taken his food directly to his place when they got back to Queen's house.

Before submerging herself into the balmy water, Eboni thought about Gunnar. It hurt her that with one call from his mother, he came back home. He couldn't make that same sacrifice for her. Why hadn't she rated as someone just as special to him?

Eboni stripped and climbed into the pink bathtub. She laughed thinking about Gunnar and his equally hulking brothers bathing in this pink tub and matching pink bathroom. Queen Elizabeth epitomized girlie.

After her bath, she dried herself and wrapped a robe around her body. She heard a light tapping against the window. She opened the blinds to discover heavy sleeting rain pelting against the glass. Something else caught her attention. Across from her, she saw Gunnar in what must be the bedroom.

He walked around shirtless. From her vantage point, it looked like he had a towel wrapped around his waist. He must have just gotten out of a bath or shower, too. His blond hair looked almost dark brown as it lay wet against his face. He pushed his hand over his hair to get it out of his eyes.

Eboni had to lick her lips as stared at his shiny body. His muscles seemed bigger and more defined. In her head, she calculated the number of steps it would take to get to his room.

In that moment, Gunnar glanced over. He did a double take when he caught Eboni staring at him. Instead of closing his blinds, he returned her stare with an intense one. He braced his hands against the window pane.

Eboni's breathing increased. She chewed on her lower lip as her body warred with her to go over to see him. Then she thought about their last conversation before he'd left to start his fighting career. She recalled him walking away from her without a thought in his head about what she had going on in her life at that time. He didn't care about her.

Eboni had to love herself more not to get caught in his life again. She reached up and twisted a rod next to the blinds to close them again. She had to stay as far away from that man as possible or she could risk another heartbreak. She couldn't go through that again.

*＊＊＊

Gunnar should be filled with a renewed spirit. After visiting with his mother last night and seeing her full of hope, he should have gone into surgery day feeling positive. Instead, he felt helpless. If he could, he wanted to be in the operating room with the doctor and staff even if wiping sweat off the doctor's brow had been his only function.

It didn't surprise him that Eboni came to the hospital. She did care about Elizabeth, almost as much as Gunnar and his brothers.

He refused to let Eboni's harsh words from yesterday cloud his mind. She assessed him based on his actions as a young, dumb eighteen-year-old who had only focused on himself. She wouldn't even give him a chance to show a different side of himself. Gunnar had to concentrate on his mother right now.

Gunnar sat in the room where his mother would be returning after her procedure. His phone and hers had not stopped ringing since the surgery had started. He reassured the parties on the other line that Queen Elizabeth would be okay and, no, she hadn't gotten out of surgery yet, but they had hope she would be fine.

Gunnar's knee bounced as he kept his stare to the floor. That same glazed-over feeling he would get during his fights happened again. He concentrated on a small dark fleck in the pattern on the tile floor. His mind went blank except for that black speck. If he allowed his thoughts to gain freedom, he would only think of his mother, the surgery, and the possible consequences.

"Gunnar!"

His name being shouted snapped him out of his concentration. He peered up and stared at Eboni who sat across from him.

"You want something to eat or drink?" She held up her purse.

He shook his head, too afraid to speak until he got confirmation of his mother's condition. Gunnar squeezed his hands into fists, trying to relieve the ache he felt in them. Right now, he would kill to have a heavy bag to work out some of his anxiety.

"What if she doesn't..." He let the words trail off.

"Hey, hey." Eboni went to him and crouched down to meet him at eye level. "Don't think that way. They don't call her Queen Elizabeth because she wears a lot of jewelry."

Gunnar peered up and stared into Eboni's soulful eyes.

"She's a strong woman. You have to think positive." She kept her stare on him as though trying to make sure he understood every word she'd said.

Crystal B. Bright

Gunnar took notice of her slender neck, her full lips, her smooth skin, all things that he shouldn't have become aware of in that moment, but he couldn't help himself. The longer she kept him hypnotized in her stare, the more he thought about their past, the kissing, the deep emotions, the intense connection.

Then he remembered last night. She'd been staring at him after he'd taken a much-needed cold shower. Gunnar couldn't get Eboni out of his thoughts. She consumed his every waking moment, exactly like when they had first dated.

Seeing her in a robe with her hair pulled up into a messy bun, he wanted to run over to the house and pull her hair down from the bun and make love to her.

He swallowed hard. His hands itched to touch her.

As he started to open his mouth to say something, anything, orderlies wheeled in the bed that carried his mother. Gunnar stood along with Eboni, who moved back from him so that they could slide her bed between the two of them.

Elizabeth remained conscious but looked tired, evident from the bags under her eyes and her pale skin tone.

"I made it." Elizabeth smiled. "That room was so cold. They were trying to freeze me."

The same doctor who had spoken to them yesterday returned.

"Looks like the surgery went okay." Gunnar smiled.

The petite woman's expression remained serious and somber. "We didn't install a stent."

The smile melted from Gunnar's face. "You were gone a while. Why didn't you do the procedure?"

"We found another artery behind her heart that is also completely blocked. Installing stents will not help. At this point, we need to talk about doing bypass surgery. At least double, but it could be triple."

Clutching his mother's hand gave Gunnar the strength to remain standing. His world spun out of control. He gazed down at her. "Ma?"

Gunnar needed to hear her to know that she would be okay.

His mother frowned. "I'm going to have a scar. I won't be able to wear my dress with the plunging neckline."

Gunnar laughed through his impending tears. He kissed her forehead. "I think that might be the least of your worries."

"I know." She became solemn as she spoke to him.

"We'll hold her for a couple of days to watch her. She'll go through a healthy heart care class."

"What?" Elizabeth's bottom jaw unhinged.

"Mom, you wouldn't go to a class like that voluntarily. Catching you while you're in bed would be the only way." Gunnar squeezed his mother's hand.

Elizabeth sucked her teeth and turned away from her oldest son.

"If all goes well, she should be home by the weekend." Dr. Patel typed something in the wall-mounted computer in the room.

"When is her surgery scheduled?" Eboni patted Elizabeth on her shoulder as she talked to the doctor.

"I'd like to do it in the next couple of weeks. I don't want to wait too long with the amount of blockage that she has." She patted Elizabeth's legs and said her good-byes before walking out.

The room fell into a deathly silence. Elizabeth put her hand to her chest.

Gunnar knew his mother and knew her statement about her scar being visible hid her fear. He patted her hand. When she looked at him, he smiled.

"Did you two work out your problems?" Elizabeth looked at both of them.

"We're taking it step by step." Eboni rubbed her fingers over Elizabeth's arm.

"That's the only way to do it. Rome wasn't built in a--" She fell asleep before finishing her statement.

Gunnar peered up. "Now I'm starving," he said in a whisper. He nodded toward the doorway.

Eboni followed him and they both went to the hospital cafeteria for lunch. When they got to a table, he wasted no time in asking Eboni questions about the salon. He didn't want to bring up his mother and have the thought of her surgery plaguing his mind.

"What are the other stylists like?" Gunnar opened one of his four bottles of water and chugged the entire bottle down within seconds.

"The stylists have changed since you were there. They aren't like me or your mother." Eboni flicked the lettuce and cucumbers around in her salad. "Other salons rent their spaces out so that stylists can be their own bosses. Not your mother. She employs these people. She feels like she can give them better benefits than if they went out on their own."

"Any problems I need to know about?" He picked up one of his sandwiches and finished it in three large bites. Good thing he'd grabbed two more sandwiches to fill him.

"Same ol' beauty-shop drama. One person accuses another of stealing their client. You know. Stuff like that. But nothing major." She watched him work on his second sandwich. "Do you have a tapeworm or something? I've never seen anyone eat like you do."

Gunnar opened his second bottle of water. "I work out a lot. I need the food for fuel." He took a couple of gulps and then wiped his mouth. "So my plan for tomorrow will be to see my mom in the morning and be at the shop an hour before it opens."

Eboni blinked. "Really?"

Gunnar shrugged. "I want to be a good boss."

Eboni shook her head.

"Supervisor."

She cleared her throat.

"Owner."

"Oh, hell, no."

"Fine. I want my presence there to be seamless. I don't want the staff or the clients to even notice that my mother is not there."

"That'll be a neat trick. But tell me, Gunnar, when you didn't talk to you mother for a long while, did you miss her?"

He laughed. "Of course."

"That's how other people are going to feel. Don't go in thinking you're her replacement. You can't do what she does."

Gunnar knew no one could replace his mother. He just wanted an opportunity. "I think I'll surprise a lot of people. You just wait and see."

Chapter 5

Eboni arrived at Press 'N Curl thirty minutes before the shop opened, her usual time to get there. She couldn't help but notice Gunnar's vehicle in the parking lot. It took up two spaces.

At least he stuck to his word. He did get there before she did. Since she'd gone back to her place after spending one night in Elizabeth's house, she couldn't watch him...not that she watched him before. Not entirely.

After a deep breath, Eboni walked through the back door of the salon. She noticed right away that certain items had been moved around. The bin for the wet towel had been moved to a space in between the washer and dryer. Of course, that meant that the washer and dryer had been moved as well, pushed over about a foot from their original spot.

The linen closet that held the brooms and dustpans now had shelves that held clean towels. Out in the main salon area, she found another set of empty shelves. She heard a rustling sound from the office. Eboni stepped inside and found Gunnar straightening that area as well.

"What are you doing?" Eboni put her fist to her hip.

"Cleaning up." Gunnar must have caught her shocked expression. He quickly amended his statement. "I mean straightening up. Putting items in logical order."

"Like the washer and dryer?"

"They're in the right spot. But the towel bin should have been put next to it. I moved some things around to make that happen." He continued reorganizing his mother's office.

In his white T-shirt and jeans, Eboni couldn't help but notice his form. When he bent over, she admired the wide planes of his back. His firm ass begged to be grabbed. She managed to bring her gaze up to his when he stood up straight. She hoped he hadn't noticed her staring at his body.

"Did you put the coffee on?" She took a couple of steps out of the office.

"Not yet." He started to head toward her.

"I got it. If I were you, I would put your mother's office back to the way it was." Eboni went to the reception desk to stow her purse and coat. Then she went to the small counter area with the coffeemaker to start pots of regular and decaffeinated coffee.

"I'm not removing anything. Just organizing."

Eboni heard him clanging items in her boss's office. "So the message you want to relay to her is that you think her organizing skills are crap and you know better than her, right?"

The movement stopped.

"Maybe I should rethink this," he called from the office.

She shook her head. As she put the filter full of ground coffee into the canister, she noticed the empty shelves. "You know we could use these shelves for something."

Gunnar walked out of the office and stood between the shelves and the coffee area. "Like what?"

Eboni cocked her head. "Remember you used to make a bunch of hair stuff back in the day?"

"Do you really want to talk about the disastrous Kool-Aid hair-color incident?" Gunnar had sworn to Eboni that he could use the lemonade Kool-Aid mixture to put highlights in her hair. It had taken four months for the garish orange color to disappear.

"No, but you used to make great leave-in conditioners and hair moisturizers. You could do that again."

"Why would I want to do that?" Gunnar furrowed his eyebrows.

Eboni smiled before revealing her proposal. "You could make those products again and sell them here. The proceeds could go toward the center."

"If I did it, I would use the money to help this place out first." He shook his head. "That place doesn't mean a tenth as much to me as this salon. I hope you understand that."

Before she could answer, the back door slammed shut.

"Whew! It is too cold and I am too cute to have on all these clothes." Shay did her trademark sway into the salon. As soon as she saw Gunnar, a smile sprang to her face.

The dark-skinned young woman stood almost as tall as Gunnar and had to be as big around as one of his legs. Her bright, white teeth gleamed against her dark complexion when she smiled. She rocked her standard short Afro puff trumpeting from the back of her head.

"Well, hello." She sauntered to Gunnar, who didn't move but did watch her. "Are you her parole officer, or did you hire security for us?"

"Shay, while Queen Elizabeth is in the hospital, her son has--"

"Son?" Shay split her attention between Gunnar and Eboni. "Since when does Miss Queen have a white son?"

"Three actually," Gunnar offered.

"How can you not know that? She talks about her boys all the time. She has pictures of them in her office."

"I just thought the pictures came with the frames."

Eboni balled her hands into fists. "This is her oldest, Gunnar Wells."

Gunnar held out his hand.

"Oh, no, honey. Any family of Queenie's is family to me." She embraced him in her slender, muscular arms. For good measure, or maybe she thought he would respond to it, she wiggled her backside.

Gunnar gave her a pat on the back and pulled away from her. Eboni hid her smile when he broke from Shay's embrace. Most single men--and even the married ones--that came to the shop fell for Shay's look and charms. Good to see one man holding strong...at least in front of Eboni.

"Gunnar, this is Shay Brownley. She does it all but really specializes in braids, twists, and natural styles." Eboni poured herself a cup of coffee and took a sip of the needed pick-me-up.

"Good to see we're doing more for our customers than just relaxers and weaves." Gunnar put his hand on one of the empty shelves.

"*Our* customers? What is he talking about?" Shay looked at both him and Eboni.

"As I was saying, while Queen Elizabeth is in the hospital, Gunnar has agreed to step into her spot." Eboni would leave off the fact that Gunnar would be leaving like he'd done in the past.

Shay blinked as though she stood in the middle of a windstorm. "What? What? What? He's going to be here?"

Eboni nodded.

"Just like old times." Gunnar smiled.

"That's going to go over like a lead balloon." Shay grabbed her purse and strutted to her station.

"Why do you say that?" Gunnar followed her.

"Women like coming to a beauty salon to talk about you." Shay pointed to him.

"Me?"

"Not you specifically. Men in general. How are they going to feel free talking about what guy stood them up or who is a bad tipper or which guy is a bad la--"

"Uh, he gets it." Eboni had to cut her off before she got too risqué. "Tillman is here."

"Oh, he doesn't count." Shay waved her hand. "Tillman has been here for a while. Anyway, how are women going to feel like themselves here? I hate to say it, but you might have to go."

Gunnar crossed his arms over his massive chest. "That's not going to happen."

"Then you had better hide out in the office for the day."

He shook his head. "I grew up here in this shop." He walked over to the doorway that went to the play area for the kids. "See these notches? That's where my mother marked my growth each year."

"So that's what those are. I thought some kid didn't want to leave the play area and they were holding the doorframe." Shay cackled as she started up her curling irons and flat irons. "Listen, folks are funny about their hair. You're going to have to do a lot to gain their trust. Being Queen's *adopted* son ain't going to cut it."

Eboni knew the *adopted* tag would get to Gunnar. Seeing his jaw flex clued her in that her assumption had been dead-on.

"Nice to meet you, Shay." Gunnar turned and headed back to the office.

"I mean for real, Eb." Shay pulled on Eboni's arm and lowered her voice. "Does he seriously think he's going to come up in here and be like Queen?"

"I did warn him that the salon now is not like the salon was back in the day." Eboni had to give the man credit. He'd put himself out there more than she had expected.

Eboni thought she heard a squeak from the back area. Sunlight streamed through the doorway that separated the back of the salon from the front working area. Within a few seconds, Tisha crept into the salon.

The slight woman walked with her head down as though unsure of her own steps. She constantly pushed up her black horned-rimmed glasses, which probably slipped down her slender nose because of the position of her head. The flowered dress she wore and the pale blue cardigan sweater swallowed her tiny frame. When she got to her station, she took off the ice cleats from her black orthopedic shoes.

"Hey, Tisha. Another wild night?" Shay poked the light-skinned woman in her side with the silver end of her rat-tail comb.

Tisha flinched and mumbled something.

Shay put her hand to her ear. "What did you say?"

"I was home all night," Tisha said in her version of a shout, which sounded more like a loud whisper.

"Leave her alone. Not everyone is like you." Eboni nudged the statuesque woman with her elbow.

Eboni noticed a look of horror cover Tisha's face before the woman grabbed a can of hairspray and sprayed it in front of her.

"Intruder! Intruder! Call the police!" Tisha managed to scream as she jumped from side to side.

Eboni looked over to where she'd sprayed the hairspray and saw Gunnar standing in the doorway of the office.

"Put the can down. He's not an intruder." Eboni took the tall, light blue aerosol can from her hand and returned it to its spot on her station. "Tisha, this is Gunnar Wells. He's Queen Elizabeth's son. He's going to be filling in for her while she's in the hospital."

"Hi, Tisha." Gunnar smiled and extended his hand just as she dropped her gaze to the floor and turned her back on him.

Eboni walked by Gunnar to get more coffee. In a whisper, she said, "Don't mind her. She does great hair but she's painfully shy."

Gunnar nodded. "Anyone else showing up?"

The back door slammed open again. Tisha jumped at the sound.

"Whooo, man! It ain't fit for man nor beast out there." Tillman strutted into the salon.

The husky man had only started working there within the last six months. Elizabeth had said she wanted to diversify the salon and had offered him a job as a stylist, which had surprised Eboni.

Tillman looked like he should have been a football player. He kept himself in pretty good shape. Eboni thought he would hit on the clients. So far, Tillman had behaved himself.

"Gunnar, this is Tillman. He's sort of our jack-of-all-trades. He does hair, nails, waxing. Whatever." Eboni pointed to the man who took off his heavy leather jacket and placed it on the coat rack by his station. "Tillman, this is--"

"Gunnar 'Guns' Wells! As I live and breathe." Tillman held out his hand and brought Gunnar in for a half hug.

"You know this man?" Shay asked as she leaned against her station.

"You don't? He's only the undefeated mixed martial arts champion. He kicks some serious butt. I saw that fight with The Shark this past weekend. Actually, I missed it. I saw him when he laid that punch on you." He pointed to Gunnar's eye. "Then I blinked and it was over." He laughed hard.

Gunnar gave him a slight smile and nodded. "My mom had called me before the match and said she was in the hospital. I had to make it quick so I could come home."

"What a coincidence. Queen is in the hospital right now."

Eboni punched Tillman in the arm. "Queen is his mother. Do none of y'all listen to her when she talks about her children or even go in her office to see the pictures?"

"I would remember seeing this cat's picture."

"She has pictures of me as a teenager with shorter hair." Gunnar jutted his thumb over his shoulder to his mother's office.

Tillman pointed to Gunnar. "Man, I can't believe you're here. So what are you doing at the salon?"

"He's filling in for Queen while she's sick." Shay shrugged and turned to her station.

"Okay, okay. Welcome to Press 'N Curl." Tillman nodded and went back to his area.

"I thought men working here wouldn't work out." Gunnar stared pointedly at Shay.

Shay took her time turning back to him. "People know Tillman. He grew up around here. He's like everybody's little brother."

"I grew up here." Gunnar pointed all around the salon. "I grew up in this neighborhood and I grew up in this salon."

"I've been here for the last five years. Where have you been?"

The question stopped him cold.

Shay pointed at him with her rat-tail comb. "Hey, since you're a big celebrity and all, maybe you could do a commercial or print ad or an interview to drum up some business around here."

Gunnar shook his head. "Not going to happen. Not my thing."

"Yeah, I don't think I've ever seen you do an interview." Tillman looked at his reflection in the mirror behind his station. He looked over at Shay. "He's not a hype man like them other MMA cats."

Shay snickered and shook her head. "Great. He's about as functional as a paperweight."

The backdoor opened again, and this time Monica lumbered inside. The short, heavy woman didn't stop when she looked at Gunnar. She made it to her seat at the receptionist area, plopped herself down, and turned to the group.

"Who is this? Health inspector?" She pointed to Gunnar.

"Queen's son." Tisha spoke a hair above a whisper.

"MMA champ, Guns Wells." Tillman pumped his fist in the air.

"Gunnar." He approached Monica's area and extended his hand.

She accepted it but gave him a suspicious stare. "What are you doing here?"

"Filling in for Queen while she's in the hospital." Shay sat in her styling chair and swung her high-heeled booted foot back and forth. "The great white hope is here to save us."

"Hey, don't do that." Eboni wagged her finger at Shay.

As much as she didn't want Gunnar there, she wouldn't stand to have him ridiculed because of his race.

"Is this everyone?" Gunnar asked again.

"This is it." Eboni walked toward the front door to unlock it.

"Before you open the door, I just wanted to say a few things. Just one second." Gunnar ducked back into the office.

Eboni hurried to the area to find out what in the world he had planned. "What are you doing?"

At that moment, she caught him without a shirt. He had his back to her. The muscular expanse of flesh had her imagining her fingernails clawing it. She chewed on her lower lip as she continued watching him get dressed.

He slipped on a black T-shirt and tossed his other one into a gym bag. "Had some dust on the other one."

Eboni smiled and nodded, unable to speak after that show. He ushered her out of the office and closed the door behind himself.

"As I was saying, I wanted to thank you all for working so hard for my mother while she's recovering. In case you hadn't heard, she was supposed to have a stent installed yesterday, but they found additional blockage in another artery."

"So what does that mean?" Shay asked.

"They're going to do bypass surgery. Double for sure, but may be triple if they find more problem spots."

Shay and Tillman covered their mouths in horror. Tisha barely lifted her head to look at him.

"I'm going to assume my mother's duties while she's gone. So look to me as you would look to her."

"You going to get your nails painted like Queen?" Shay laughed so loud Tisha jumped at the sound.

Gunnar smiled. "Funny. I also wanted to propose something." He glanced at Eboni before continuing.

Eboni felt her eyebrows draw together at his unexpected announcement. The brief stare started her heart. She put her hand to her chest and looked at the other employees to ground herself.

"The Oceanfront Community Center is in need of some money to make necessary repairs. What do you all think about opening the salon on Mondays and have all the money made on that day go to the center? Are you all in?"

The room fell quiet. Gunnar hadn't mentioned this plan to her before springing it on the group. Unexpected anger bubbled in her gut. Then Shay broke the silence with her cackling laughter.

"You are too funny. Open up the salon so that we can make some money. I have a client coming in a few minutes." She scratched the inside of her Afro with her pinkie nail.

"So you don't want to do it?" Gunnar crossed his arms.

"If it's not paying my bills, I'm not paying no mind." Shay shook her head. "I'm not coming here on my day off to work for *free*. Are you crazy?"

"Yeah, man. Sundays and Mondays are our weekends. We work here Tuesdays through Saturday. I like my weekends." Tillman shrugged.

Tisha glanced up, mumbled something and turned around.

When Gunnar brought his attention to Eboni, she hoped he caught her genuine surprise. "I'm going to unlock the door, and then you and I need to talk." She walked to the door. "Let's open."

Once Eboni unlocked the door, she stormed to the office and waited for Gunnar. He followed right behind her, closing the door for privacy.

"What was that out there?" Eboni asked.

"What? Didn't you want some support for the center?" Gunnar felt an intense headache stabbing the middle of his forehead.

"Yes. Support. What you did was so halfhearted, you practically dared them to accept it. You might as well have laughed with them." Eboni crossed her arms over her chest.

"I need some air." Gunnar grabbed his coat and swung the office door open. He stomped outside.

"Where is he going?" Monica asked.

"He needs some space." Eboni strolled out of the office.

"Damn, the first customer hasn't even come in yet and he's already bailing." Shay shook her head. "Didn't think he would last. No one can fill Miss Queen's shoes. No one."

Eboni felt no need to go after him. She'd made the center her baby. He didn't care about it…or her.

Her sensible side whispered in her ear that his plan had been solid. Had the employees been on board, they could have raised a lot of money.

As she started to walk by Shay, the woman grabbed her arm and pulled her close to her.

"So what's the story?" Shay asked under her breath.

"What do you mean?" Eboni shrugged out of her boney grip.

"Are you and Gunnar hitting it?" Shay punctuated her question with an obscene thrust.

"No." Eboni shook her head. "We did date when we were in high school. Then he left."

"Without you?"

Eboni nodded, feeling no need to rehash that old story.

"Honey, he's got to be a millionaire now. Are you going to go after him again?"

Eboni shook her head. "Too much drama from our pasts. Too much for me to get over."

"So you wouldn't be upset if I went after him, right?"

Eboni regarded Shay for a moment. She imagined Shay and Gunnar together and her stomach compressed. Why would she even care if Gunnar dated someone else? She assumed he'd done that and more in the ten years since he'd left.

"Be my guest."

Shay smiled as a customer walked into the salon. "I'm going to have that man wrapped around my finger, toe, and eyelash before I'm through. I can't believe you're willing to let him go. White or black, he's fine. He needs to get rid of that ponytail, but other than that, he's hot. He's got a great body. And, again, he's probably rich. What else do you need?"

Eboni didn't tell her misguided coworker that commitment meant everything above all of the superficial items she'd mentioned. Instead, she took a step to the side to let her customer get to her. "I thought you were seeing someone else?"

Shay waved her hand at her. "I can handle more than one man. Don't worry about Miss Shay. Or is that jealousy I hear?"

Eboni shook her head. "Whatever."

Gunnar Wells had his own agenda. Eboni wouldn't get fooled again.

* * * *

Gunnar had managed to walk down the street about half of a mile to a corner store he used to go to when he was a teenager. Except for being dirtier and smaller than he remembered, the convenience store looked the same.

He took a deep breath as he thought about the fact that not everything had changed. This store still had its candy aisle in the middle. Then and now, Gunnar figured out that they situated the candy that way so that little kids wouldn't be tempted to steal...like he had.

Gunnar walked into the store, thankful for the lack of customers inside. He poured himself a cup of coffee for the long walk back to the salon. He paid for the drink with a twenty-dollar bill. When the cashier tried giving Gunnar his change, he walked away.

"Keep it. I owe you." He walked out and headed toward the salon.

The employees at Press 'N Curl, including Eboni, had given him the cold shoulder. Shay had been the most obvious and vocal about her feelings toward him. Tillman had remained polite but still came off as unsure. Tisha...he couldn't figure her out. Monica looked like she wanted to do her job and go home.

As Gunnar got closer to the salon, he hurried his steps. He hadn't given up on a fight in the past. These folks would not break him either.

Gunnar walked in the front door of the salon to the surprise of the two customers that sat in Shay and Tisha's chairs. The chatter that he'd heard from outside stopped when he crossed the threshold.

A young African-American woman sat in Shay's chair. She scanned Gunnar from head to toe and pursed her lips as he passed her. An older African-American woman sat in Tisha's chair. Her bottom lip hung down as she watched him.

After hanging up his jacket, he went back out to the front desk where Eboni sat with Monica. "May I have a word with you, please?"

Eboni wouldn't even look at him. "Not right now. I'm working. I have to refill some supply orders." She glared at him. "Queen normally does that, but I wasn't sure when you would be coming back."

That dig cut him to his core. Gunnar opened his mouth to insist that she talk to him in private when she picked up the phone receiver and began dialing.

Gunnar released a long, exasperated sigh through his nose. Eboni would not be making this easy on him.

The front door opened with a slam and a teenage boy strolled inside. "Ladies, ladies, ladies!"

Tillman cleared his throat.

"Oh, and my man right here." The young man held up a bag. "I'm a high school student and I'm selling chocolate to raise money to go to band camp. Anyone want to buy some Snickers or Kit Kats?"

Gunnar walked up to him. "What's your name?"

The boy looked at him for a split second before his eyes went wide. "Oh, shit! You're Guns!"

"Watch your language. There are ladies present." Gunnar blocked the teenager from moving any farther into the salon. "Your name?"

"My friends call me T-Lite." The white boy did a single stiff-legged strut toward Gunnar.

He tried pulling Gunnar into a half hug but Gunnar didn't budge.

"You come into this establishment, I expect you to remove your hat." Gunnar pulled at T-Lite's black wool cap.

"Hey. Don't touch." T-Lite adjusted his hat low over his eyes.

"Wear clothes that are your size, not ten times too big." Gunnar tugged at the young man's oversize camouflage jacket. "And you cannot have your pants down around your hind parts."

"Dude, am I in the *Twilight Zone*? Some fighter is telling me how to dress?"

"No, I'm telling you what I expect of people in my establishment."

Eboni walked up behind him. "Gunnar--"

He held his hand up to her. "No. I've seen your kind before. I saw you outside of the community center during the day. Why aren't you in school?"

"Damn, man. I'm just trying to sell some candy."

Gunnar felt flames engulfing his head. He grabbed the young man by his collar. "I asked you to watch your language. Now you need to go." He pushed him out of the door. "Don't come back until you learn some manners."

"Fuck you!"

Gunnar pulled the door closed. He didn't expect to run into Eboni.

"You were rude to that kid." She pushed against his chest.

"What? That boy came here with baggy jeans and a disrespectful mouth. I'm not having that here in my shop."

"This is not *your* shop. Get that straight now."

The movement in the salon stilled at Eboni's blunt words. Gunnar stared at Eboni for a moment to see if he could find the woman who had captured his heart so many years ago. She no longer existed.

He shook his head. "I'm going to go check out some things and I'll be right back."

Gunnar needed air and space before he could sit Eboni down to talk to her. Eboni couldn't stay busy for long. Whether at the salon or after work, he would get to talk to her.

Gunnar decided to run over to the flower shop. He found it open and his mother's long-time employee, Victor Dabu, working hard as usual. Sharing the news with the man he saw as an uncle hurt him when he saw Victor's worried expression.

"You know my mother," Gunnar began. "She's strong."

Victor nodded and seemed relieved, especially after Gunnar shared that after the Super Bowl, Gideon would be coming back home to help run the shop.

Gunnar hit the clothing boutique as his next stop. In the door read a sign that said that the shop would be closed until the beginning of March. That would buy him some time to track down Thane to help run that business.

Since he had time on his hands, Gunnar continued his drive and headed back to the hospital. Even though he'd seen his mother earlier that morning, Gunnar felt the need to visit her again. He knocked on her partially closed door.

"Enter," his mother said regally.

Gunnar smiled at her response as he entered the room. As soon as she saw him, Elizabeth's face lit up like a Christmas tree. When he thought that he may not see that smile again if something went wrong with the surgery, he pushed the idea out of his head.

"You're back." She opened her arms to hug him as he planted a kiss on her cheek.

"How are you doing?"

She scanned her area. Magazines now covered her bed and tray. Eboni must have brought them for her.

She sighed. "Okay. I would love to go home."

"I came to give you some updates. The flower shop is going well." Gunnar sat in a chair next to her bed. "Victor sends his love and will be up to visit when the shop closes."

Elizabeth nodded. "He's always been a good man." She pushed her magazines off to the side and removed her reading glasses. "How's the salon?"

Gunnar gazed down before answering. "I'm sure Eboni has it all under control without my help."

He hated that Eboni couldn't let the past go. He had returned for a reason. Moreover, he'd tried to help her.

"What happened?"

Before Gunnar could spout any lies about everything going okay, he made the mistake of looking his mother in her eyes. Ever since that one fateful day she'd put her life on the line for him, he could never lie to her.

"Ma, I'm trying to help. I swear. I straightened up the shop." He saw his mother's eyes get wide. He continued talking. "I reorganized your office." Gunnar winced as soon as he used the word reorganized.

Eboni had warned him against even touching her office. Evident from Elizabeth's gasp, she must agree.

"You went into my office and moved things around?" Elizabeth sat up taller in her hospital bed, which prompted Gunnar to fluff up her pillows behind her.

"Just a little. Not that much." He would have to put her stuff back the way she had it before the day ended. "I even had an idea to help raise money for that center she keeps talking about."

"And she didn't seem happy about it." His mother stared at him with such love in her expression.

"No. She acted as though I was trying to wreck the place or something." Gunnar lowered his head. He felt his mother tuck a strand of his hair behind his ear.

"Have you two talked about your breakup?"

Gunnar lifted his head. He started to open his mouth to tell her yes when she stopped him.

"I don't mean her calling you insensitive and you telling her you're not. I mean, did you two *really* talk about your choice?"

He chuckled and shook his head. As he leaned back in his chair, he said, "I get sick and tired of people telling me that my leaving was just my choice. She had a say in the situation. She could have come with me. I asked her. No, I *begged* her."

"Darling, no one wants to be seen as an accessory or as a piece of luggage when you're talking about the rest of your lives."

Gunnar crossed his legs at his ankles as he stared at his mother. "What are you talking about?"

"Why didn't you ask her to marry you?"

Now his mother sounded like Eboni.

"God, not you too." He covered his eyes with his hand. "Did you ever think that maybe I would have asked her once we got to Vegas?"

"Did you ever think that she would have wanted to know your full commitment before leaving?" His mother posed the query with a soothing voice. When Gunnar didn't respond, she continued. "My darling, if you want to move forward, you're going to have to address the past."

As much as Gunnar didn't want to admit that fact, he couldn't deny his mother knew the answer. He had to rip off this Band-Aid and allow the wound to be exposed to heal.

"And if you want the employees there to like and respect you, you're going to have to get to know them." Elizabeth offered a soft smile. "I'm not telling you to get all in their business. Figure out what makes them happy. Nothing deep. You'd be surprised what listening to people will do for them and for you."

"What would I do without you?" He leaned forward and held her hand.

"Be a mess." She smiled. "But you'd be my mess." She straightened herself up and looked at the TV monitor in the corner of the room. "Now, you want to watch *Judge Judy* with me?"

"You'll watch that but you don't want to watch me fight?"

"Honey, she doesn't shed any blood."

He laughed at his mother.

Gunnar managed to stay with his mother until about eight that night when she forced him to go back to the shop to help them close.

With great reluctance, he left her and returned to Press 'N Curl. By the time he arrived, the employees had the floors swept and their stations cleaned. Monica accepted payment from the last customer before she locked the front door.

"What a day." She fanned her round face as she waddled back to the desk. When she saw Gunnar, she blinked. "You came back. Didn't think I would see you again."

"I promised my mother I would help her. I can't do that if I'm not here." He watched Monica struggle to get her coat on so he ran to her and helped her. "Need to be walked to your car?"

"Nope. Been walking even before you were alive, and no one is going to mess with me." She walked out the back door.

"Wasn't a bad day for a Tuesday."

Gunnar turned to Shay when she spoke. Her smile lit up the corner where she had her station.

"Want to go for a drink?" she asked him.

Gunnar shook his head. "No, heading home. Thanks for the offer."

"That's okay." She walked up to him and lowered her voice. "There will be other offers on the table." She winked before leaving. "See y'all tomorrow."

Gunnar hardly even noticed when Tisha left. She walked out as quietly as she walked in that day.

"Hey, man, I told my boys that you were in town. Hope you don't mind." Tillman put on his heavy jacket.

Gunnar did mind. He never understood why people regarded him as a celebrity. He fought for a living. He didn't get wrapped up in the hype.

"I wanted to lay low while I was here. It's not about me. It's about my mother."

Gunnar's words must have come out a lot harsher than intended. Tillman simply nodded and walked out without another word.

Gunnar heard a door open behind him. Eboni appeared from the bathroom. She scanned the area, probably to see if anyone else remained besides Gunnar. When she realized she had been left alone with Gunnar, she started packing up her things.

"Now you have time to talk." Gunnar followed her to the front desk.

"Um, sure." She put on her coat and wrapped a scarf around her neck. "I would hate for you to manhandle me like you did that kid earlier."

"Do you really want to save that community center, or did you just tell me that to mess with me?" He glared at her as he waited for her answer.

"What? You think I would say that as some sort of joke? You saw the place."

He saw her honey-brown complexion turn crimson before his eyes. Good to see her passion. He wished she had displayed that earlier.

"I don't know. I throw out this suggestion about working on Mondays and you get bent out of shape about it. I thought you'd be happy about the idea. I thought you would be happy that I am trying." The fact that she looked so shocked surprised him considering how passionately she'd talked about this center. "I'm used to fighting. And I'm used to fighting by myself. I thought you would have my back, and you left me hanging. I can't want this more than you. If this whole thing was a joke, then I don't think it's funny. You made me look like an idiot and you wasted my time."

Eboni's jaw tightened even more. When she didn't say anything, Gunnar shook his head and marched toward the office.

"Go to hell."

Those three words stopped him in his tracks. Gunnar turned and gave her his full attention.

"First you come back out of nowhere to be by your mother's side after all these years. Did you ever think to come home to visit me? Maybe even call me? My number has not changed since you hopped on that bus to Vegas." She wrapped her scarf around her neck until she thought she would choke herself. "Then you come back like some knight in shining armor ready to fix everything. You can't, and do you know why?" She peered up at him. "Because in a week or two or even in a couple of months, you'll be gone again. You'll get everyone rallying around you like some great hero, then when Queen Elizabeth is all better, you'll pack up and go back to your home." She turned off the salon lights.

Gunnar followed her out of the shop. She locked the back door before heading to her car, careful to not slip on the ice.

When she turned back to him before getting into her car, Gunnar noticed the pink color that shaded the whites of her eyes. She wiped the back of her gloved hand over her eyes.

"You expect these people to follow your every word when the fact of the matter is that they don't know you. If Tillman hadn't said anything about your career, you probably would have kept that a secret, wouldn't you?"

"Did you tell them that we used to date?" Gunnar managed to ask in her tirade.

"I told Shay because she asked." She unlocked her door and threw her purse and bag inside.

"Exactly. If there's anything they want to know about me, they can ask."

Eboni shook her head. "Really?" She stared him in his eyes. "Why did you leave?"

Gunnar opened his mouth to explain. He hated to do it in the middle of a parking lot, but the situation called for it. Then his cell phone rang. Hoping the call came from Thane, he pulled it out of his pocket to check.

"It's Chuck." When he caught her confused expression, Gunnar remembered that Eboni had missed the bulk of his professional life. "He's my manager and trainer. One second." Gunnar answered the call. "Yeah?"

"Guns, what's going on with your mom?" From the noises coming from behind him, Gunnar knew Chuck had to be in the gym.

He heard clicking of the steel plates from the weights being slapped together. Gunnar also caught the sound of rope cutting the air like a jump rope being twirled around.

"She's still in the hospital." Gunnar glanced up at Eboni. She stayed as he talked.

"That's terrible. Is it bad?" Chuck asked.

"She'll have to have bypass surgery."

Chuck whistled. "Tough break. When is that going to happen?"

"Not sure."

"So you can come back and train for your fight with Seamus?"

Flames encircled Gunnar's head. "You want me to come back to train?"

Eboni groaned. "No shock. Running again. I'm out of here." She ducked into her car.

Now he felt like a heel. He didn't want to upset her. He needed Eboni to hear his side of the whole situation.

"Hold on, Chuck." Gunnar knocked on Eboni's window. After a beat, she powered it down. "Would you like to go out to dinner to talk about other fund-raising options?"

"No." She got out with an ice scraper and attacked her windows. "Sounds like you have other plans. Plus, I don't think it would be a good idea."

"What do you mean? It's just dinner." He attempted to follow her around the car to keep up the conversation.

Eboni remained quiet until she finished removing all the ice from her car. Before getting in, she pointed to his cell phone. "Finish your conversation. Your future is calling you."

"That's not fair. You don't know what this is about." He held up his phone.

"I know what it isn't. It isn't you planning on making a life here." She powered the window back up and drove home, leaving Gunnar by himself.

He put the phone back to his ear. "Look, I'm not leaving here until my mom has the surgery and she's one-hundred percent."

"Guns, you can't do that. You have a contract."

Gunnar could hear the tightness in his manager's voice as though he talked to him through gritted teeth.

"I also have a family. When my career is over, my family will still be here." Gunnar disconnected the call. He walked to the edge of the property and watched Eboni's car lights disappear into the night.

Maybe he deserved the cold shoulder from her. He wouldn't stop trying to regain her trust again.

Chapter 6

Eboni stormed into the apartment she shared with her cousin and aunt and slammed the door behind her.

"Hey, hey, hey." Craig shuffled out of the kitchen wearing his standard uniform of long denim shorts, a throwback basketball jersey, dingy sport socks, and sandals.

Her lazy cousin carried a large bowl filled with multicolored cereal and milk.

"Don't start with me, Craig." Eboni slammed her purse on the couch and ripped off her coat. "I had a rough day."

"Who's making all that noise out here?" A young woman padded out from one of the bedrooms. The dark-skinned woman wore one of Craig's T-shirts and nothing else.

Eboni hoped she came from Craig's room. Eboni hadn't met this new woman Craig had in his life. She wondered how a man with no job could manage to meet and attract anyone.

"Cuz had a bad day." Craig pushed his way past Eboni and plopped down on the couch. "Eb, this is Tryna. She's going to be staying here for a little bit."

Eboni glared at the woman with the micro braids slung over her shoulder. Before Tryna sat down next to Craig, Eboni snatched her purse and coat from the couch.

"What's a little bit?" Eboni split her glare between the duo.

"Why?" Tryna screwed up her face.

"I need to know if I should be getting money from you and splitting the rent." She turned her attention to Craig. "Or you can just pay her share."

Craig paid no attention to Eboni. His stare remained on the TV behind her. "I think my mom's social security check covers enough." He smirked and nodded.

Eboni stayed with her long-suffering aunt and her cousin to make sure Craig didn't rob the woman blind. Her Aunt Bettie had raised her after her mother passed away. She felt obligated to care for her. Too bad none of her other children felt the same way.

"Word on the streets is that your dumb-ass ex is back in town." Craig glared at Eboni. "True?"

Eboni crossed her arms over her chest. "Gunnar is not dumb."

She never thought she would be defending Gunnar.

"If he tries to jump me again like he did at the community center, I'll straighten his ass out." Craig scooped more cereal from the bowl and shoved it into his mouth.

Seeing Gunnar fighting her cousin had hurt Eboni to her core. Her love and her family had gone after each other with such hatred. For years, Craig had said that Gunnar jumped him for no reason. When she'd heard Gunnar say that he'd beat up someone who'd talked about his family, she'd started to rethink part of her resentment toward Gunnar.

"That was years ago, and the two of you were teenagers." Eboni took off her shoes as she spoke to her cousin. "You can't get over that after all this time?"

Craig didn't wait until he'd swallowed his food. He said, "No. He used to walk around the neighborhood and stuff like he was hot shit because Queen adopted him. I wanted to knock him down a peg or two."

Eboni shook her head. "God, Craig, grow up. He's moved on. So should you."

Even though she didn't like Gunnar's decision to leave, one thing she knew for sure. He'd never lied to her. Good or bad, he'd always told her the truth.

"Get a job and get a life." Eboni stomped back to her bedroom.

"Mind your business!" Craig screamed after her.

Eboni stewed in her anger throughout the night and into the next morning. Going home to Craig and his new houseguest hadn't helped her headache either.

She got dressed and headed out to the salon. When she pulled into the parking lot, she spotted Gunnar's vehicle as she'd suspected she would. She got out and marched to the back door. If he wanted a second or third round with her, she would be ready.

As soon as she stepped into the salon, an unusual aroma hit her. She took in a deep breath and thought it smelled like roses. Until she saw the two huge bouquets sitting on the front desk, she wondered where the scent emanated.

Gunnar walked out of his mother's office. As usual, he had his hair pulled back into a ponytail. He wore a plain blue T-shirt this time along with his jeans and black boots.

"Good morning." His low voice rumbled over her.

"It's morning." She pointed to the flowers. "Who are they for?"

"One is for the group."

Eboni poured herself some coffee. "Tillman will like that." She laughed.

That brought a smile to Gunnar's face. "The other is for you."

She wanted to be impressed. She should have been impressed. She shook her head. "So you went to your mother's flower shop and got a couple of vases of roses for free and think that that's going to impress me." She shrugged.

"Would it help to tell you I arranged them myself?"

As Eboni got closer to the arrangements, she saw signs of his handiwork. Broken stems left some rose buds drooping to the side. The baby's breath all looked bunched to one side instead of spread out throughout the plants. The ribbon wrapped around the vase looked like her three-year-old cousin had tied it.

Eboni turned back to Gunnar.

He shrugged. "Gideon has a knack for those things. I wanted to show you and everyone else that I'm here to help. Although I can't commit to the future, I'll do whatever I can while I'm here."

She bit her lip to keep from falling for his charms. "Thank you."

"Wow." Gunnar framed his face with his hands and dropped his bottom lip. "That must have hurt to say that."

"Yes, it did. Don't expect to hear that from me again to you." She gave him a jab in his side as she headed to the front desk.

"I know I screwed up in the past. I'd like an opportunity to explain my actions. Will you please go out to dinner with me so that I can tell you what I was thinking?"

Eboni stared at him, trying to see if she could figure out his motive. "I still don't think it's a good idea. We work together and I'm cool with that. But we can't do dinners or lunches."

"What about breakfast?" His voice dropped to a dangerously low octave.

Eboni swallowed. "Let's just concentrate on work."

One by one, each employee showed up for work except for Shay. The closer it got to opening time, the more Eboni realized the flighty woman might be a no-show.

As of late, Shay had gotten better with getting to work on time. Looked like she'd started to slip back into her old habits.

"Where's Shay?" Gunnar stood by Shay's station.

Tisha shrugged and turned her back on him. Tillman and Monica exchanged glances.

"What's that? You two know something?" Gunnar approached the duo.

"Shay does what Shay wants." Monica left her glasses resting at the end of her bulbous nose. "We were lucky these past few months that she showed up to work at all, let alone on time."

"I don't know why Queen keeps her." Eboni shook her head. "Yes, she does great work, but she has to be reliable."

"She has a lot on her plate. Don't judge her until you walk a mile in her shoes." Tillman pointed to Monica with his curling iron.

"Oh, no." Tisha covered her mouth with her small hand as she looked out the front of the building.

"What's wrong?" Eboni asked. Then she turned to the front door. "Damn."

Gunnar stared outside. "What's up? Are you all talking about that woman?"

"That woman is the devil's little sister. Shay is the only one who has managed to make her happy besides your mother. Neither one of them are here. Mrs. Pratt is going to raise holy hell up in here." Monica rubbed her temple.

"Don't be ridiculous. She can't be that bad." Gunnar went to the door and unlocked it. "Good morning."

The short woman, who looked like she wore a gray wig under her large church hat, barreled into the salon. Tillman and Tisha turned their backs to her, pretending to busy themselves at their stations.

Eboni watched the ball of fire in her green velvet tracksuit march toward Shay's station. When she got there and discovered Shay missing, she turned to the group.

"Where is she? Where's my girl?" Mrs. Pratt stomped around the salon.

"Monica is trying to call her now." Eboni peered down at Monica who only stared at Mrs. Pratt like an oddity. Eboni had to kick Monica's chair to get the woman to move to action.

"Calling her right now." Monica started dialing numbers.

"With the weather and road conditions, she may have had some car trouble or have been in an accident." Eboni kept the smile on her face to keep the woman on her side.

No such luck.

"I have an appointment. I demand to get my hair done today." The customer pulled off her hat, which removed her gray wig as well. She uncovered a wig cap that hid her real hair. "Where's Queen Elizabeth?"

"In the hospital still." Eboni spoke slowly and in a low tone.

In that moment, two other customers came in for Tillman and Tisha. Relief covered both of the stylists' faces as they got their clients into their chairs.

After taking a deep breath, Eboni said, "I'd be more than happy to do your hair, Mrs. Pratt."

The elderly woman assessed her from top to bottom. Then she shook her head. "Too much weave in your hair. You won't know what to do with me."

Eboni blinked at her blunt assessment. She didn't think she had so much weaved-in hair that it would turn off customers. She felt the sting of embarrassment fill her cheeks.

"We can call you when Shay shows up if you don't want to wait." Eboni tried not to let this woman see how her words had bothered her.

"I am not leaving." To prove her point, Mrs. Pratt occupied Shay's chair. "Y'all had better figure something out."

Gunnar stepped forward. "I'll do your hair."

Silence filled the salon. Even the other customers looked over at Gunnar as though he'd grown a second head.

He approached the woman. "But I'll only do it if you apologize to this young woman here. You insulted her when she only tried to help you." He crossed his arms over his chest. "So what's it going to be?"

Mrs. Pratt's mouth hung open until she gathered her wits about her to speak. "Who the hell are you?"

Eboni stood next to Gunnar as a show of solidarity. "Ma'am, this is Queen's son, Gunnar. He's here to help around the salon while she's recovering."

The customer stared at him for a moment before she pulled off her taupe-colored wig cap. "Do my hair."

Gunnar sank his crossed arms deeper. "Not moving until you apologize."

Eboni touched Gunnar's arm. His muscles felt like steel coiled under his flesh. "She doesn't have to do that."

He turned to her. "She absolutely does. We don't insult our customers. She had no right to be insulting to you or anyone else here." He returned his attention to the woman. "What's it going to be?"

Mrs. Pratt mumbled something under her breath before she glanced at Eboni. "Sorry." Then she huffed before she returned her gaze to Gunnar. "Now will you do my head?"

"That's better. Let me get you a towel and drape. Meet me at the sink." Gunnar went to the closet and pulled out a pink cover-up for his client and a couple of towels.

Eboni and the rest of the staff as well as the clients watched Gunnar work. Like he'd done it a million times, he wrapped a towel around the back of Mrs. Pratt's neck before lowering her onto the edge of the sink. He soaked her short gray hair, pumped some shampoo into the palm of his large hand and worked the cleanser into her hair until it formed into a white, sudsy lather.

As much as she didn't want to stare, Eboni couldn't break her attention. Not only had he managed to keep Mrs. Pratt quiet, he handled her like a true stylist.

After rinsing her hair, he applied a deep conditioner.

As he covered her hair with a plastic cap, she fussed at him. "I didn't ask you to do a deep conditioner."

"You also didn't tell me how damaged your hair is." He brought the short towel she had around her neck up to her ears and signaled for her to hold it for him. Then he wrapped her hair with a mesh netting head wrap, capturing the towel in the netting. He tied it off so that it protected her neck and ears.

"I'm tender headed. Don't put the heat on high." She sat under a bonnet.

Gunnar lowered it and adjusted some settings before engaging it. "I've got it on a cooler setting. You let me know if it's too hot for you."

The elderly woman nearly let a smile peek through before he walked away. He went to an empty station and prepared it. Eboni took that opportunity to approach him.

"What are you doing?" she asked in a low tone so that Mrs. Pratt, nor any of the other customers in the salon, could hear her.

"Doing a customer's hair." Gunnar didn't stop moving as he set out a comb, brush, a spray bottle of a leave-in conditioner, and a hair cream. "The cart with the hair curlers still in the same spot?" Before Eboni could answer, he peered over her and spotted it in the corner.

Gunnar went to it and pulled it over to his station. His station. Since when did this mixed martial artist have a hair-styling section in a salon? In what universe did this happen?

Gunnar rinsed out the conditioner from Mrs. Pratt's hair. After a roller set, he left the mature woman with silvery, crisp, shiny small curls over her head. She looked polished. She looked good. The style looked like something Queen Elizabeth would have done. Eboni couldn't hide her astonishment.

"Finished." Gunnar twirled his client's chair so that she could look at herself in the wall-length mirror.

Mrs. Pratt admired herself after a small gasp escaped her lips. She raised her hand to touch her hair but stopped. "Beautiful work." She stood and faced Gunnar. "I would expect nothing less from Queen's boy." She reached into her pocket and pulled out a folded bill. While pressing the tip into his hand, she said, "You haven't lost your touch."

"He's done your hair before?" Eboni knew Gunnar had worked in the salon as a teenager. She didn't remember him doing hair.

"Long, long time ago. I didn't recognize him until you mentioned he's Queen's son. She taught you well."

"Of course. I always listen to my mama." He smiled as he ushered her to the front desk.

"Next time, don't be so heavy-handed with the oil-sheen spray."

"Just tell me I'm good at what I do."

The woman they had dubbed as the devil's sister laughed. "You know you are. Will I see you here next week?"

Eboni held her breath until he answered.

"I'll be here for as long as my mother needs me."

That answer must have pleased the client, who smiled even wider. She paid for her services and left.

"What the hell just happened? Am I dreaming?" Tillman curled his client's hair with a curling iron as he stared at Gunnar. "For as long as I've been here, that woman has never been nice. Shay is the only one who can put up with her ornery ass."

"Watch your language. There are ladies present." Gunnar stared at his mother's employee until Tillman broke the stare first to concentrate on his client.

To see Gunnar take control gave Eboni hope that he had changed. If she could only know the reason why he'd left her, left their life, she might be able to fully forgive him.

"My mom has done Mrs. Pratt's hair ever since her shop opened." Gunnar went to Monica. "The first hair I did was Mrs. Pratt's."

Tisha gasped.

"Yeah, talk about trial by fire. She was rough on me as a kid. Yelled at me. I learned that if you treat people the way you want to be treated, they'll meet you halfway." He addressed Monica. "Any money I earn doing hair will go to Eboni for the center."

"What?" Eboni wanted to move closer to Gunnar but her feet remained cemented to the ground.

Gunnar strolled over to her. She noticed his confident gait. Her heart pounded out of control.

"I don't want to be a distraction. I really want to help." He took her hand and pressed Mrs. Pratt's tip into it. "You won't take my personal money. You can at least take the money I earn here as a stylist. Deal?"

Eboni couldn't move. She could barely blink. In that moment, everything changed on its head.

The front door crashed open. Gunnar blocked Eboni's body as he faced the door. That move garnered him more cool points in her book.

She peered around him and breathed a sigh of relief when she saw Ant at the door.

"What are you doing here?" Eboni made her way around her protector.

"I heard Guns was here." He stared at Gunnar and hopped around like a lovesick teenager. "Man, I thought you were lying." He pointed to Tillman. "I love you, man." He ran up to Gunnar and pulled him in for a half hug. Then he scanned the place. "This is a beauty salon."

"You're quick." Eboni laughed and got the others to do the same.

"I thought with you being here and running things and with a name like Press 'N Curl, you'd turned the place into a gym."

This time, Gunnar laughed. "This is my mom's spot. I'm just helping her out." He approached the short man with the wild Afro. "If you want, I can hook you up." He touched Ant's hair. "Maybe some braids. Or I can shape up your 'fro or just cut it down all together."

Ant ducked away from him. "Are you crazy?" He patted his hair like a beloved pet. "I'm not getting you to touch my hair. Maybe Tillman."

"I don't know, man. He does good work." Tillman shrugged as he put on the finishing touches to his client's hair.

As much as she didn't want to admit it to herself, Eboni started to get that same feeling.

"That's all right." He headed to the door. "Good to see you here."

She liked having Gunnar at the shop. She couldn't let him back into her life that easily.

* * * *

Gunnar found himself developing a rhythm at the salon. He stayed out of the stylists' way unless they needed something. Then he became Johnny-on-the-spot. He even noticed Eboni staring at him a bit more.

Styling Mrs. Pratt's hair had gotten him noticed. He still felt Eboni remained guarded around him. By giving Eboni some space while being available to her, her walls started coming down. Gunnar would have to thank his mother for the advice. He wanted to get closer to Eboni, and her plan had worked.

Shortly after lunch, a young white man walked into the salon carrying an African-American toddler on his hip.

"I don't have an appointment." The slim man waved his hand in the air. Both he and the little girl wore the same style fur-lined coat. "I need help." He sat the child on the reception desk counter.

"Don't set that baby up here." Monica pointed to the customer who'd styled his hair to mimic a rollercoaster ride. He had it stiffened with enough hairspray and mousse to withstand any hurricane or tornado.

"Easy, Monica." Gunnar walked up to the customer. "How can we help you?"

The customer grabbed his child and took a couple of steps back from Gunnar. "Look, I'm not here to be ridiculed."

Gunnar scanned the area around him. "What are you talking about?"

"I've encountered guys like you before. Big, tough guys. Think it's funny calling me names like fag or gay boy or wanting to talk about me having a black daughter."

Gunnar raised his hands in the air. "Sir, I've never met you. I would never be disrespectful to you or your child. I'm here to help."

"I don't want *your* help." When the little girl wiggled too much in his arms, he placed her on the floor to run around. "Terral is so much better with this than me." The man covered his eyes with his hand.

Gunnar thought he heard him sobbing.

The girl walked up to him and patted him on the leg. "No cry, Dada." Her hair had been styled in two disheveled Afro puffs.

Yes, this man definitely needed help. Gunnar could tell that guys that looked like him had picked on this man for his lifestyle. To Gunnar, it didn't make a difference.

Eboni brought over a cup of water to the customer. "How can we help?"

He dabbed under his eyes and brought his child over to him. "My husband's is out of town. He normally does Alicia's hair. That's her name. Alicia after Alicia Keys."

"Very pretty name for a very pretty girl." Eboni crouched down to get eye level with the child.

"Thank you. I'm Marc, with a C."

"Nice to meet you, Marc. You need us to do her hair?"

The customer nodded. "She won't sit still for me. She won't let me wash it. She won't let me comb it. Her hair is a little, um, challenging."

Monica squeezed out an, "uh-huh," through her nose.

"Monica." Gunnar shook his head at her.

"Let me give her a try." Eboni opened her arms up to see if the child would let her pick her up.

"No!" Alicia ran to the other side of her father.

"Maybe it would be best if you held her while I did her hair?" Eboni stood.

"Come on, baby. Come to Daddy."

The child, in her pink tights with matching white dress with pink flowers over it, jumped into her father's arms. He walked her over to Eboni's station.

Gunnar strolled over to the cart with the hair curlers and searched the bottom shelf for his mother's secret box. She kept it for children like Alicia.

He watched Eboni attempt to remove the hair ties from the child's jet-black hair. Alicia twisted and turned her head so much that watching her could make a person seasick.

While Marc attempted to hold Alicia on his lap, Eboni managed to remove one rubber band from her hair.

"Oh, not good. Shouldn't use rubber bands on her hair." Eboni threw it away.

"I didn't know. Like I said, Terral normally does this." Marc reached up to remove the other rubber band.

As soon as it was removed, Alicia's wild hair made a halo around her face.

"Okay, let's get started." Eboni pulled out a wide-tooth comb.

As soon as Alicia saw it, she started crying and hugged her father around his neck.

"She does the same thing with me." Marc patted his daughter on the back. He looked like he wanted to shed some tears himself.

Gunnar had to help them out without pushing himself on them. Marc had made it clear that he didn't like Gunnar's kind.

In an exaggerated fashion, Gunnar plopped down in one of the chairs that sat under the hair dryer. Alicia, Marc, and Eboni turned to him.

Gunnar carried his mother's box in his hand. He backed his head up and bumped it against the hairdryer bonnet. He pretended the intentional ding hurt him so much that he had to rub the back of his head.

Alicia giggled and pointed to Gunnar.

Gunnar rubbed his head and then opened the box, being sure to keep the contents hidden from Alicia's prying brown eyes. He removed a pink plastic hair barrette shaped like a bow from the box and slipped it into the side of his hair.

Again, Alicia giggled. She wriggled off Marc's lap and padded over to Gunnar, being sure to stay a couple of feet from him.

Gunnar pulled a long yellow ribbon from the box and wrapped it around his ponytail holder. Then he retrieved a hair band with pink butterflies on it and put it at the front of his head. He realized that he'd made a fool of himself. In doing so, Alicia approached him.

He finally turned the box around so that she could see the contents. The dark-skinned beauty reached into the box and pulled out a white barrette. Gunnar turned his head for her and she attached it to the end of his ponytail.

"Pretty?" he asked her.

She nodded. Then she pointed to her hair.

"I could do that to you if you want. Can I try?"

Alicia nodded.

"Good. I'll do you like my mama used to do her clients." Gunnar slid down to the floor and rested his back against the chair.

The child, as though she'd done it before, sat on his lap as she busied herself playing with another barrette from his box.

Gunnar turned to Marc. "Are you okay with this?"

Marc, with his mouth agape, could only look at Eboni, who also looked as shocked. Then the customer finally nodded.

"Good." Gunnar pulled out a paddle brush and started brushing Alicia's hair.

The entire time he styled her hair, Gunnar told her stories and kept the child talking. By the time he finished, Gunnar had put eight cornrows in her hair and secured the end with a hair clip that Alicia had chosen. As long as he talked to her, she stayed still for him.

"All done, baby girl." Gunnar lifted the child to her feet and stood up himself.

Alicia ran to Marc and held her arms up to him. Marc admired the work and then looked over at Gunnar.

Before Marc could say anything, Gunnar said, "Wrap her head at night. She should be good with this style for a few days. If you need help with her hair, don't hesitate to come by the shop."

"Thank you so much. And I'm sorry for what I said to you before. It's just--"

"I know." Gunnar held his hand up. "I did the same thing to a kid who came in here." He glanced at Eboni, hoping she had caught his remorse. "I'm not one of those guys."

Marc nodded. "What do I owe you?"

"I didn't do a perfect job on her hair. Her parts are not straight. I could have made the rows a little tighter. No charge for this one as long as you spread the word to your friends to bring business here."

Marc helped his child on with her coat. "Done." He shook Gunnar's hand. "I don't know how to thank you."

"Keep your business with us." Gunnar looked down at Alicia. "Bye, Princess Alicia." He gave her a courtly bow.

"Bye-bye, Gun-Gun." She laughed at him as she walked out with her father.

Gunnar turned around and saw a sea of stunned faces staring back at him. "What?"

"How did you do that?" Monica asked first. "I have five daughters. I've never gotten them to be as good as that girl was for you."

"My mom taught me the secret." He pulled out the hair accessories he'd used to lure the child in to trust him. "Get down to their level. Make them laugh. Make them be a part of their hairstyle choices. Doesn't always work. For her, it did."

Gunnar walked by Eboni who stepped into his path. She stared at him but didn't say a word.

She cleared her throat. "Um, forgot one." She unclipped the white barrette Alicia had put in his ponytail. "Here." She handed it to him.

"Thanks." He hoped with the child and everything he'd done today that Eboni saw him as a different man.

When he gazed back at her and she smiled at him, he had a feeling he had begun to win her over. Getting to know Eboni again went beyond his mother's advice of sitting down with each employee and talking to them. Eboni started to look at him the way she used to when they'd first dated. Those stares alone ignited the smoldering flame that existed in him, the fire for her that had never been extinguished.

Chapter 7

At the end of the day, Gunnar helped clean up the salon until only he and Eboni remained. He had a feeling from the way she dragged out folding the clean towels that she'd planned it that way. When he thought about being alone with her, he felt like a teenager again and his stomach fluttered. He wondered what kind of damage they could do in her Smart Car.

As soon as Tillman walked out, she eased over to him in Elizabeth's office.

"Did I thank you for donating your money to me, I mean, the center?" She sat on the edge of the desk as he sat behind it watching the security monitors.

"It wasn't my money. I told you I would do what I could while I was here." He turned in the chair to face her. "Guess I'm not as cruel and heartless as you think."

"I deserved that."

Even with her working hard all day, Eboni glowed. Her golden skin tone brightened the dim office.

"Why?" Eboni started to chew on her thumbnail, a habit he hadn't seen her do since her junior high days. "Why was it so easy for you to come back for your mom?"

Gunnar stared at her for a moment, considering the ramifications of letting her get that close to him, that close to the truth, the ugly truth.

"My birth mother was a really bad drug addict and alcoholic." He spoke slowly and evenly so that she could absorb his words. "Gideon was too young to remember a lot of what she did. She used to beat us for no reason. Some boyfriend left her, she would hit me. She couldn't get her beer or wine for the night, she'd smack Gid." He raised his arm and showed her a small circular patch of discolored and rippled skin near his inner elbow. "See that?" He glanced up at her. "That's where she put out her cigarette on me because the store wouldn't sell me beer for her and they called social services. I was only eight."

Recalling that moment, Gunnar could feel his birth mother's cold hand wrapping around his wrist, pulling him forward, and stamping out her smoldering cigarette into his flesh. He covered his arm when his imagination got the better of him and he could feel the burning sensation over again and smell his scorched skin.

"I didn't know." Eboni attempted to stroke his face but he leaned back, not wanting compassion or pity right now.

"No one knew. I didn't tell anyone. I didn't even share this with Thane, who was a baby at the time. The three of us got bounced from foster home to foster home. Sometimes together. Sometimes not. It wasn't until the three of us landed with Miss Elizabeth Wells, as she was known when she took us in, that we started to have some stability." He recalled the moment he walked into her home. He distinctly remembered the doilies. She had them everywhere. He remembered how much he'd hated them back then. Now, whenever he saw one, it reminded him of her.

"She took you in. That was a good thing, right?" Eboni moved closer to him.

"Absolutely. As a kid, I didn't see it that way. I had been with people who'd taken me and my brothers in for the check. I lumped my mother into that category. So I made her life a living hell in every way possible. I screwed up at school. I stayed out late. I drank. I smoked pot. If I was offered drugs, I took them. I wanted to be out of this woman's house and this world." Gunnar saw the look of horror grace Eboni's face.

She wanted truth. He would give it all to her.

"When I got older, maybe twelve or thirteen, right before you and I met, I became uncontrollable. I stole from my mother. I treated my brothers like crap. They didn't get it. They didn't understand my pain because I didn't understand it. My mother did all she could to help me. She took me to church. I would steal money from the offering plate and sleep during the sermons. One night, I started to leave the house to hang out with this group of friends who were the dregs of society. Real pieces of crap. They were who I thought I deserved."

"What happened?"

"My mother tried to stop me. She told me not to leave the house. I told her--" Gunnar paused in this hurtful part of the story. His throat started to feel scratchy. He cleared it and barreled through the rest of the tale. "I told her that she wasn't my real mother and I cursed at her. I left the house and got up with my buddies. One of them points out a crazy lady in heels walking toward us. I turn. It's Queen Elizabeth herself."

Eboni smiled. "She followed you?"

Gunnar nodded. "She said in front of my friends that I was her son and that she loved me. She said that she had no problem showing me off to her friends and that she hoped I had that same feeling and wanted me to introduce her to my friends. When I told her I couldn't do that, she said that if my friends weren't good enough for me to introduce to my mother, then they aren't the people I should associate with."

Eboni nodded. "Sounds like something she would say."

"One of my friends got the bright idea that he was going to rob my mother in front of me. In that moment, something clicked. No one, and I do mean no one, had ever stuck their neck out for me. She did that. She actually cared enough to put her life on the line. I knew a few of those guys had weapons on them. Knives, brass knuckles, guns. They could have hurt her. As soon as one tried going after her, I jumped on him and beat him down. If she hadn't pulled me off of him, I would have seriously hurt him. I straightened up then. I went to church. My grades in school improved. I followed her teachings to the letter. When she told me to respect women, I did it."

Eboni chuckled. "You were and are the only guy who ever opened my door for me."

"My mother, the woman who raised me, will always be number one because she made me and my brothers a top priority in her life. I can honestly say I wouldn't be where I am today without her. She taught the three of us a good work ethic when she made us work in her businesses. That's when I met you I think."

She shook her head. "You don't remember?"

Gunnar racked his brain but couldn't recall the exact moment.

"You were at Oceanfront with your friends playing basketball. My girlfriends and I were doing double Dutch and some boy took our ropes. You ran after that kid and he screamed for dear life."

Gunnar laughed. "Yeah, I had a temper back then."

"You caught up to that boy and got our ropes back. You handed them to me and stared at me." She glanced at him. "Kind of like the way you're looking at me now. And you said--"

"I believe these belong to you." He remembered that moment now. He also recalled the softness of her skin.

"You said you liked watching me jump." As soon as she said it, her bottom jaw unhinged. "You pervert."

Gunnar laughed. "At least I was honest."

"Thanks again for taking on Mrs. Pratt."

He started to stand. "You didn't think I could handle her, did you?"

"She is a lot to take."

"It's okay. She probably recognized that I could do hair better than you." He shrugged.

"Excuse me?" She crossed her arms over her chest. "You had one good day with one or two clients and you think that that means you're a better stylist? Get real."

"I've only been here for two days and I've done more hair than you. All I've seen you do is slap your gums around." He made a talking mouth motion with his hand.

"Great of you to say that when there are no clients left to show you."

Gunnar raised his hands in the air. "I'm here." He took out his hair tie to allow his hair to fall freely about his neck and shoulders. Chuck would have hated to see it. "Work your magic on me."

Eboni snickered. "Are you serious?"

"Sure." He walked by her to the main salon. He wrapped a towel around the back of his neck and assumed the position. Of course, he had to scoot down in order to get his head into the bowl. "Work your magic."

"Okay. Just don't start crying when I make you look fabulous."

"I'll try to reserve my tears."

* * * *

Eboni couldn't believe Gunnar's challenge. She ran the water in the sink, testing the temperature with her fingertips before sluicing the water over his hair. She ran her fingers through it to make sure to fully saturate each strand.

Yes, that excuse sounded good in her head instead of the real reason of wanting to run her fingers through his silky tresses.

She started to choose the standard shampoo that all the stylists used but stopped herself and instead chose one with a flowery scent. As soon as she rubbed it in his hair, Gunnar opened his eyes.

"Don't think I don't know what you're doing." He screwed up his lips.

"You relax, Mr. Wells. I'll have you in and out in no time." Eboni had to bite her bottom lip to keep from laughing.

After rinsing the shampoo out, she covered his hair with creamy conditioner. Gunnar kept his eyes closed while she slathered the product.

"Sit up, please."

Gunnar did as instructed while keeping the towel wrapped around his neck. Eboni picked up a wide-tooth comb and started combing his hair to detangle it.

"Sharing time." Gunnar kept his head still while she combed. "I opened up about something personal. Time for you to do the same."

Eboni stopped combing for a moment. "Depends on what you want me to share."

"Your look. Why did you change it so dramatically?"

That question hit her out of left field. She stopped combing and rinsed off the comb as she collected her thoughts to answer. "I thought I looked good until Mrs. Pratt made that comment."

"I don't get your need for the fake hair. Your natural hair, from what I remember, was so full and healthy on its own." He attempted to turn around to look at her, but Eboni stopped him.

"Time to rinse your hair. Lean back into the sink again." She patted his back and helped guide him down.

She took her time rinsing the conditioner from his hair in hopes that he would forget his question about her hair.

"I think all the conditioner is out now." Gunnar opened his eyes.

"Who's doing the hair here?" To tease him, she sprayed water in his face.

He jerked his body and sat up. "You're going to pay for that one."

Eboni covered his head with a towel and patted his hair dry. "Just remember. I'm doing your hair."

She picked up a blow dryer and got his blond hair dry. After a few passes to the back of his head, she noticed something green and blotchy on his scalp.

"What's that?" Eboni attempted to part his hair to look at it.

"Hey, dry the hair, okay? It's nothing."

Gunnar's serious expression clued her in that it meant something more. Eboni wouldn't push him. He'd revealed so much already.

As his hair dried, she noticed how soft it became. She used a round brush to give him a slight curl.

"Really?" Gunnar gave her a sideways glance.

"You're supposed to trust me, right?"

Once done, she put her styling tools down and used her fingers to fluff out his hair.

"Can I see it?" He tried turning his chair, but she held the back of the chair.

"Not yet." Eboni needed this time to touch him without remembering his vanishing act.

"By the way, I agonized about coming back home." He lowered his voice. "My decision wasn't easy."

"Why?" She stopped styling to concentrate on his words.

"I couldn't face how I failed the most important people in my life." He stared at her. "You think it was easy for me to come here?" He shook his head. "It wasn't. I was afraid of what you would say to me. I think I would have rather you slapped me or kick me than tell me I'm a loser. I know that I am. I can't take it if I hear you say it."

Eboni couldn't break her stare from Gunnar until he tried to stand. She spun his chair around so he could see his reflection. "Okay. Now you can look." She fluffed his hair. "What do you think?"

Gunnar looked at his image. He turned his head from one side to the other. Then he stared at Eboni. "Looks okay."

"Okay?" She plucked the back of his head with her finger. "I made your hair look healthier and softer."

"Softer?" He cringed as he stood up. "Not a good way to describe a fighter."

"I think you should keep your hair like this. It makes you look--"

The word sexy got caught in her throat.

"Look like what?"

Eboni remained quiet. She mustered enough courage to speak again. "Not like a loser."

Gunnar stalked toward her. "What do I owe you?"

"Um, just keep working here and that'll do it."

"That's one way."

Eboni's back met with the counter. He stood directly in front of her.

"Here's another way." Gunnar cupped her cheek.

As though happening in slow motion, he lowered his head and pressed his lips against hers. The initial contact felt like nothing she remembered from their kisses in the past.

His breath offered her a bit of sustenance as he leaned in more to capture her mouth. As soon as his tongue slipped into her mouth, she wriggled away from him.

"This is a mistake." She ran to the reception desk to get her coat and purse.

"Wait. Let's talk about what happened. Let's go to dinner." He followed her around.

"No. I'll see you tomorrow." She ran from the salon and slipped and slid the entire way to her car.

Her heart pumped faster than her feet could carry her. Eboni hadn't expected to kiss Gunnar. Worst yet, she'd liked it. Loved it. To feel his warm lips on hers felt familiar. Her body still tingled as she thought about it while speeding home.

"What he must think now." Eboni shook her head.

She had been so firm on her feelings for him, or rather against him. He had walked away from her to pursue a career and hadn't looked back. Now her body fought with her mind.

Eboni pounded her fist on the steering wheel as she waited at a traffic light. Frustration overwhelmed her senses as she thought of ways to explain her actions. Maybe she would tell him that she'd kissed him because she thought he had been so sweet with that little girl earlier. Her mind tripped over thoughts of him caring for their daughter.

"Damn, snap out of it, girl."

A car horn blared behind her to prompt her to move when the light turned green. Instead of going to the center like she usually would after work, she headed home. She arrived at her apartment and nearly sprinted to her unit.

As usual, Craig and Tryna occupied the couch. Aunt Bettie, who sat at the glass-top kitchen table, busied herself putting together a jigsaw puzzle.

"You're home earlier than I thought you would be." Her aunt looked at her with her light brown eyes.

"Decided to come straight home instead of going to the center." Eboni left out the part about Gunnar.

A knock sounded at the door.

She glanced at Craig. "Expecting anyone?"

Craig shook his head. "You're standing."

"Such a gentleman." Eboni strolled to the door and peered through the peephole.

The person standing on the other side kept their head down. She saw the top of a hat but nothing else.

"Who is it?" she asked through the door.

A pause lingered before the person said, "Eboni, open up, please, so we can talk."

Eboni's heart stopped and dropped to the floor. Gunnar had followed her home.

"Who is it?" Craig asked from the couch.

Eboni ignored him. She whispered into the door. "Go home. I'll see you tomorrow."

"No. We need to talk right now."

Eboni heard something rustling behind her. By the time she turned around, she saw Craig in his pajama pants and a different basketball jersey stomping up behind her.

"Move out the way." Craig grabbed the doorknob.

"Don't open the door." Eboni grabbed her cousin's arm and tried pulling him back.

No such luck. Craig opened the door. She watched him blink as he stared at Gunnar. It took her cousin a hot second before Gunnar's identity registered.

"I can't believe you have the nerve to show up to my home." Craig adopted a fighting stance where he stood with his feet apart, his fists raised and his head bobbing back and forth. He looked ridiculous.

"I came here to talk to Eboni. You and I have no business together." Gunnar stood his ground. Once he made his statement to Craig, his full attention returned to Eboni.

Eboni couldn't look into his eyes. Each time she did, she remembered the kiss that turned her insides into mush.

"If you're bothering my cousin, it's my business." Craig took a step forward.

Gunnar didn't move. "Cousin?" He brought his stare back to Eboni. "I didn't know you two were related when--"

"Go home, Gunnar. We can talk tomorrow. I have to take care of my aunt." Eboni nodded behind herself.

"Shut that door. Y'all are letting the cold in." Tryna threw a blanket over her bare legs.

"Yeah, that's all that's getting in here. Go home, man. And don't you ever talk to my cousin again." Craig started to close the door.

"I think the last time you tried telling me what to do, it didn't go so well for you." This time, Gunnar did take a step forward. "Like I said, you and I have no business together." He gazed at Eboni. "I'll see you tomorrow."

Craig managed to slam the door in Gunnar's face before Eboni could respond. "I can't believe he came here like anybody would want to see him." He lumbered back to the couch. "Now that old boy has some money, I should say that he hurt me bad in that fight so I can collect some of his dough." He laughed along with his girl.

"Not funny, Craig." Eboni put the chain on the door and turned the deadbolt. "Drop it. It was a long time ago."

"Have you dropped it? I didn't see you running into his arms like you'd missed him."

If Craig only knew.

"You don't get it." Craig plopped down on the couch. "Yes, it was years ago, but we fought hard. That dude was trying to kill me over what? Some dumb-ass comments about his brothers and shit? If I'd had one more minute with that fool, I could have knocked him out. I could have ended him and you wouldn't have anything to worry about now."

"Stop talking." Eboni rubbed her temple. "I'm so tired of hearing about this old grudge." Too bad she didn't mean the one between Craig and Gunnar.

She hid herself in her bedroom. Now Eboni had an entire night to run over arguments to keep from kissing Gunnar again. As it stood, Gunnar had managed to lower her defenses.

Chapter 8

"I hear you're going to be able to come home today." Gunnar held his mother's hand.

He'd gotten used to visiting her before going into the salon. Today, he really needed to talk to her.

"Yes, darling. I'll get to come home finally until it's time to do that awful surgery." His mother patted his hand.

Gunnar stared at the floor. He couldn't get the kiss with Eboni out of his mind. Following her to her home had been a knee-jerk reaction to wanting to get an explanation. Did she like the kiss as much as he had?

"What are you thinking about?"

Gunnar snapped out of his thoughts and brought his gaze up to his mother. "Nothing. Thinking about salon stuff."

"You know I can always tell when you're lying. Tell me the truth."

Gunnar sat up straight. He took a deep breath before speaking. "I kissed Eboni yesterday." He glanced at his mother to check her reaction.

Elizabeth remained stoic.

"She freaked and ran home. I wanted to talk to her, but she wouldn't even let me in her apartment." He squeezed his mother's hand.

"So go to work today and ask her out to dinner tonight."

Gunnar shook his head. "I've been asking her out to dinner since I got back. She's turned me down flat."

Queen Elizabeth picked up her nurse call button and pressed it frantically.

A beep sounded before a voice came through a wall speaker. "Yes, ma'am?"

"I'm feeling a little flushed. I think something is going on."

Gunnar stood. "What?"

"We'll be right there."

"Ma, what's wrong? What can I do?" Feeling helpless, Gunnar fluffed up her pillows and tried to make her comfortable until the nurses showed.

"You want to help me? Act like I'm sick so I can stay here another day."

Gunnar blinked. "What?"

"You need a day to spend time with Eboni without me being there to cramp your style."

"Ma, I--"

"Quiet." She winked at him. "Get your girl."

When the nurses arrived, Queen Elizabeth put on a show, clutching her chest and putting the back of her hand to her head in typical swooning fashion. Although the EKG didn't support her claims, the nurses and doctor all agreed that she would have to stay another night for observation.

Thanks to his mother, Gunnar had an extra night alone. Could he get Eboni to the house? If he did, what would he do in a confined space, especially now that he knew she wanted him for more than just a fundraiser or a business owner?

* * * *

For the first time since working at Press 'N Curl, Eboni contemplated calling in sick. She couldn't get any sleep just thinking about Gunnar's firm lips. God, that kiss. It ignited feelings in her that she hadn't experienced in years, not since before Gunnar left for training.

She waited for as long as she could before stepping into the salon. As usual, Gunnar had already opened the place. He had the coffee going. He'd opened the blinds to allow the sun to stream inside. As soon as his gaze fell on her, he stopped moving.

Eboni opened her mouth but nothing came out. She wanted to tell him to stay in his spot and not get closer to her. Gunnar started walking toward her until the back door opened. He stopped when Tillman entered the room.

"Another day, another dollar." He patted Gunnar on the back as he headed to his station.

Tisha came through next, being as quiet as a mouse as usual.

Eboni put her purse and coat in the office. By the time she turned around, she found Gunnar blocking the doorway.

"We need to talk. Go to dinner with me tonight." Gunnar didn't ask.

"We shouldn't."

He started to move into the office when the back door slammed again. Eboni saw a hand on Gunnar's shoulder. He turned around to reveal Monica standing behind him.

"The diva is out in her car." Monica nodded her head behind her.

"Who?" Gunnar asked.

"Shay?" Eboni suspected who Monica meant but wanted to be sure.

Monica nodded. "She won't talk to me. Maybe you two can do something with her."

Eboni started toward the door but Gunnar stopped her.

"I got this. This is part of my responsibilities, right?" Before Eboni could answer, Gunnar walked out.

She breathed a sigh of relief, thankful that Shay's drama would give her a little break from the tension between them. She would just have to figure out a reason she couldn't go to dinner with him.

* * * *

Gunnar walked out to the back parking lot. As soon as he caught Shay sitting in her red sedan, she turned her head away from him. He came up to the window, trying hard not to show his irritation.

He'd had Eboni cornered. Gunnar had felt her starting to melt, starting to yield to him. Now he had to deal with some temperamental employee.

Gunnar knocked on the window. "Come on out, Shay."

Shay kept her face away from him. "Go on back in to the salon. I'll be in there in a minute. I just need to get myself together."

Gunnar sighed. This must be the internal problems Eboni had alluded to when he asked her about the salon and the staff. He really didn't have time for this. As he thought that, his mother's words rang through his head. She would have told him to get to know each person.

"Shay, what can I do to help you get out of the car?" He crouched down next to the window.

The fact that she wore sunglasses made her look like a diva. "I told you I'm fine. Go in the salon. I'll be in there in a minute."

Gunnar looked at his watch. He really didn't have time to play her games. "If you aren't in there in five minutes, I'll be back out here again."

Shay put her hand up to the window. "Whatever."

Gunnar stood and went back into the building. He noticed Tillman leaning against his station.

"Couldn't get her out of her car?" Tillman asked.

"Does she do that often?" Gunnar went directly to the coffeepot to get something to warm himself up.

"Every once in a while." Tillman dropped his gaze to the floor. "Not in a long time though. Just recently."

Instinct told Gunnar that Tillman knew more than he had revealed. "Do you have any appointments this morning?"

Tillman glanced at Monica. "Anything on the books?"

Monica glanced at the computer screen. "Nope. Free as a bird until after lunch."

"Waiting for walk-ins."

"Want to catch some breakfast? My treat." Gunnar grabbed his jacket from the office.

"For real? Hell, uh, heck yeah." Tillman slipped on his jacket and walked out the back door with Gunnar. "Queen never did this with us."

"I figured this will be a good way to get to know you." Gunnar glanced at Shay, who remained in her vehicle.

She turned her head as soon as she spotted him.

"I'll drive." Gunnar unlocked his rental.

"Is this Hummer your ride?" Tillman jumped into the vehicle.

"I'm renting it while I'm in town." Gunnar got into the driver's side and started up the vehicle to warm it up as fast as he could. "Is the Providence Restaurant still open?"

"Yeah. I thought you would want to go somewhere fancy."

Gunnar shook his head. "I'm not that kind of guy."

Gunnar drove over to the small restaurant at the end of a shopping strip close to the hair salon. The waitress sat them in a booth in the corner. After they'd received their drinks and placed their orders, Gunnar started in with his questions.

"So how long have you been working for my mother?" Gunnar took a sip of his jet-black coffee.

Tillman blinked. "Man, it's still wild to me that Queen is your mom."

"I've been getting that most of my life."

"Yeah, I can imagine. I've been working at the salon for only six months. It's cool. I didn't go to barber school, so most barber shops wouldn't give me a chance." Tillman leaned back against the bench in the booth and chuckled. "I remember I had lied to your mom about my experience. I knew how to do hair because my grandma and my mom did it out of their homes for years."

"So you learned the same way I did." Gunnar smiled.

Tillman nodded. "No one would hire me without some piece of paper saying that I could style. Queen interviewed me and I told her that I went to cosmetology school. Of course, she asked me which one. I lied again and made up some place so that she couldn't do any research, but your mom is smart."

"That she is." Gunnar had been caught in many a lie back before he'd reformed himself.

"So she called me on my lie. I thought she was going to show me the door. Instead, she gave me an opportunity. She allowed me to style one customer." Tillman held up his index finger. "If the customer and your mother liked it, I could stay. If the style was whack, I would be out of there." He held up his hands. "As you can see, I'm still here today."

"Did you ever get your license?" Gunnar didn't ask to bust the guy.

"Of course. Your mom put me through school while I worked for her. She's a smart, cool lady."

Gunnar nodded. "She absolutely is. Always willing to give people a chance."

By the end of his story, the waitresses brought their breakfasts. Gunnar had picked this place because he knew they made their food quickly.

"Do you see yourself working in a salon the rest of your life?" Gunnar asked.

Tillman shook his head. "Eventually, I'd like to do what your mother did and own my own salon. I'd like to think that one day your mom will make me manager, but no one can get by Eboni. She's her girl."

Just hearing Eboni's name prickled Gunnar's skin. He had managed to get her out of his mind during breakfast. Now the kiss invaded his thoughts again.

"Does that bother you that my mom relies on Eboni so much?"

Tillman shook his head. "I haven't earned that spot yet. Eb's been with your mom for years, and she works hard. She's one of those sisters that you know will do something special with her life. When she's not working, she's usually at that center. If she's not there or at the salon, she's taking care of her aunt. That woman is focused."

Gunnar knew that from being with her before. Now he wanted to kick himself for letting her go.

"Don't worry, man. I won't go after her." Tillman raised his hands in the air as he laughed.

"No worries. I know you won't."

The waitress collected their empty plates and left their check.

"How are you so sure about that?" Tillman wiped his mouth and finished off his sweet tea.

Gunnar chuckled. "Because you know. You're gay."

The smile slipped down Tillman's face. He grabbed his jacket and jumped out of the booth.

Gunnar managed to throw some money on the table and paid the check with the cashier while keeping Tillman in his sights. He chased after Tillman who stomped down the street.

"Tillman, wait. Did I say something wrong?" Gunnar wriggled into his coat as he chased the big man.

Without a word, Tillman stopped and turned around to him. "Did someone say something to you?"

Gunnar shook his head. "No."

Tillman leaned his head toward him. "Then how did you know?"

"I've been around enough closeted guys to recognize the signs. Although I don't have a problem with anyone's sexual preference, I have noticed you staring at my ass when I look in the mirror at the salon."

Tillman put his hands behind his neck and leaned his head back. "Fuck. If you know, I wonder if anyone else knows."

"I'm guessing you haven't come out yet."

Tillman shook his head.

"Want to come back to the truck? We can talk there where it's warmer."

Tillman waved his hand in the air. "I don't want to talk about it. Not with you. You wouldn't understand."

"I wouldn't understand feeling out of place and being different?" Gunnar cocked his head. "Come on. I won't say a word to anyone. It's your business. As far as I'm concerned, it doesn't change you as a person."

Tillman snickered. "Wished my family felt that way."

"If they love you, it won't matter who you fall in love with."

Tillman wagged his finger in Gunnar's face. "If you say a word to anyone, I'll beat your ass."

Gunnar squared off in front of the man. "I won't say a word. Now get your finger out of my face before I break it and your hand."

After a quick beat, Tillman lowered his hand.

"Come on back. As far as I'm concerned, we had a great breakfast." Gunnar nodded toward his vehicle. "Let's get you back to work."

Tillman said nothing on the walk back to the truck or on the trip back to the salon. After Gunnar parked, Tillman grabbed Gunnar's arm.

"Thanks."

"For what?" Gunnar turned off the vehicle.

"I don't know a lot of straight guys, especially guys like you, who wouldn't have ridiculed me. You're pretty cool."

Gunnar shrugged. "I don't feel that way sometimes. But I'll take the compliment."

"So these closeted guys you know, any of them MMA fighters like you?"

Gunnar chuckled. "If you want me to hook you up, just ask."

"Hook a brother up."

Gunnar laughed. "First thing's first. Get your life in order before you try involving other people."

Tillman grabbed the handle to the backdoor of the salon and opened it. "Taking that advice yourself?"

Great question. Gunnar couldn't answer that. Luckily, he wouldn't have to right now. As soon as Gunnar walked into the salon, he felt the energy in the room. The place had been empty when he and Tillman had left for breakfast. Now the waiting area overflowed with clients.

"What in the world is going on?" Gunnar asked.

"It's about time you two came back," Eboni snapped. "As soon as you left, all of these people showed up." She pointed at Gunnar. "All of them looking for you."

Tillman leaned over to Gunnar. "Gonna break her finger?"

"All of these people can't be here because I'm here." Gunnar saw more women than men.

"There he is," a woman squealed.

Oh shit.

"Why are they here?" Gunnar removed his jacket and headed to the office.

"Marc posted on his Facebook page about this hot guy working at this salon who did wonders on his baby's hair," one woman said as she stared directly at Gunnar. "He was so right."

"We need help." Desperation filled Eboni's eyes.

"I'll get to my station." Tillman went to his area and quickly accepted the next client.

"If there are no empty stations, I'll take over the shampoo station." Gunnar stood by the sink.

"Are you serious?" Eboni asked as she put curlers in a woman's hair.

"I'm here to help." Gunnar hoped Eboni believed that.

"It would have helped if you and Tillman hadn't gone out for breakfast." Eboni glared at Gunnar and then brought her attention back to her client.

Gunnar didn't want to start a fight in front of a roomful of customers. He would play nice until he could get her alone. He'd had enough of her frosty attitude.

* * * *

Eboni had never seen the salon look so busy, not since the salon's heyday when the main road had gone by the place. As much as it bothered her to have Gunnar here, she had to admit his presence brought in customers. With customers, the salon would bring in a lot of money. She could use her money for the center.

With all the business, Eboni still had a way to keep her distance from Gunnar. She needed the space. The more he asked her to dinner, the more she wanted to tell him yes. Between his accommodating nature and the kiss, she found it hard to resist him. If she couldn't rebuff his advances, she would make him not want her anymore. Being difficult with him seemed to do it.

"I'm ready to shampoo the next person." Gunnar wiped his hands on the white terrycloth towel he had draped over his shoulder.

"I have one for you here." Monica pointed a woman in Gunnar's direction.

Gunnar reached up to get a towel to wrap around the woman's shoulders. "Looks like I'm out of towels."

"Great." Eboni stomped by him. "So professional." She ducked behind a curtain that separated the main salon from where their supplies and washer and dryer hid.

Right now, the washer had a full load of towels in it, probably thanks to Gunnar.

"Hey." Gunnar followed her into the area. "Is there a reason you're giving me a hard time out there? I'm doing the best I can."

"Maybe you need to do more." Eboni reached up to retrieve clean, folded towels.

She heard the wobbly shelf creaking before it started to come down. Gunnar pressed his body behind hers and held the shelf before it toppled on top of her. In his position, he had her pinned between his rock-hard body and the vibrating washer.

"What are you doing?" Eboni swatted him with her free hand.

"I'm trying to keep this shelf from falling on your head. Stay right there." He used his other hand to brace the shelf against the wall, which pushed his body into her even more.

"I've been here longer than you and know about this shelf. It falls off the wall all the time. Move." When Eboni tried wiggling from under him, Gunnar's hand slipped and he nearly dropped the shelf.

"Will you stop moving? You're going to make me drop this on you. Stay right there!"

"I'm a lot tougher than you think. I will not break if this shelf falls on me." She pushed her back against his chest. "Move."

"Stay right there." Gunnar pushed his body forward. "I almost have it."

As though wanting in on the combative exchange, the washer hit its spin cycle. The sudden vibrations sent a rippling feeling throughout Eboni's body, enough that she had to brace her hands on the lid. Between the steady tremors and the feeling of Gunnar against her ass, she closed her eyes and imagined the two of them in bed, limbs intertwined, and Gunnar deep inside her.

He must have felt something as well. Eboni felt the length of him through his jeans. It pressed against her hip until he moved around and got it between her cheeks.

"Move." This time Eboni said it for a different reason. She wanted to feel Gunnar move his hips and slide the length of his manhood between her cheeks.

He must have felt the same way. Gunnar thrust his hips ever so slowly and accompanied the motion with a low groan. "Stay right there."

He managed to hold the shelf against the wall with one hand. He wrapped his free arm around her waist.

Eboni gripped the hand he used to hold her. The vibrations from the old washer increased in intensity. Or maybe Eboni imagined it. Either way, she didn't want this sensation to stop.

"Move," she said with a harried breath.

"Stay right there," Gunnar quickly followed.

He brushed himself against her. When she felt his chest against her back, Eboni didn't want the feeling to end. His warm breath feathered over her ear and cheek.

Eboni leaned her head back and closed her eyes. When he moved his hand around her waist, she let him. She pushed her back against him and undulated her hips.

She had the smooth corner of the washer nestled between her legs, vibrating against her now-throbbing clitoris as her former lover rocked his body back and forth. Her nipples hardened and strained against her lace bra. Her heart pounded so hard, it sounded in her head.

Gunnar's staggered breathing pattern matched hers. Again, she imagined her and Gunnar entwined in bed, and him giving her the hot, hard sex she'd been missing for years.

The washer continued its mad gyrations, screeching and squealing like an active sexual partner. Gunnar exhibited so much control. Not only did he continue supporting the wobbly shelf, he kept his arm around her body, protecting her, controlling her, driving her crazy like only he could.

He eased his hand up her body until he stopped under her breast. Gunnar swept his large thumb under her sensitive tit, now heavy with need. He continued grinding against her ass, which, in turn, rubbed her clit against the washer.

Eboni's body trembled. She gripped his hand, interlacing her fingers with his oversized digits in an effort to ground herself. She felt his head lowering down to the side of her face.

"You feel so good." The rumble of his chest vibrated her body.

Between the washer and Gunnar, Eboni didn't stand a chance. He cupped her breast. He circled her hardened nipple with his thumb, a brazen move considering only a thin curtain separated them from a roomful of clients.

Gunnar's breath warmed the shell of her ear. As soon as she felt his lips touch her face, Eboni emitted a small cry.

Damn, did she just come from a touch and a washing machine? The spin cycle ended and it sobered Eboni to her situation.

"Oh my God." She put her hand over her mouth.

"I didn't mean to--"

Eboni turned her head away from his view. "I need to--"

"Go get yourself together. I'll take care of things out there." Gunnar released his hold on her and used both hands to carry the shelf down from its position on the wall. He set the board on top of the washer and dryer.

"Are you two making the towels or something?" Shay burst through the curtain. Since she still wore the same sunglasses from this morning, she really pushed the diva envelope.

"The shelf was falling off the wall. Almost hit Eboni." Gunnar moved away from Eboni and allowed her to run to the bathroom.

"Get yourself together, girl. We have a roomful of folks who need their hair did." Shay disappeared back through the curtain.

Before Eboni could duck into the bathroom, Gunnar said, "We're going out to dinner tonight. I'll pick you up at seven."

This time, Eboni decided not to fight it. She nodded before going into the bathroom. In one fell swoop, Gunnar had proved he could have her again.

Chapter 9

Gunnar hadn't meant to rub his body against Eboni's like some horny teenager. She'd felt so good and smelled even better. That still didn't excuse his bad behavior.

He dressed in jeans and a black pullover sweater. He pulled his hair back in a ponytail. When his cell phone rang and he saw Chuck's name across the screen, he ignored the call. The last time Chuck had called, it had killed the vibe between Gunnar and Eboni. He wanted this night to be perfect.

Gunnar arrived at Eboni's apartment right on time. It surprised him to see her waiting for him outside.

"I would have gone up to your apartment to get you." Gunnar opened the passenger door for her and helped her into the tall vehicle.

"I know. My cousin is acting a bit crazy. I didn't want any drama tonight." Although she had her hair styled in a high bun, she'd left one tendril to fall down the side of her face. She tucked her hair behind her ear.

Gunnar closed the door and went over to the driver side of the vehicle. After he got inside, he wasted no time in telling Eboni how he felt.

"You smell wonderful." He smiled as he put on his seat belt.

"Thank you. You clean up well yourself."

"I try." Gunnar drove down to a quiet section of Virginia Beach to a strip mall. The parking lot area had a few cars.

After parking, Gunnar jumped out and went over to her side. He helped her out and kept his arm around her waist to help her navigate over the ice in her heels. He wanted her to feel secure in his arms again, like when they had dated before. He protected her like no one else he had ever been with, like a man should.

At one point, Gunnar felt her hand on his side, like she wanted to push him away. Fortunately for him, she allowed him to hold on to her. She must have loved the contact as much as he did.

"What is this place? Eboni peered around the lot. "I've driven through this area before, but very quickly."

"Amoré. Some of the best Italian food in Virginia Beach." Gunnar opened the door to the dimly lit restaurant.

The intimate space had a few patrons at various tables. Candles illuminated each one. The young waiter seated them at the back of the restaurant, away from the front window as Gunnar had requested.

"I've never heard of this place before." Eboni sat down in the chair Gunnar held out for her.

"Back in the day, this used to be the spot." Gunnar sat across from her. "Mom used to bring me and my brothers here for lunch after church to teach us about table manners."

Thinking about his mother telling him and his knucklehead brothers to sit up straight and use their napkins made him laugh.

"What's so funny?" Eboni crossed her legs.

"My mom. Can't believe what she made us do when we were younger."

After they gave the waiter their drink order, Gunnar didn't want to waste another moment without telling Eboni what had been running through his mind since that afternoon.

"Before we go any further, I want to apologize." He held up his hands as though surrendering.

"Apologize for what? We had the most profitable day at the salon that we've had in months. Morale seems to be up. I think I even saw Monica smiling." She laughed.

"You know what I mean. The thing between us and the washer." Gunnar remembered the sensation so vividly that he had to adjust himself in his chair when his cock started to get hard. "I started out trying to save you from getting hurt and ended up grinding and groping you like I was sixteen again. It was inappropriate and I'm sorry."

"You're not sorry." Eboni shook her head.

Gunnar sat up taller. "I am--"

"Nope. You *apologized*. But there's nothing sorry about you." She smirked as she sat back in her chair.

Gunnar laughed. "You think you're clever, don't you?"

"I have to keep up with you." She twirled her finger around the flower pattern on the tablecloth. "I was with you the entire time. I could have told you to stop or pushed you back." She dropped her gaze, waited a moment, and then reconnected to his stare again. "I liked feeling you against me."

He leaned forward and lowered his voice. "In case you're worried, I erased the security-camera footage."

"You did? I didn't even know that was possible."

"I've learned a lot of little tricks these past few years." He winked at her.

The waiter dropped off their drinks to Gunnar's relief. After Eboni's salacious look and response, he needed something to help him cool down. He downed his ice water and handed the empty glass back to the waiter with a request to bring another along with a pitcher.

The young waiter disappeared again after Gunnar ordered a caprese salad. He glanced up from his menu and found Eboni staring at him.

"Why are you looking at me that way?" Gunnar asked.

"You. You're different."

"Different than what? Other men?" A strange tingle went up his spine as he thought about Eboni with another man.

"Different from when I knew you." Eboni kicked her foot back and forth, showing off her long legs and her sexy black booties.

"I was a boy when you knew me. I didn't know my head from my a--, uh, foot." Gunnar closed his menu and kept his full attention on Eboni. "When I left to go train, I wasn't running from you. You know that, right?"

Eboni pushed her menu to the side. With her jaw set in, she looked defiant. "I didn't know what was going on. One minute, you were saying you would be by my side. The next minute, you were telling me this fighting thing was something you had to do."

"It was. It is. I had no real skills. My only job prospect was construction or working in my mother's salon for the rest of my life."

"You say that like it's a bad thing." She crossed her arms over her chest. "Why do you act like I needed a million dollars to be happy?"

"Because you *deserve* it. I couldn't ask you to marry me if I couldn't support you and a family."

"You never asked me to marry you."

"Because my plan was to make a success of my life and then ask you." Gunnar thought about his plans from years ago. He saw his life turning out so differently.

"So what happened? Last I checked, you're the champion."

"I thought you didn't follow my career."

Eboni pursed her lips.

"By the time I'd made something of myself, too much time had passed. I didn't think you would want me anymore."

"You know what would have been nice when you're planning *our* lives? If you'd allowed me a little bit of input." She looked away from him.

That hurt him more than him leaving.

"You're right." Gunnar waited until she looked at him again before he continued. "I'm so used to making my own way. I never wanted you to feel shut out. I'm sor--" He caught her glare. "I apologize." He put his hand out on the table. "Can we at least try to be friends again?"

Eboni looked at his hand for a while before she finally put hers in his. Gunnar squeezed her hand. If this was his last intimate moment with her, he wanted to cherish it. Too bad the waiter returned with a large plate of salad and two smaller plates.

Ready to get their dinner orders, the young man stood by with a smile and an expectant expression.

"If you don't mind, I would like to order for you." Gunnar proposed.

"After the conversation we had? Really?" Eboni cocked her head.

"Trust me."

"No. I got this." Eboni lifted her menu.

"Say what you want to order and I'll say what I would have ordered for you on the count of three." Gunnar held up his hand with his middle three fingers sticking up prominently. "One." He smiled and brought down his ring finger. "Two." He lowered his middle finger so that only his index finger remained in the air.

"This is ridiculous. We won't order the exact same--"

Gunnar cut her off and said, "Three."

At the same time, they both ordered a salmon dish with a side of bread. Even the waiter couldn't keep a straight face. Eboni jutted her menu to him.

Gunnar ordered spaghetti with clams and mussels, his usual order.

As soon as the waiter walked away, Eboni asked, "How did you know that's what I wanted?"

Gunnar smiled. "I know you."

"You are so full of it." She leaned back. "You probably saw what page I was on when I was looking through the menu."

"Lots of items on one page. How could I have guessed exactly what you wanted unless I really knew you?" With great reluctance, Gunnar broke from her grip to serve up the salads. "This is part of the reason I love this place. They make all of their mozzarella. So fresh and delicious."

Eboni gave him a suspicious look until she took a taste. When he saw her eyes roll to the back of her head, he knew she'd experienced what he had so many years ago.

"It is really good." Eboni rubbed her stomach.

It was then that Gunnar had noticed her outfit. Eboni wore a Japanese-inspired long-sleeved black satin dress that had satin-covered buttons going from the neck down between her breasts and off to the side over her waist to her hip where it stopped at the top of an almost obscene slit. "If I haven't told you already, you look gorgeous tonight."

"You can thank your mother." Eboni scooped more salad on her fork. "She made this dress for me a few years ago. I haven't had an opportunity to wear it." She smoothed her hand down her side.

Gunnar had to look away otherwise he would topple the table and pull her on to his lap to finish what they had started earlier.

"So tell me about you. I feel like I've been dominating the conversation here. Any secrets you want to share?" Gunnar finished his first plate of his salad and went in for more.

* * * *

Did Eboni have any secrets? Plenty. Had she told Gunnar one crucial secret, he wouldn't look at her like he wanted to rip her clothes off her body. He would be calling her the monster, a coward. Part of the reason she had been so short with him lately had everything to do with not getting him back into her life. If he hated her, it would make it easy for him to leave…again.

Then they'd kissed. They'd shared that strange but steamy moment by the washer. Here at dinner, the tension hung thick between them. She couldn't tell him. Until she knew he would forgive her, she would keep some secrets to herself.

"There's not that much to tell." Eboni picked at her salad. "I'm still taking care of my Aunt Bettie."

"Is she Craig's mother?" Gunnar asked.

Eboni nodded. "He doesn't work. If I left her alone with him, he would take all of her money, and she gets so little of it to begin with. A couple of weeks before you left, she had a stroke. I make sure she takes her meds, goes to her doctor appointments, and eats right."

"That's pretty awesome. How did I not know you were doing that when I was here?" He finished off his second plate of salad and offered Eboni some more.

She shook her head, barely through her first plate. "You had a lot of stuff going on. I didn't want to burden you."

Gunnar dropped his fork. "Wait a minute. You jump all over me about me making decisions for us, but you don't share something this important with me? It's the same thing."

"No, it isn't."

"It absolutely is. You made a decision about us." He ran his hand over his head. "Good thing I'm in a forgiving mood."

"Ha-ha. You're so cute."

"Not as half as cute as you."

The laughter subsided at the table. Fortunately, the waiter showed up to remove the empty plates and refresh their drinks.

"So you never dated anyone else after me?" Gunnar asked.

"I never said that." Eboni liked teasing Gunnar.

He sat up taller. "Well?"

"I dated here and there." She kept her stare on her drink, only peering up at Gunnar on occasion. "Nothing serious."

If Eboni wasn't mistaken, it looked as though Gunnar breathed a sigh of relief.

"I went out with Grover Maddox once."

Gunnar's eyes went wide. "You dated Mad Maddox? That dude was crazy."

"We didn't date. We just had lunch after church one day. He seemed nice." She shrugged. "He was the first guy who didn't immediately tell me he could help me forget you. Little did I know that church boy had a million and one hands."

Gunnar balled his large hand into a fist.

Eboni had to diffuse this bomb before it went off. "He tried to touch me and I made him cry like a girl. Don't ask me what I did."

"Do I need to go down and talk to him?" Gunnar's knee bounced like he wanted to fight.

"Calm down. This was almost nine years ago." She held up her hand. "That man is married with seven kids of his own now. I guess he can't keep his hands off his wife either."

"He wouldn't have approached you if I hadn't left."

Eboni got quiet. Luckily, their dinner arrived and she didn't have to confirm what he already knew.

She took a bite of her fish. The buttery, flaky flesh danced on her tongue before she swallowed it. If Gunnar had planned on ordering this meal for her, he certainly knew her tastes.

Halfway through the dinner, Gunnar started up their conversation again.

"If you weren't at Press 'N Curl, what would you be doing?"

Eboni shrugged. "I would be doing something for the community center. That place really saved my life. It gave me a place to go when things got rough at home."

Gunnar nodded. "I could see you as a teacher. You would be so good with children."

Eboni grabbed her water and took a hefty gulp.

"You're very patient and open." Gunnar smiled at her.

She didn't respond except to match his smile with one of her own.

"Hold on." Gunnar picked up his napkin and wiped the corner of her mouth. "Got it."

He sure did. She loved his touch. The way he looked at her really started her heart. Her skin tingled. Each time she looked into his eyes, her nipples hardened. Deep in her heart, she knew this moment should be the one to share her secret, her pain.

Gunnar had revealed himself to her and told the truth about what had broken them apart. She started to tell him, but the words had gotten choked in her throat. The evening had gone by so well, Eboni didn't want to break the easy flow. She would have to reveal the secret later.

At the end of the meal, Eboni had to collapse back in her chair. "So much wonderful food. I would have never stopped at this restaurant if you hadn't brought me."

"Never judge a book by its cover." He winked at her.

After paying for the meal and leaving a sizeable tip, Gunnar stood and held his hand out for Eboni. She accepted it, hoping he didn't notice how her knees buckled when he touched her.

He helped her put on her coat before walking her to his rental.

"It's so strange that they had to keep Elizabeth for an extra day." Eboni climbed into the SUV with Gunnar's assistance.

After getting inside, Gunnar turned up the heat. "Not really." He sort of snickered before he said, "She said she wasn't feeling very well so that she could stay another night." He glanced over at Eboni when she didn't say anything. "It was Mom's way for me to ask you out tonight. She was giving me my space by faking a medical condition."

Got to love Queen Elizabeth.

Eboni grinned. "Can we have some coffee at your place? I don't want to go back to my apartment right now."

"I'm sure my mom has coffee or tea in her kitchen." Gunnar remained quiet as he drove the nearly empty Virginia Beach streets. "You could spend the night if you wanted."

"I didn't bring a change of clothes." Eboni wrung her purse straps. "But with it being so late, I think I'd like that."

"I'm sure my mother has something in her closet that can fit you."

Eboni didn't think about what other clothes she could wear. She wanted to get out of her attire and figure out a way to get Gunnar naked as well.

After a rocky start to dinner, it sure looked like it would end smoothly.

Gunnar pulled the truck around to the backside of the house in front of the detached garage. As he'd done all night, he jumped out of the truck and got her door for her. Eboni could get used to this chivalrous behavior.

He unlocked the back door and let her inside. "Let me get your coat."

Eboni shrugged out of her black coat and let Gunnar hang it up in the closet along with his own. "I've always loved Queen's house. It feels so inviting."

"Funny. I feel the same way." Gunnar went into the kitchen and knocked around, looking for mugs and some tea or coffee. "Found some instant coffee. Is that okay?"

Eboni strolled around the living room, looking at pictures of Queen with her boys. "That's fine. Just need something to warm up my bones." She didn't think Gunnar would be keen on warming her up with his body, although the heat between them challenged her assumption.

She walked toward the kitchen. Gunnar had catered to her all night. The least she could do would be to help him. Besides, she liked looking at him and being close to that incredible body.

She stood in the doorway. "Anything I can do to help?"

Gunnar glanced at her. He shook his head. "You go relax. I found some chocolate chip cookies. I should have known Mom would have had those around here. They're her favorite."

Eboni sauntered into the kitchen. She picked up a cookie from the plate and took a nibble. "Homemade."

"Yes, she loves to bake." Gunnar moved over to the other side of the kitchen.

"Did you taste one?" She followed him to where he stood.

"No. Not yet."

Eboni held up the cookie she'd just tasted. "Take a bite."

He shook his head and went back to the stove. "No, I'll wait to have one with my coffee."

She watched him carefully. "Are you avoiding me?"

Gunnar crossed his arms over his chest. "Why would you think that?"

"Because whenever I get close to you, you move away from me." To prove her point, she walked toward him.

"I need spoons." Gunnar went to a drawer on the other side of the stove...away from her.

"See." She laughed.

Gunnar turned toward her. "Okay, fine. So you caught me." He took a deep breath.

"A big MMA fighter is afraid of little ol' me. Why won't you get near me? Afraid I'll bite you?"

"I wish." He braced his hands on the counter with his back to her before he finally turned around. "I want you so badly. I'm afraid if you get too close to me, I'm going to make a fool of myself somehow."

"A fool how?"

"I want to kiss you again." He stared at her lips. "If I kiss you, I'll want to touch you. If I touch you, I'll want to--" Gunnar stopped himself before he finished his thought.

Eboni licked her lips. "Then I think we need to talk."

She didn't really want to talk. She wanted her man. Her body ached to have him touch her, move inside of her, connect with her in a way she hadn't felt in years.

The kettle whistled on the stove, and Gunnar turned off the gas and moved it from the heat. "I think I need to take you back home."

Chapter 10

Eboni shook her head. "No. I don't want to go home. I want us to talk." She approached Gunnar and put her hand on his arm.

That simple touch sent a surging heat through his body. Although Gunnar stayed in his spot, he couldn't stop his heavy breathing. "You don't understand what you're doing to me."

"Tell me." She moved closer to him.

"It's like dangling steak in front of a starving man." He billowed the front of his sweater to get some cool air against his chest. "You want to know the last time I had sex? It was the last time *we* had sex." Gunnar motioned his hand between their bodies. "I haven't dated anyone else. I haven't had any other type of sex either. You were right about the groupies. There were plenty of them willing to do whatever I wanted." He shook his head. "I didn't want any of them. I don't even watch porn. I wanted to stay focused on training and fighting. All night, hell, all day I've thought of nothing but having sex with you."

Eboni blinked and took a step back. "Wow."

"Yeah. Lack of sex makes a man angry."

She snickered. "No wonder you remained undefeated."

"I thought I'd be okay. But having you here and looking the way you do and smelling so good, I just keep thinking about--"

"What?" she interrupted him. "Tell me."

"I wouldn't be gentle. I would rip every one of those buttons off your dress to get to your body. I'd destroy your panties just to get to you."

"How do you know I have any on? I might not be wearing any."

"Christ, don't tease me." He moved by the doorway of the kitchen and pulled a chair in front of his body.

Gunnar felt himself trembling and hoped Eboni didn't notice. He gripped the top of the chair so hard he heard the wood crack.

"It looks like we have a great opportunity here. It would be a shame to turn our backs on it." Eboni looked like she glided toward him.

Gunnar held up his hand. "What I don't want is for us to do something that we'll regret. I can't have you hating me again."

Eboni remained quiet, regarding him for a moment. Then she spoke. "I never hated you. I just didn't understand." She took a deep breath. "There's a difference between now and then. First of all, we'll be going into this with eyes wide open. I know when Queen gets better that you'll be going again. No surprises this time. You have a career. You have to defend that title. Second, I want you, too. We're adults. I think we can handle a little fling without it being something more."

Gunnar shook his head. "I'm not going to treat you like a fling."

She moved in closer to him again. "Good. Then don't. Treat me like a woman you truly care about."

Gunnar approached her.

Eboni halted him with a hand to his chest. "And treat me like a lady. You may have had my body years ago. I'm going to make you appreciate it now."

He framed her small face in his large hands. "Baby, I'm not a virgin. You know that." When he pressed his lips against hers, everything stopped. He didn't want to pull from her when he did.

"Every dog can learn a new trick." Eboni smiled.

"Let me get your coat."

She furrowed her eyebrows. "You still want to take me home now?"

"No. I want you to keep warm when we walk over to the apartment over the garage. I can't do what I want to do to you in my mother's house."

Eboni went to the closet to get her coat. "What about yours?"

"I'm hot enough." Gunnar put some cookies into a plastic storage bag. When he turned to Eboni, he held them up. "For later."

After locking up the main house, it didn't take Gunnar long to walk Eboni over to the garage. He unlocked the door and ushered her inside. As he climbed the stairs behind her, it took every bit of strength for him not to strip out of his sweater and start undoing his jeans.

He wanted to feel her skin next to his. He wanted to touch every part of her body.

* * * *

Eboni's skin felt electrified as soon as she stepped into Gunnar's apartment. He took her coat and hung it on a coat rack next to the door. Then he took no time in commanding her mouth again.

Gunnar put one arm around her waist and another hand to the side of her face as he kissed her. Eboni couldn't help but touch his chest. She brushed her hand over his hard nipple through his soft sweater.

He moaned and slipped his tongue into her mouth. Eboni touched the tip of her tongue against his. She lifted the hem of his sweater and found his nipple again. As soon as she touched it, he broke from the kiss.

"How do we get you out of this dress?" Gunnar put his hand on her shoulder.

It felt as though it weighed a ton. The heft of it reminded Eboni of Gunnar's size. He'd gained what looked like a good fifty pounds of muscle since last she seen him.

"This is where patience comes in to play." Eboni took a step back.

Gunnar, accepting her challenge, started undoing each button, starting by her neck. By the time he got down to her breasts, she felt his hands shaking.

Eboni thought for sure he would give up being Mr. Patient and just rip open her dress as he had stated earlier. After a breath, he continued down her body. Once he undid the final button, Gunnar breathed a sigh of relief.

"Very nice, but you could have just unzipped me." She turned her back on him to reveal the hidden zipper that went all the way down her back.

"Oh, you are going to get it for that." Gunnar removed his sweater and tossed it to the floor.

Eboni imagined the wild expression he carried scared many of his opponents. To her, she desired him even more. As she backed from him, she slipped her dress down her arms and placed it on the living room couch. She watched Gunnar scan her body.

She imagined that he enjoyed the view of her new black lace bra and matching thong panties. From the way he kept his stare down at her body, and from the prominent bulge in his jeans, she felt she guessed correctly.

Gunnar stalked Eboni. She didn't want to appear like she fled from him. When her back met the wall, she realized she had blown her cool demeanor. He didn't blink. Gunnar picked her up and wrapped her legs around his body as he held her under her backside. He carried her to his bedroom.

With great gentleness, he placed her on his bed. From her vantage point, she caught the view of his erection. Before she could give him relief by undoing his pants, he grabbed her ankle and removed her bootie. Then he did the same for the other foot. When Eboni started to pull off her stockings, Gunnar shook his head.

"Keep them on." He gave her a sly smile.

As though giving her a striptease show, Gunnar kept his stare on her as he undid his jeans. Eboni licked her lips as she anticipated the view. She hadn't seen his penis in more than ten years.

Gunnar sat on a chair in front of her and took off his boots. She scooted to the edge of the bed as she watched him. With his boots off, he stood again.

"Come here." Eboni curled her finger at him.

Gunnar stood and strolled to her. When she reached for his jeans to push them down, he held her wrists. She brought her attention up to his face.

"Let me appreciate your body first." Gunnar released her and undid her bra.

He slipped the garment down her arms and tossed it on the floor. When he reached down for her panties, Eboni moved back to the center of the bed. Gunnar slipped her thong down her legs.

He growled as he admired her. "I didn't think it would be possible for your body to get any better than the last time we were together."

"Stop it. I was fat back in the day."

He shook his head. "Then and now, I saw you as this incredible beauty. Don't ever put yourself down."

His compliment had Eboni looking at Gunnar like the man she'd always wanted. It took her a moment to start breathing again.

Gunnar crawled over the bed and hovered his body over hers. Eboni writhed under him. She damn near begged him to touch her. As though reading her thoughts, he lowered his head and arrested her mouth with his firm lips.

Eboni snaked her hand behind his head. With her nimble fingers, she removed the band holding his hair back in a ponytail. His soft hair flowed around his face and tickled hers.

Gunnar moved his body down hers, kissing her cheek, her neck, and the center of her chest. He cupped her breasts in his large hands.

Her breathing increased. He used his thumbs to circle her hard nipples. With the pleasure he gave her with his hands, she found it hard to believe that he used these same hands to inflict pain or even render opponents unconscious.

"Mmm, Gunny." Eboni arched her back.

Gunnar took that moment to cover her nipple with his mouth. He flicked his tongue over her hard, sensitive pebble. With each pass, Eboni's body jerked.

He kissed over her chest as he made his way to her other breast. He licked and suckled it like he'd done the other. When he sucked her whole breast, she thought she would climb out of her skin.

Eboni gripped a fistful of his hair. That sensation kick-started a reaction she didn't expect. Gunnar gave her playful nibbles over her stomach before making his way down between her thighs. She had to let his hair go but she didn't mind this release.

He pushed her legs apart. Eboni felt her juices flowing from her pussy, thinking about what would happen.

Being the tease she remembered, Gunnar first blew his warm breath over her. The sensation sent her body into a shivering fit. She'd become the addict getting reintroduced to the drug she'd spent years weaning herself off of and swore to never do again.

Tingles rippled over her body when he kissed her inner thighs dangerously close to her core. If Gunnar didn't relieve her soon, she would be taking care of herself in front of him. She preferred him over her own hand.

Gunnar didn't disappoint. He swiped his tongue the entire length of her vagina, ending the sweet trip at her hardened clitoris.

Eboni sucked air between her teeth and gripped a handful of his comforter. "Feels so good."

He pushed his tongue inside her as far as he could while he circled his large thumb over her clit. The sensation forced her to sit up. Her legs shook. She didn't want to come yet. She didn't want to be the first one to break. Then again, she'd broken simply feeling him and an old washer going through a spin cycle.

Eboni held the back of his head as she released a scream. When she thought he had finished, Gunnar moved his mouth up to her clit. He twirled his tongue around it as he let a finger delve in her moist channel.

He brought one hand up to her breast and held it as he continued pleasuring her with his mouth. Eboni thought for sure Gunnar had become an octopus at that moment.

Her gyrating hips pressed her mound into his face until, once again, he made her climax.

"God, stop. You're killing me." Eboni relaxed against the bed.

"I'm not done appreciating your body." Gunnar stood and pulled down his jeans.

"It was a suggestion, not a dare." Eboni propped her upper body on her elbows as she admired his firm ass.

When he turned around to her, she had to blink. Eboni didn't remember Gunnar being so long and thick. As he made this way to the side of the bed to get in, she stopped him. She sat on the edge and put her hands to his hips as she looked up at him.

"If you do it, I'm going to come right now."

Eboni offered a grin. "You may not like it." She grabbed the base of his shaft. "I may not be any good." She swiped the tip of his weeping cock with her tongue. The saltiness of his essence hit her tongue. "You may be begging me to stop after a while."

She covered his thick mushroom tip with her mouth and held him there. Unable to fit him entirely in her mouth, she continued to hold him around his base as she moved her mouth down to her hand. When she brought her mouth back up to the tip, she heard Gunnar emit a long, low groan. His shaky thighs gave her enough indication that he liked what she did.

Eboni brought her mouth down on him again, tightening her lips around his shaft. She felt a subtle throb pulsating in her mouth, against her tongue. Her fisted hand brushed against the nest of his sandy-blond pubic hair.

She used her free hand to cup his tightening balls.

"Sweet Jesus!" He held her shoulders.

Eboni increased her speed, moving her mouth up and down the full length of him. Gunnar's breathing became loud, quickened, and erratic. Until he put his hand on her head, she thought she could make him climax.

Eboni didn't want him touching her hair, feeling her imperfections, the tracks of her weave. She pulled back and peered up at him.

"I have condoms in my purse." She winked.

"I'll protect us both." He bent down and kissed her quickly before he went to the dresser.

There, he pulled out an all-black box. Eboni watched him opening the box and ripping one of the packages from the string. He opened it and rolled the condom down the length of him.

Eboni rolled to the side and patted the bed. "On your back, King Kong."

Without argument, Gunnar positioned himself on his back. Eboni straddled him, holding his cock. She braced her free hand on his muscular chest. To tease him, she brushed the tip of his dick back and forth between her wet nether lips.

Gunnar held her hips. She felt him trying to pull her down as he rose his hips up. To control this, Eboni eased the tip of him inside her and stopped. The connection halted Gunnar's movements for a moment. When she brought herself down all the way to the hilt, he exhaled.

"Bigger than I remembered." Eboni rocked herself back and forth on him.

"Tighter than I remembered."

He held her upper arm and pulled her down to him. When her chest met his, he wrapped his arms around her body and thrust his hips up to impale her deeper.

"Yes!" Eboni framed his face and kissed him hungrily, nipping his lower lip.

Gunnar moved one hand down to her ass and squeezed it. In that moment, Eboni felt so connected to him.

He turned her over onto her back. It didn't take the giant long to take over the situation. The first thrust hit her deep but felt so good. To encourage him, she wrapped her legs around him.

"Waited so long to do this again." Gunnar made his thrusts slow and even.

Eboni grabbed his ass and pulled him in to her. "More. I need you."

Just saying the words exposed her vulnerabilities. Eboni didn't want to need Gunnar. As he penetrated her, she felt open.

Gunnar increased his speed. She removed one hand from his ass to claw his back. When he curved his hips, the tip of his penis hit a sweet spot.

"Yes!" Eboni coiled her arms and legs around his body and froze as she absorbed the intense orgasm. She could die at this moment and be happy.

Gunnar, on the other hand, needed more. He scooped her under her back and sat up on his knees. He kept her on his lap as he positioned himself at the edge of the bed. The control and power he had over her body made her feel lightheaded and desired all at once.

She leaned her head back, which allowed Gunnar to kiss her neck. He licked the column of her neck up to her chin as he continued pumping into her.

Wanting more, needing more, Eboni brought her face up to connect her gaze to his. She pressed her forehead to his as she stared into his eyes.

"Yes. Yes. Yes!" Despite the light dusting of snow floating down outside the window, Eboni felt sweat rolling down her back between her shoulder blades.

Gunnar held her breast and gave her a slight pinch on her nipple.

"Wait." Eboni grabbed his hair, now slick from sweat. "Not yet. Please."

Gunnar nodded, nonverbally letting her know she could let go. Treating her like she weighed as much as a feather, he stood and carried her to a waist-high dresser. He pumped into her. He shook the dresser, banging it against the wall until they both screamed in absolute pleasure.

Eboni felt him stumble once as he moved back to the bed. After falling back, Gunnar released a loud chuckle that shook his body.

"Damn, that may have been worth the ten-year wait." He ran his hand over his head.

Still with him connected inside of her, Eboni leaned forward and rested her head on his chest. She had to tell him or never do this again. Having sex with him opened her heart up more than she had expected.

"What now?" she asked in a whisper.

"I don't know about you, but I'm ready to go again." He gave her a playful slap on her backside.

"Sounds great. You have to promise me one thing." Eboni lifted her head and stared at him. "We shouldn't tell anyone about this."

Chapter 11

After a sleepless night, Gunnar remained in bed, staring at the wood beams, trying to figure out the woman next to him, who seemed to have no problem getting her sleep. It still stunned him that Eboni wanted to keep what they had done a secret. Not that he'd planned on telling the world that they'd had sex. He had hoped that she would at least acknowledge she still had feelings for him.

Gunnar peered over at the digital clock next to the bed. With it being a few minutes after six in the morning, he knew he didn't have a lot of private time left with Eboni. They both had to get dressed, and he had to take her home. Plus, he hoped that they would be letting his mother go home today.

"Wake up, Eboni." Gunnar nudged her shoulder.

She moaned and snuggled down deeper into bed. As a result, her ass brushed against his dormant cock. The touch alone woke it up.

Gunnar thought about tasting her again. He loved her sweet but almost salty flavor. Thinking about it made his dick hard. The tip of it brushed against Eboni's ass cheek.

"No more." Eboni shook her head. "Too sore."

Gunnar chuckled and kissed her temple. "No sex."

"No?" she asked with her eyes closed. "Just a little?"

Gunnar peered behind him at the other nightstand. He found the remaining string of condoms. "Make up your mind, sweetie." He ripped open a package. "You want it or not?" He rolled it on him underneath the comforter.

"Slow," she murmured.

Gunnar kept her on her side and swept her top leg over his body. "Slow."

"Gentle."

He nodded even though with her eyes closed, she wouldn't have seen him. "Gentle, I promise."

"Good."

Gunnar wrapped one arm underneath her and held her tit. The other hand he used to guide his cock to her still-wet pussy. He slid inside of her so slowly it felt like neither one of them breathed until he'd fully seated himself.

"Mmm, yes." Eboni blinked her eyes open as he made his slow thrusts.

"Good morning." He tightened his hold.

Gunnar could die at this moment. He didn't care about going to work. He could care less if he never fought again. He could give everything up for her. Too bad Eboni didn't feel the same way.

Stroking in and out of her felt like he touched heaven. Her silken folds welcomed him. It surprised him how quickly her body responded to him. He had expected her to be stiff or reserved. Instead, as soon as he touched her, she melted.

So why did she want to hide how she felt about him? Eboni seemed to dismiss him without much thought. To make sure he stayed on her mind, Gunnar deepened his strokes. He moved over to her ear. He swiped his tongue over the shell of it before dipping it inside. For that move, he received a throaty moan.

"You're addicting." She caressed his arm that held her and brought his other hand down to her clit.

"Just tell me what you want." He joked.

As soon as he brushed his fingers on the hardened nub between her legs, her body ignited. Eboni undulated her hips to drive him more into her. In an attempt to keep her controlled, he tightened his hold around her body. Gunnar stroked his thumb over the side of her tit.

Eboni coiled her outer leg around him more. She clawed his arm. Having sex with an older Eboni allowed him to experience how a real woman moved. She enjoyed her body and his. Gunnar hoped she knew he desired her for more than sex. Damn if it didn't feel good though.

"I thought you wanted it slow and easy." Gunnar slid her clit between his fingers.

The slick nub eased in between his digits. With each pass, Eboni writhed with a complementing moan. When she nibbled on his arm, giving his skin slight nips, he knew he had her.

"Please." She reached up and grabbed his head.

"Please, what?"

"Hard."

Gunnar didn't need to hear anything else. He turned her over on to her stomach, brought her up on her hands and knees, and pounded her from behind. The sounds of their slapping bodies echoed in the room.

"Yes! Yes!" Eboni pushed back against him.

He held her waist as he moved in and out of her. The tightness of her slick inner walls would forever be imprinted in his thoughts.

"Come with me." Gunnar put his hand on her back.

Eboni nodded as he stroked faster and faster. As hard he tried, as soon as Gunnar dropped his gaze and saw her true hourglass figure, her broad shoulders that went down to a slender, tapered waist and out again at the soft curves of her succulent hips, he knew he wouldn't have long. His pounding heart and panting breath supported his thoughts.

Gunnar squeezed his eyes shut, but it didn't help. He increased his speed. The combination must have been enough for Eboni. He felt her inner walls tightening around his shaft. Each time he pulled back, her tightness drew him back inside.

When Eboni screamed, he grunted. The only thing that could have made this experience better would be to come inside of her. No condom. No barriers. He would take what he could get for now. At this moment, he had his woman back. Could he keep her?

As soon as he pulled out of her, Eboni slid back down on the bed. She curled her arms under a pillow that she used to rest her head. She completed her heavy sigh with a smile.

"You're an evil, evil man." She laughed.

"You didn't like that wake-up call?" Gunnar brushed her hair from her face and kissed her.

"Loved it, but I'm going to be so stiff today. Can I call in sick?" She rolled on to her back, showing off her firm breasts.

Gunnar had to back away from her to prevent himself from reaching out and touching her again. If he touched her tits, he wouldn't get out of bed for the rest of the day.

"I thought you said I wasn't the boss." Gunnar stood and removed the used condom. "You really need to be at the salon today."

"Why?"

"Because I have to pick up Mom."

Eboni sat up. "You're not going to tell her, are you?"

The same queasy feeling that had hit Gunnar last night when Eboni had made the same request washed over him again. "Yes. I had planned on telling my mother with heart problems that her oldest son brought a woman home and had sex with her in the apartment over the garage."

When Eboni's mouth hung open, Gunnar saved her.

"I'm kidding. No, I hadn't planned on saying anything. Why are you so concerned about that? You're the one who said last night that we are two consenting adults and we're going into this with our eyes wide open." He crossed his arms over his chest.

"I don't need the chatter going on at the shop."

Gunnar felt in his bones that Eboni had another reason behind her request, but he allowed the subject to drop. He held his hand out for her. "You take a shower. There's an extra unopened toothbrush in the medicine cabinet and towels underneath the sink. I'll run over to the house and get you another outfit."

Eboni accepted his hand and stood on wobbly legs. "No. That's okay. I can go home in the outfit I wore last night."

Gunnar cocked his head. "Your family will still figure out you weren't eating dinner all night even if you wear a different outfit home."

"I'm fine."

"Okay. Then I'll make you breakfast."

"You're not joining me?" Eboni nibbled on her bottom lip as she backed into the bathroom.

Gunnar strolled up to her. He wrapped his arm around her body and gave her ass a gentle squeeze. "If I do, we'll never leave this place." He gave her a quick peck before guiding her into the bathroom.

Although he loved everything he'd done with Eboni last night--and that morning--Gunnar wanted more than just his short trip home. Before he went back to Vegas, he had to convince her to give up life in Virginia and join him.

* * * *

Eboni almost didn't accept the good-bye kiss from Gunnar when he dropped her off at her apartment. With the quick brush against his lips, she confirmed she wanted what they had rekindled hidden.

Being a gentleman, he opened the vehicle door for her. Eboni had to stop him when he offered to walk her to her building.

"See you at the salon," Gunnar said as she ran up to her building.

She unlocked her door and ran inside. Her cousin remained asleep on the living room couch. Until he could smell food cooking, or until his girl of the moment wanted sex, he didn't move.

Eboni started down the hallway to go to her bedroom when she ran into her aunt. "Oh, hey, Auntie. Have you had breakfast?"

Her aunt gave her a suspicious glare. "Isn't that the same dress you wore last night?"

"Yeah. I just spent the night at a friend's." She hadn't lied. "Let me change and get you something to eat."

Eboni hurried to her room to change.

Behind her, she heard her aunt say, "Craig said that boy you used to date is back in town. Is that right?"

As she stripped out of her dress, Eboni answered. "You mean Grover? He never left town, and he's married." She knew exactly who her Aunt Bettie meant, but Eboni needed some time to come up with reasons why associating herself with Gunnar Wells again wouldn't be damaging to her soul.

"Don't be cute. You know exactly who I'm talking about."

Eboni got dressed in her usual work attire of a black turtleneck, black slacks, and comfortable black flats. Now that business had increased, she needed to be as relaxed as possible.

"Who are you talking about?" Eboni ducked into the bathroom to put on some lipstick and redo her hair.

Going to work with obvious morning-after-sex hair wouldn't be sexy. Plus, she could almost hear Shay's cackling if she showed up with signs that she had been with a man.

"That fighter boy," Aunt Bettie said. "Garth."

"Gunnar." Eboni walked into the kitchen. She poured some prune juice into a glass and placed it on the table in front of her aunt.

"Is it true?"

"Yes. He's back in town. He came back to help his mother. She's not doing well." Eboni prepared her aunt's oatmeal and toast breakfast.

"You're staying away from him, right?"

"Aunt Bettie, I'm a grown woman. The mistakes I made when I was a teenager won't happen again." At least Eboni had hoped not.

"I hope not. Losing that baby might have been a godsend."

Eboni rushed to her aunt and pointed in the living room at Craig who looked to still be asleep.

"Let's not revisit the past. Let's move on. Lord knows, I have." Her aunt's toast popped up. Eboni quickly slathered some butter and a bit of jelly on it before serving it.

"I don't want to see you hurt again." Aunt Bettie shook her head and wiped her eyes.

How could Eboni be mad at the only relative who cared about her? When the microwave dinged, Eboni removed her aunt's hot cereal and gave that to her.

"I appreciate you being there for me." She leaned down and gave her aunt a hug. In a whisper, she said in her ear, "And I really appreciate the fact that you have kept my secret after all these years." She kissed her aunt on her cheek. "I have to go to work. I'll see you all tonight."

"Okay. See you later. Love you, baby."

"Love you." Eboni grabbed her coat and purse. As she walked by her lumbering cousin, she glanced his way and thought she caught him closing his eyes.

She hoped he hadn't listened in on her conversation with her aunt. She didn't need her cousin revealing the secret she'd kept from Gunnar for all these years before she had a chance to explain.

* * * *

"Hey, Ma." Gunnar beamed as he strolled into her room. He gave her a kiss on her cheek and held her hand.

After regarding him for a moment, Queen Elizabeth proclaimed, "You've had sex."

The nurse in the room taking Elizabeth's vital signs snickered.

"Mom." Gunnar felt his face get hot. "Why would you say something like that?"

"Because it's true. A mother always knows. I knew it when you lost your virginity." She tapped the nurse on her side. "He skipped through my house like he had ants in his pants."

The nurse giggled and split her attention between the machine calculating Queen's blood pressure and Gunnar.

"I really don't think this is an appropriate conversation to have right now."

His mother pulled on the nurse's arm to bring her down closer to her face. When she bent over, Elizabeth said in a not-so-quiet whisper, "Did you notice he didn't deny it?"

The nurse burst into laughter. Gunnar sat on the couch that doubled as a bed.

His mother at least waited until the nurse walked out of the room before she continued with her questioning.

"So?" She sat up in her bed and pressed a button to bring her head up even more.

Gunnar waited for the whirring sound to end before he answered her. "So what?"

"Don't be cute. Did you have sex with Eboni?"

"You know this is an awkward conversation for an adult man to have with his mother, right?" He leaned back on the couch and stretched his feet in front of him.

Elizabeth sighed. "You're really not going to tell me anything, are you?"

"Wasn't it you who told all of us that it's impolite to talk about our intimate relationships in public?"

"Did you take her to Amoré?"

His mother's fishing expedition had no end.

"Yes. I took her there for dinner." Before his mother could ask, Gunnar quickly supplied, "And we talked about everything in the past. I think that's all resolved now."

"Really?" His mother gave him a quizzical look.

He nodded to reassure her. "Yes. We agreed to remain friends."

"Then you took her back to the house and had sex."

Gunnar laughed. "I love you, Mom."

"Did you at least use protection?"

"I love you."

"Did you tell her you love her?"

Gunnar didn't have time to answer that question before the doctor came in the room. He wanted to kiss the petite Indian woman for the intrusion.

"Queen Elizabeth, how are you feeling today?" The doctor nodded to Gunnar and then turned to his mother.

"Much better. Looks like I might be missing some excitement at my house." Elizabeth winked at Gunnar.

Gunnar sprang to his feet. "Nothing exciting happening at her house. She's kidding. Can my mother go home today?"

"Yes. She can change and we'll be sending her home today. The discharge nurse will come in to give instructions on what she needs to do when she's at home. Hopefully, they'll set up the schedule for your surgery today. If not today, we'll call you at home when a date and time has been set up."

The joy drained from Elizabeth's face. Gunnar held her hand and smiled as he nodded at her to try and reassure her.

"Of course, if anything changes when she's at home, please don't hesitate to bring her back here."

"Thanks so much. I appreciate everything you've done for her." Gunnar shook the doctor's hand before she left.

He noticed after the doctor walked out and closed the door that his mother squeezed his hand.

"I'm scared, son."

Gunnar embraced her without a word. If he could give her a part of his physical strength, he would. "I'm here for you. Gideon and Thane will be here for you, too. You've got nothing to worry about."

"Thank you, baby." As soon as Gunnar pulled back from her, Elizabeth said, "You smell like you've just had sex. Did you do it before you came here?"

"Mom."

"You did foreplay, right? I told you about how it takes a woman a while to get her engine going." Elizabeth even chugged her arms like a train to illustrate her point.

"Mom," Gunnar said more sternly.

"You didn't spank her, did you? I don't know who came up with that. It's never okay to strike a lady."

"*Mom*. Will you please stop it?"

Elizabeth smiled. "I'm going to miss teasing you like this."

"No, you won't. You'll be here. You dealt with three businesses, three ornery boys and an ex-husband not worth mentioning. You'll outlive all of us."

A tear managed to escape her eye. Queen Elizabeth quickly wiped it away before she finally nodded to agree with her son.

"If anything ever happens to me--"

"Mom."

"No. Hear me out. If anything happens to me, promise me you'll keep the family together."

Gunnar would give his mother anything. Corralling Thane into the mix would be the hardest thing. His baby brother had a way of dodging his calls.

Gunnar smiled at his mother. "I promise."

She sniffed. "Hand me my makeup bag, please. I need to fix my face before I leave."

"Yes, ma'am."

If Gunnar could trade hearts and arteries with his mother, he would. The woman had given him the world. She'd given him an opportunity when no one else would. He would move heaven and earth to do the same for her.

Chapter 12

Eboni acted like she didn't notice when Gunnar arrived to work around ten in the morning.

"Sorry I'm late." He put his coat in the office and came back out. "Great news, everyone. Our beloved Queen Elizabeth has been discharged from the hospital and is resting comfortably at home."

The staff and clients all applauded and whistled their excitement over the news.

"She wanted me to bring her here today, but the doctor said no stress." Gunnar glanced at Shay who still wore her sunglasses.

"Why did you look at me?" Shay pointed her curling iron toward Gunnar.

"Because you're a handful, that's why," Gunnar shot back.

"You know that's right," Monica said and laughed.

"Forget you." She pointed to Gunnar. "And forget you." She pointed at Monica. "I'm nothing but positivity and light."

Tisha even giggled at that one.

"And forget you, Mouse." Shay pointed to Tisha.

"Don't call me that," Tisha said.

"Barely hear a peep out of you until you want to laugh at someone." Shay continued styling her client's hair.

As soon as she finished her client, Tisha ran to the back room.

"Tisha--" Eboni started to go, but Gunnar stopped her.

"You have a client in a chair. I'll go." Gunnar ducked into the back room.

* * * *

Gunnar found Tisha standing in a corner. When she spotted Gunnar, she turned her back on him.

"Hey, come on out, Tisha. You know Shay didn't mean it." Gunnar kept a safe distance away from her but remained in the room until he could gain her trust.

"Yes, she did. Shay hates me." She gradually turned around and kept a guarded stare on Gunnar.

"To be fair, I think Shay hates everyone." Gunnar smiled to calm her.

It must have worked. Tisha took a step out of the darkened corner toward him. "I hate when people call me mouse or squeak or Tinker Bell."

"I know what you mean."

She shook her head. "No, you don't. No one teases you."

"Are you kidding? I've been called a beast, a wall, a bully, and Thor because of my size and how I look. It used to bother me."

"It did?"

Gunnar nodded.

"What did you do?"

"Fight."

Tisha blinked. "I can't fight."

"And you shouldn't have to. Shut people up with your skills." Gunnar sat at the break-room table. He hoped Tisha would join him.

She pulled out a chair across from him and sat down. "You really were teased?"

"Yep. All my life. I bet you if you go online and pull up videos and websites about me, you'll find that people post the nastiest things about me. They'll call me a loser or a cheater or old or mean."

"How do you deal with that?" Tisha nibbled on her thumbnail as she waited for his answer.

"I pay no attention to it. Those people don't know me. The only reason people tease you is because they're insecure." It felt strange spouting the same speech his mother had given him when he kept fighting other boys in school who had made fun of him and his family.

"Shay is tall, thin and beautiful. What does she have to be insecure about?"

Gunnar shrugged. "I don't know. But I'm sure she has something. The trick is to not worry about what she says about you. You worry about being your best. From what I can see, you're an amazing stylist. I've watched your work since I've been here. You do great hair."

Tisha smiled and pushed her glasses up her nose. "Thanks. My mom calls me the hair whisperer." She giggled with a snort. "Your mom took a chance on me. I came in here fresh from cosmetology school with my certificate. She allowed me to style hair in the chair by the window."

Even Gunnar had to blink at that bit of news. He knew what it meant for a stylist to get the window chair. His mom must have seen something special in Tisha.

"My mom is an amazing woman." Gunnar glanced to the side and noticed a postcard on the refrigerator being held up by a pizza delivery magnet. "Have you thought about going to a hair show?"

"To watch it? Yes, I love going to hair shows. They're so informative and theatrical at the same time."

"No." Gunnar stood and removed the postcard. "I mean participate. You could represent Press 'N Curl at the next hair show in Atlanta. Do you want to? I'll pay for you to go and I'll foot the bill for the registration."

Tisha's mouth hung open until she shook her head and lowered her gaze. "I can't do that."

"Why not? I'm not asking you to win. I just want you to have the experience."

"I can't go alone."

Gunnar looked down at the date. With the event being two months away, he didn't know if he would be in town to be able to go. "Who would you want to go with you?"

Tisha thought for a moment. "Eboni. She's so organized and smart."

Tisha left out sexy, but he knew she wouldn't say that.

"I would also like Tillman to go with me."

"Another good choice." Gunnar nodded.

"He's so cute. I want him to ask me out, but I don't think I'm his type." Tisha had no idea.

"It might not be a good idea to date your coworker." Gunnar tried defusing the situation before feelings got hurt. "If things don't work out between the two of you, it'll make working together awkward."

"Oh, yeah, I guess you're right." Tisha lowered her gaze.

"Besides, you don't have to keep your romantic choices confined to this salon. Go out and meet people. Live a little." He held up the postcard. "Go to the hair show."

Tisha took the card from his hand and stared at it.

"Let me know if you're interested." He stood and headed back out to the main salon.

Before he could cross the threshold into the main area, he heard Tisha say, "I want to go."

Gunnar glanced back at her.

"This butterfly needs to spread her wings."

"Very good. After work, I'll register you and see if anyone else would like to go." He held the curtain open for her. "Ready to get back to work?"

Tisha stood and stuffed the postcard in her oversized sweater pocket. "Yes, sir." As she walked by him, she stopped and hugged him around his waist.

He glanced over at Eboni, who cut him a strange look before attending to her client.

"Shay, you owe Tisha an apology for hurting her feelings." Gunnar stood in between the two women's stations.

"She doesn't have to say anything." Tisha shook her head vigorously and turned her back on Shay as she cleaned her station.

"Yeah, she knows it was a joke. All we have here in the salon is jokes." Shay pumped up the chair that her client sat in and turned the woman around to style her hair.

"She didn't find it funny. Apologize." Gunnar crossed his arms over his chest as he faced Shay.

"You can't be serious."

"I am. Apologize now or go home."

Shay shook her head. "Damn crybaby. I'm sorry, Tisha, that you can't take a joke."

"Did that hurt?" Gunnar went over to the shampoo station.

"Yes, it did. This is what I meant about you messing up the flow in here. We women can't be women in here. We should be able to tease each other and talk about things like S-E-X." She licked her lips.

"I don't care if you talk about sex, so long as there aren't any kids around."

"Okay." Shay scanned the area. With a waiting area filled with women and no visible children around, she continued. "So, Big Guns, do you have one?"

Gunnar called over a client to the bowl. "One what?"

"You know." Shay bounced up and down and simulated having something large between her legs. "Do you have a big gun, and I'm not talking the one with bullets either."

Several women laughed, including the one who came over to his bowl to get her hair washed. The client sitting at Eboni's chair screamed in pain.

"You burned me!" the woman said as she rubbed the back of her head.

"Sorry." Eboni glanced at Gunnar and turned her back on him.

He still caught her looking at him in her mirror. "None of your business. Whatever happened to you women saying it's not the size of the ship but the motion in the ocean?"

"Honey, we only say that to guys who are like this." She held up her hand and placed her thumbnail against the upper section of her pinkie finger. "That way we don't hurt their little feelings, and I do mean little feelings."

The women in the salon laughed.

Gunnar wrapped a towel around his client's shoulders and lowered her to the bowl. "If you love someone, size shouldn't make a difference."

"Says a man who saves himself for his wedding night and reveals his tiny package to his new wife." Shay put her hands in prayer form and bent her knees. "Please, honey. Don't mind my little dick. I love you." She pushed air through her lips. "I'm used to working with long, hard things." She held up her curling iron. "I can't go from this to tweezers."

The women in the salon erupted in laughter.

"Hold on. Eboni, you said you and Mr. Guns here had a thing back in the day. Tell us. Was he packing or pretending?"

Eboni glanced at Gunnar before she looked at Shay. "I'm not talking about that here. It's not right."

"That's code for a little winky." Shay waved at Gunnar with her pinkie finger. "Or you can prove me wrong and join me for a drink."

Gunnar filled his hands with shampoo and scrubbed the solution into a foamy lather in his client's hair. "So you think that a night of drinking and I'll jump into bed with you?"

"Why wouldn't you? You're young and hot. And, well, look at this?" She showed off her body. "How could you resist?"

"I can resist by respecting you as a woman. I don't know you. Therefore, I'm not going to jump right into bed with you. Plus, I tend to go for women who have more going on for themselves than what they can offer me between their legs."

"I'm liking this guy more and more each day," Monica said before she answered the phone.

"Whatever. He's no different than any other man. That I know for sure." Shay turned her back on him and continued doing her client's hair.

"Let's get off me." Gunnar rinsed off his client's hair.

"Haven't gotten on you yet." Shay blew him a kiss.

"As a man, I'd like to know what you women want in an ideal man."

"A big dick!" a group of women said simultaneously.

Even Tillman laughed at that response. "You asked for it."

Gunnar helped his client to a chair where he applied a deep conditioner to her wet tresses. He covered her hair and then moved her to a hair bonnet next to the wall.

"Put it on a low setting. I want to hear this conversation," his client said and winked.

Gunnar adjusted the setting and turned to the main salon again. "No, really. What do you women want from men? Monica? You're married. What did you look for in your husband?"

Monica remained quiet for a while before a smile spread over her face. "He knew how to dance. I never liked dancing at the school dances. But he could always get me out on the floor. He was patient. And he could move. He swept me off my feet then." She chuckled. "I guess he's still sweeping me off my feet now." She picked up the desk's phone receiver. "Let me give him a call."

"My husband knows how to make me laugh," a client chimed in. "Granted, his jokes are always corny. But it tickles him so much to tell the joke that you can't help but laugh with him."

Gunnar turned to Shay. "Shay? What do you want? And don't you dare talk about anatomy."

"Whatever. Men don't have much to offer besides the sex." She adjusted her sunglasses. "Maybe security."

"Financial?" Gunnar asked.

Shay didn't answer.

"What about you, Tisha?" Tillman asked.

Tisha's face turned every shade of red known to man.

"I'll tell you what I like," Eboni said.

Gunnar gave his full attention to her.

"Good dancer just means he's good in bed." Eboni directed that statement to Monica.

The older woman poked her head up but continued with her phone conversation.

"Good sense of humor is great, that way when things get rough, the two of you can somehow laugh about it." Eboni styled her client's hair but seemed to get lost in her own thoughts. "My ideal man has to have those things and be honest. Honesty will give me security. He has to be intelligent. If I can't hold a conversation with him, there's no use for us to be together."

A chorus of umm huhs sounded in the salon.

Eboni continued. "He has to be a great listener. I hate it when you tell a man about your day and they want to fix things for you. Like if I say that

I burned my tongue on a Starbuck's coffee, don't tell me what I should do next time. Just hold me and kiss me. If I talk about a bad day at work, I want him to listen. Don't ask what you can do to help."

"We can't help it." Gunnar put his hand to his chest. "Men are expected to fix things. We automatically go into fix-it mode, especially when it comes to someone we love."

When Eboni glanced at him, Gunnar had no problem staring back at her, almost daring her to make the next crucial step. She wanted to keep their new relationship quiet. Would she?

"So apparently, your need to be a fixer caused the two of you to break up years ago, huh?" Shay posed as she pulled the drape off her client.

"I guess so." Gunnar summoned another client to him to the shampoo bowl. "Guess I'll know better for the next relationship."

The client Gunnar put under the hairdryer lifted the face shield. "Are you all going talk about sex again?"

Laughter filled the salon again. Too bad Gunnar found nothing funny in losing the most incredible woman he'd ever known. After last night, he had to figure out a way to get her back. He needed Eboni, and he needed to leave Virginia.

* * * *

At the end of the day, Eboni helped Gunnar lock up the salon.

"Are you going to come over?" Gunnar asked. He held his hands up as if to surrender. "To see Queen Elizabeth. I don't want you to think that I want you for one thing only."

"I know you better than that." Eboni headed to the office to get her coat and purse. "I would love to see Elizabeth. I have to make a stop first."

"Where?"

Eboni turned to him as she put on her coat.

As though answering a question she wanted to ask, Gunnar quickly supplied, "I just wanted to know if it's a place where you would like my company or if it's someplace private." He walked into the office. "You don't have to tell me if you don't want."

Suddenly, the space felt confining. Eboni swallowed. She wished she had made it to the doorway before Gunnar entered the office. All day, she'd thought about his body and what he'd done with it with her.

Just thinking about the sex, Eboni felt phantom pressure against her inner thighs, as though Gunnar had positioned himself in between them again. Her nipples hardened just from her looking at his mouth.

She broke her gaze from him to pull herself out of the spell. "I was going to stop off at the center to check on some donations."

"I'd like to go with you, if you don't mind." Gunnar reached behind her and picked up his coat.

"Really? I didn't think you liked the center. The last time I took you, you damn near bolted out the door like you'd seen the devil." Eboni tried to maintain eye contact with him.

"I'm trying to appreciate things that are important to you."

The closeness of their bodies caused Eboni to sigh.

Gunnar must have picked up on her lusty exhale. "Or we can stay here. I'm sure there's a load of laundry I can put in the washer."

"You are so funny." She pushed against his chest and made it out to the main salon. "You can come with me if you want."

"That's my preference." He winked at her.

Eboni didn't comment on his salacious statement. If she did, they would never leave the empty salon. "I'll meet you there."

"You don't want to ride with me?" Gunnar opened the back door for Eboni and locked it.

"No. I'll drive myself." She got to the driver's side of her car. Before she got inside, she felt Gunnar standing behind her, pressing his massive body against hers.

"I promise to behave." His warm breath felt good on the back of her neck.

"You mean like now?"

He put his hands on the roof of her car, surrounding her with his arms. "I haven't touched you at all today. I barely looked your way, which killed me. If getting some alone time with you means driving you ten minutes, I'll take it."

Eboni turned around and faced him. "It means that much to you to be with me?"

His eyebrows furrowed. "Are you kidding? I realized in one night what a fool I've been for the last ten years. I want to spend every waking moment with you."

"Until?" Eboni wanted to hear the answer to that crucial question.

"Until we can figure out where *we* go from here."

She dropped her gaze. "Perhaps where we go is just around here. When you leave, that'll be it."

Gunnar shook his head. "Not good enough. But it's too cold to talk about something so heavy out here. I'll see you at the center." Before parting, he gave her a kiss on her forehead. He turned to his truck, stopped and turned back around. "Oh, hell." He wrapped his arm around her waist and pulled her close to his body.

As soon as Gunnar's lips touched Eboni's, her body became alive like a million and one firecrackers ignited all at once. She couldn't deny that she missed this intimate connection with him. If she had been honest with herself, she would admit that she wanted more.

Gunnar broke from the kiss long enough to say, "I'll see you at the center."

Eboni could do nothing but nod.

Once she got into her car, she stayed in it. She would have been content to have her heater and defroster remove all of the ice and snow from her windows. Gunnar felt differently.

Before she knew it, Gunnar had come to her car and scraped her windows while she sat inside getting warm. He gave her a smile and wink as soon as he finished his work. Then he worked on his truck.

Eboni opened her door. "Let me help you now."

"Get back in your car and stay warm. I'm fine."

Gunnar Wells certainly fit every category of fine in the dictionary.

While everything progressed so well for them, Eboni decided holding off revealing her damaging news to him until he prepared to go home would be best. He would want to go once she shared it.

As soon as Gunnar gave her a nod, Eboni led them to the Oceanfront Community Center. He parked next to her car, and they walked to the building in silence.

Inside, Eboni went straight to the business office where she knew Drew would be. Drew had been the manager there since Eboni had gone to the center as a teenager. No one had more passion about the place than him. He worked day and night to keep the place going.

"Hey, Captain. What's shaking?" Eboni smiled, hoping he would match the expression.

The older white man pursed his lips and exhaled. He shook his head and Eboni got her answer.

"No donations?" She clasped her hands together and hoped for a miracle.

"None," he answered.

Damn.

"I thought for sure that local dairy would come through for us. The donations they promised would have been enough to fix the pool." Eboni rubbed her forehead.

"I know." Drew glanced up at Gunnar. "Can I help you?"

"Oh, I'm sorry. Drew, this is, um, my friend, Gunnar Wells." Finding a tame way to introduce him became complicated considering what they'd done. "Gunnar, this is Drew Pausini. He's the manager here, but I like calling him Captain."

"She's the only one I let get away with that." Drew smiled and shook Gunnar's hand. "Nice to meet you. Any friend of Eboni's is a friend of mine."

"Ditto." Gunnar stared at Eboni. "She's pretty special."

"Yes, she is." Drew stared at Gunnar for a moment. "You look so familiar."

Eboni watched Gunnar draw his shoulders back.

"I used to come here back in the day along with Eboni." Gunnar clenched his jaw as though expecting a confrontation.

"Hell, I barely remember what Eboni looked like when she first came here. No, I've seen you elsewhere."

"He's a fighter," Eboni quickly supplied.

"Like boxing?" Drew held up his fists.

"Mixed martial arts," Gunnar said.

Drew's dull brown eyes widened. "Oh yeah. I heard the kids talking about you around here. Guns, that's what they call you, right?"

Gunnar nodded. "I'm home to help my mom."

"I'm trying to convince him to help promote the place." Eboni nudged Gunnar on his side.

From the glare he gave her, he didn't find anything amusing in her admission.

"That would be awesome. The kids would love seeing a local celebrity talking up this place." Drew rubbed his hands together. "And we could certainly use the publicity."

"I'm sorry. I don't do commercials or promotions." Gunnar held out his hand. "Nice to meet you." He glared at Eboni. "I guess I'll see you at the house." He left the office.

"Did I say something wrong?" Drew asked and shrugged.

"No. I think I did. I'll talk to you later." Eboni rushed out to the parking lot in time to see Gunnar stomping to his truck. "Gunnar! Gunny!"

He stopped at the driver-side door and turned to her. As soon as she got close enough to him he unloaded on her. "Why did you do that? Why did you try to make me feel guilty about not doing some promotion for this place? I told you I don't do commercials."

"I didn't mean to make you feel trapped." Eboni tried making eye contact when she found Gunnar looking elsewhere. "Hey, will you at least tell me why?"

"What I do. The fighting. I see it as a job. I find it ridiculous when guys get on TV and talk about how they're going to beat me up and hurt me. Show me. You don't go around to other salons and tell them you do the best hair and that Press 'N Curl is going to run them out of business."

"No. But I have done radio spots and promotions at local hair shows. Unlike you, we don't have a built-in audience. We also have way more competition. We need to shout from the rooftops how good we are, like this place needs someone to be a voice for them and talk about how great this center is. The news has covered us a couple of times, and we'll get some donations, but it isn't enough."

Gunnar balled his hand into a fist but kept his gaze away from Eboni. After a beat, he finally looked at her. "My mom used to have this husband who used to brag all the time what a big man he was. When she would have dinner parties, he would tell their friends what a great provider he was. To his boys, he talked about how much my mom couldn't keep her hands off him. Truth of the matter is he didn't work and he had a problem keeping his hands off her."

With Gunnar's somber expression, Eboni knew what he meant regarding Queen's ex-husband. Eboni moved in closer to him.

"I can't stand people who go on and on about themselves and what they can do, because the majority of the time they're lying. If I feel that way, I'm sure other people do. So, no, I'm not going to do any promotions. If people want to know what I can do, they can come see me."

Eboni regarded him for a moment, digesting his statement. Then it hit her. "You don't think people will believe you, right?"

Gunnar glanced at her. "No, it's what I said. Drop it."

"Gunny, you are not that shady little kid who used to steal and lie all the time. You're a fine man. A good man." She gravitated closer to him. "An honest man."

He shook his head. "When I tried being honest when I was a kid, people didn't believe me. Why bother now? If I say I can beat someone in a fight and I lose, I look stupid." He stared at Eboni. "If I promote this place as a safe haven for the community and something happens, no one will trust my word. It's taken me a long time to build it back up. I need to protect it."

"The difference between then and now is intention. Because you are selective with what you say, your word will go a long way. People will know that you care about something." Eboni held Gunnar's hand. "I didn't know about Queen and how you really felt. I shouldn't have gotten Drew's hopes up and obligated you."

"Apology--" Gunnar stopped and looked at something over her shoulder.

She turned and saw a man with a shaved head coming toward them.

"I had to get a coat to come out to this place. No snow in Vegas." He stared at Gunnar. "We need to talk."

"Who are you?" Eboni kept herself between Gunnar and this stranger.

Gunnar put his hands on her shoulders. "This is my manager, Chuck. He's about to tell me why he came all the way out here from Vegas when I told him I was taking care of my mother."

Chapter 13

First Eboni had tried to obligate Gunnar to promote the center, and now Chuck had showed up to make demands of his own. Gunnar couldn't wait to hear this.

"Eboni, go on to the house. I'll see you there." Gunnar kissed her temple and nudged her toward her car, all the while keeping a careful eye on his manager.

He tried keeping his temper in check by smiling, but inside, he had to count to one hundred in the hope of dousing the fire in him.

"I don't want to leave you." Eboni held on to his arm even though he continued moving her toward her car. "I haven't seen you fight recently, but back in the day, you had that same look in your eyes when you were about to get into it with someone." She peered down. "Your hands are in fists." She glanced at Chuck. "So are his. I thought you said he was your manager."

"He is." He shook out his hands to calm her fears. "My hands are cold."

"Okay, can you explain why you look like you want to knock his block off?"

He couldn't verbalize it. Too bad she'd picked up on his displeasure to see his business associate here and now. "I'll be fine." Gunnar raised his hand to Chuck. "He's my manager. I'm sure he only has my best interest in mind, right?" He gave her a quick peck. "Go see my mom. I'll be right behind you."

"Are you sure?" Eboni split her attention between Gunnar and Chuck. "He looks, I don't know, angry."

"He's passionate. We all are, right?" He nodded. "I wouldn't lie to you."

"I suppose if you're introducing me to him, it means he's your friend."

He blinked at her statement. She remembered the situation when Queen had followed him when he'd met up with his gang. He glanced at Chuck again and realized why she worried.

In his stance, he looked ready to rumble. His trainer kept his hands tightly balled into fists. He had a wide stance to maintain his balance. At one time, Gunnar thought he heard the man snort like a bull. He felt his gut tightening, but he had to remain cool for Eboni.

She wrapped her arms around his neck. In his ear, she said, "If you're not at the house five minutes after me, I'm coming right back."

Gunnar chuckled. "There's my tough girl." He patted her back. "Go. I'll be home shortly."

Eboni shot a glare to Chuck before she got into her car. She sat in it for a couple of minutes, probably warming it up again. The entire time, she kept her stare on Chuck.

Gunnar couldn't remember Eboni being this staunchly loyal before. He liked it. He really liked it. Had Chuck not been there, he would have shown her how much he liked her strong stance. Right now, he had another problem on his hands.

After Eboni pulled away from parking lot, Gunnar addressed Chuck. "What the hell are you doing here?"

Chuck leaned back with his arms outstretched. "You don't seem happy to see me."

"I'm not." Gunnar crossed his arms over his chest to prevent Chuck from seeing his fists.

"I'm thrilled to see you. I thought you had fallen off the face of the earth. I call and you don't answer. I tell you that you have an upcoming match and"—Chuck scanned him—"it doesn't look like you've been keeping up with your training."

Gunnar shook his head.

"And now I see you hanging out with some woman who--"

"Don't go there. You don't want to do that." Gunnar wouldn't take to him or anyone else talking about Eboni.

Chuck cocked his head and smiled. "Oh, I didn't know you were in love so quickly. I mean, are you going to ask her to marry you? Is she knocked up with your kid already?"

Gunnar stormed toward Chuck, who stumbled backward. "I told you I needed some time away to take care of my mother."

"Really? I checked with the hospital. She was discharged today."

Gunnar stalked his manager. "You have some big brass ones. She still has to have surgery. I'm staying here until she has it. If it takes her six months or a year to recover, I'll be with her."

"You can't do that, Guns. You've got upcoming matches. Hell, you're the titleholder. You're obligated to defend it."

"My only obligation is to my family." Gunnar jutted his finger in front of Chuck's face. "Before you, before the training, before the fights, my mother and brothers had my back." He turned to his rental. "If you'll excuse me, I need to go be with my family."

"Don't walk away from me, Guns. If you do--"

"What? What's going to happen? You're going to have my title stripped from me? You'll talk shit about me to the association? I'll never fight again? I don't care. You do what you have to do, and I'll do what I have to do. When I'm ready to get into the ring again, I'll call you."

Chuck studied Gunnar for a moment before he spoke. "I can't figure it out. Are you scared or tired? Which is it, Guns? Are you afraid Seamus is going to beat you, or are you tired of fighting?"

Gunnar wouldn't answer that question even though he'd thought about it a lot lately. He enjoyed being able to sleep when he wanted and not have to train every minute of the day. The idea of quitting had crossed his mind. He wouldn't be sharing that information with Chuck until he needed to reveal it. Right now, he would take advantage of this break.

Gunnar pointed down the street. "Get your ass on a plane and take yourself back to Vegas. There's nothing for you here."

Chuck tsked and lowered his head. "I wished you hadn't said that. You leave me no options."

Uninterested in hearing what else Chuck had to say, Gunnar got into his truck and sped out of the parking lot. He pounded his fist against the steering wheel to work out some of his aggression.

Gunnar still couldn't believe his manager had come all the way to Virginia to convince him to fight again. How could Chuck think that he could leave his mother now?

When Gunnar thought about the fear in Eboni's eyes when Chuck had showed up, he had to grip the steering wheel again. He never wanted her to worry about him. He had to show her and his mother he could be a changed man. No one defined him but him. No one.

* * * *

"Darling, will you sit down, please." Elizabeth spoke from her seated position on the couch.

Since arriving at her house, Eboni had planted herself at the living room window, waiting for Gunnar to come home. She glanced at her watch again, counting down the seconds until it reached that critical five-minute mark.

"I want to make sure Gunnar gets back okay." Eboni chewed on her lower lip.

"He'll be fine. I thought you said you came over to visit with me."

Eboni turned to her friend. "If you saw this guy and how Gunnar looked at him, you would be concerned."

"Chuck? That's Gunnar's manager. He's harmless, well, except for the need for the man to make a buck. But that's all managers, right? They'll squeeze every dollar they can out of you."

Eboni turned to Queen. "You don't. You're a great boss."

"I'd like to think I motivate you all in different ways." Elizabeth patted the seat next to her on the couch. "Come sit with me."

Eboni turned back to the window. "Aren't you worried about Gunnar?"

"Every day of my life. I worry about all of my children. I consider all of you at the salon my kids too. Come sit down."

Queen Elizabeth's soothing voice lulled Eboni to the couch next to her.

"Take a deep breath." To show Eboni what she meant, Elizabeth took a deep breath first. When she exhaled, she smiled. "You'll feel better."

"I'll feel better when Gunnar comes home."

Queen held Eboni's hand.

When she did that, Eboni broke from her guard duty to address her. "How do you manage to remain so calm?"

"Oh, honey, when the boys were younger, they put many a gray hair on my head. Thanks to Miss Clairol, you don't see that."

Eboni smiled.

Queen continued. "Through the years, I've found that I have raised really good men. All of them are so responsible. I don't worry about Gunnar because he has never given me a reason to worry." She thought about her statement and quickly added, "As an adult. You'll see when you get married and have children."

Eboni took in the weight of her words. She didn't think the anxiousness that riddled her body would go away if she married Gunnar, especially if she had children.

As soon as she saw a flash of headlights beam into the living room, Eboni darted to her feet and ran toward the back door.

"Eboni, a lady never runs," Elizabeth called after her.

Eboni didn't care. She burst through the door.

As soon as Gunnar stepped out of the truck, she jumped on him and wrapped her arms around his body.

"Whoa! I've only been tackled like this in the ring. What gives?" Gunnar laughed and held her.

"I didn't like that guy." When her body trembled, Gunnar held her closer. "He gave me the creeps."

"I told you I would be okay. We talked. That's it. I do all of my fighting in the ring now." He ran his hand up and down her back. "Let's get you inside. You're shivering." He slammed his truck door and walked her back into the house.

"Is that guy gone?" Eboni asked.

"I told him to go back to Las Vegas and that I would call him when I'm ready to work again." Gunnar walked into the living room where his mother sat. "Right now, I'm not ready to go back to work." He leaned over Queen Elizabeth and gave her a kiss on her forehead. "How are you doing, Ma?"

"I would be better if you hadn't scared the pudding out of this girl." She wagged her finger at Eboni. "Tell her you're okay."

"I did." Gunnar took off his jacket and hung it in the closet.

"Do it again so that I can see it."

Gunnar smiled and faced Eboni. "I'm sorry for--"

Elizabeth cleared her throat.

"Oh, that's right. I apologize for making you worry about me. I'm fine."

"Now kiss her."

When Gunnar said, "Ma!" Eboni exclaimed, "Queen!"

"Oh, come on. I know you two had sex. It's obvious." She turned to Eboni. "You wouldn't be so worried about him if you hadn't."

"I don't know what you're talking about. Gunnar and I are just--"

Before Eboni could finish her statement, Gunnar wrapped his arm around her waist, held her face and pressed his lips against hers. She closed her eyes and fell into the sensual expression.

When he pulled back, Eboni opened her eyes. She found Gunnar staring at her.

"Mama knows best." He helped her to a chair. "I'll get dinner started. Any preference?"

"Pasta." Elizabeth smiled.

He nodded and headed to the kitchen.

Elizabeth leaned over toward Eboni. "It's all he knows how to make really well."

Eboni laughed. She found that the more she hung out with Gunnar, the more she realized how much he had changed. Why was she pushing so hard to keep their relationship hidden? She put her hand over her heart. Since she'd given him permission to leave, starting anything with him again would break her heart in a million pieces.

Gunnar poked his head out of the kitchen. "Next Sunday is the Super Bowl."

Elizabeth clapped. "We need to have a viewing party." She pointed down. "It needs to be here at the house with everyone from the salon and the flower shop. We have to support Gideon."

Gunnar's face looked tight at his mother's suggestion.

"Lighten up, grumpy bear. It won't kill you to be hospitable for a day."

He growled before saying, "Yes, ma'am."

Elizabeth held Eboni's hand. "Will you help me plan it?"

"Of course." She glanced at Gunnar. "I would do anything for you and Gunnar."

He smiled before disappearing back into the kitchen. Eboni hoped he knew that about her. She shouldn't have had sex with him. Now she wanted to figure out a way to keep him home…with her.

* * * *

After dinner and a few card games, Gunnar's mother started yawning more and more.

"You want me to help you upstairs to your bedroom?" He held her hand.

"No. It may take me a while, but I'll get there." She stood from the table. "You two don't stay up too late. You both have early days tomorrow, right?"

Both Gunnar and Eboni said at the same time, "Yes, ma'am."

"But once I get to sleep, I won't hear anything. You could scream and shout, and I won't catch any of that."

"Mom!" Gunnar bolted to his feet.

"Good night, baby." She smiled as she crept up the steps.

Gunnar didn't know about Eboni, but his face felt like flames surrounded it. He finally glanced down at her and found her looking serene with a cat-that-ate-the-canary smile.

"She teased me about us too." Eboni motioned between herself and Gunnar.

"I'm chalking it up to the medication the hospital gave her." Gunnar returned the playing cards to the junk drawer in the kitchen.

"Then it has been a while since you've been home." Eboni stood. She sauntered into the living room and grabbed her coat.

At the sight of her getting her coat and purse, Gunnar's heart sank. He hadn't really expected a repeat performance of last night…although in his head he'd prayed several times over for it to happen.

Gunnar approached her and helped her put on her coat. "You want me to warm up your car for you?" He could still be a gentleman despite the fact that he hated to see her go.

"Why? Are you pulling my car around to the back of the house?" She smiled and headed to the back door. She hit the door opener to the garage. "See you in your apartment."

Gunnar felt like Eboni had thrown him a sucker punch with her brazen attitude. He wasted no time before joining her. After making sure to secure his mother's house, he strolled over to the garage, trying his damnedest to look cool. His insides jumped up and down like a sixteen-year-old kid's.

He locked up the downstairs garage before taking the steps by twos up to the apartment. He found the living room and kitchen areas dark. He did notice a light coming from his bedroom under the closed door.

Gunnar approached the door and pushed it open. Inside, he found Eboni sitting on the side of his bed wearing nothing but one of his fight T-shirts. For several reasons, he had to get that shirt off her body.

"I didn't think you would want to come over here with Queen Elizabeth next door." Gunnar stood in front of her but refrained from removing any clothing. Not just yet.

"She pretty much knows how we feel about each other." Eboni crossed her long legs.

"How's that?"

She stood. "We fit. We have history." She ran her hands up his chest.

Gunnar arrested her wandering hands by holding her wrists. When she brought her attention to his eyes, he asked, "Nothing more than that?"

"I don't know. Is there anything more?" she baited.

Unable or rather unwilling to answer the question, he silenced her by brushing his lips against hers. When he pressed them against hers more firmly, Eboni moaned. The vibration of her lips sent a ripple down his spine.

Gunnar broke from the kiss long enough to say, "I didn't want you to think that all I want from you is your body. I do respect you."

Eboni nodded. "I know." She took a step back from him and removed his T-shirt. "You still want my body?"

Gunnar tossed the shirt to the floor. "What do you think?" he asked as he stalked her.

She reached for his jeans and started undoing them. "I think if I don't get you naked in a few seconds, I'll be shredding your clothes with my fingernails."

"Can't have that, can we?" Gunnar opened his dresser drawer for his condoms.

As Eboni reached in his boxers to pull out his erect cock, he opened a package. He found that his hands had a steadier touch than Eboni's, which shook as she touched him. After rolling the thin membrane over his shaft, Gunnar scooped Eboni under her firm ass and placed her on top of the dresser.

Eboni pulled down her thong panties and kicked them to the floor. He pushed his jeans and boxers down to his knees and hooked one arm under her leg as he guided the head of his dick to her awaiting, wet channel. Before plunging himself inside, Gunnar teased her, rubbing the tip up and down her slick nether lips. The sound of her wetness cut in between their panting breaths.

Eboni stared directly into his eyes. She embedded her fingernails into his shoulder. She used her other hand to remove the ponytail holder keeping his hair back. His hair fell around his face. As long as it didn't block his view, he didn't care.

He eased himself inside so slowly he thought he'd stopped breathing for a moment. He enjoyed every titillating inch he managed to slide into her. From the way her legs coiled around his body, Eboni must have liked it as well.

She moved the hand she had on his shoulder down to his ass cheek, squeezed it and held him close, as though anything could have pulled him back from her at this point. Gunnar braced one hand on the top of the dresser as he gave her slow and easy thrusts. Although they'd started kind of franticly, he wanted to make this experience last.

Gunnar cupped her breast. Still keeping his stare on her, he rotated his thumb around her nipple, which caused her legs to thrash.

"So good." Eboni kissed the side of his neck.

He felt her slick channel constrict around his shaft, which prompted him to increase his speed until he heard the telltale hitch in her breath. Eboni clutched his shoulders and released a cry that she tried muffling against his arm.

For that, Gunnar couldn't help but laugh. "I don't think you were loud enough for my mom to hear you."

Eboni smiled. "Then don't stop until all of Virginia Beach can hear me."

Gunnar, still inside of her tight core, lifted her from the dresser and carried her to his bed. "Don't dare me." He placed her on her back while staying nestled between her succulent thighs.

If she could just break away from what held her here in Virginia Beach, Gunnar would love her to be with him.

"I love--" The words choked in Eboni's throat.

Gunnar's heart raced as he stared into her eyes.

She continued. "I love the way you make me feel."

His heart broke into a million pieces as he plastered a fake smile on his face. "Then let's not stop."

Gunnar didn't just mean for the night. For now, he would take that.

Chapter 14

Eboni had hoped to get away from Gunnar, get away from his bed, his apartment, his intense hold over her and her heart, without him noticing. In the still of the night, just snowflakes dancing over the windows, she lifted his sizable arm from around her body and scooted to the edge of the bed.

No time for a shower, she threw on her discarded clothing that had landed on various parts of the floor. By the time she pulled on her sweater, a voice stopped her in her tracks.

"I know you weren't going to leave without saying good-bye."

Eboni didn't want to jump, but she did. She turned around and saw Gunnar propped up on his elbow.

"I have to get home." She continued on her quest to find her personal items. As she slipped on her coat, she said, "I can't leave my aunt two days in a row." She turned to him. "I'm sure you understand."

Gunnar moved to the edge of the bed. Even in the darkness of the room, and with his blond hair twisting wildly over his head, he looked sexy. Damn. She had to get away from him or she would strip down again and let him have her.

"I do understand. But if you think I'm going to let you go out in this weather alone, you're crazy." He stood.

In the small apartment, he appeared so immense.

"I've driven plenty times in the snow." Eboni turned her back on the nude man to keep herself from staring at his cock.

Determined to keep to her goal to get out of his apartment, Eboni grabbed her purse from the couch. She didn't expect Gunnar to wrap his arm around her waist.

She didn't want to touch him. She kept her hands occupied by holding on to her purse strap.

"Wait for me to get dressed, and I'll take you home."

She felt his deep rumbling voice through her coat. She hoped he couldn't feel her heart racing. She swallowed hard.

"That's crazy. You need your sleep. I'll be fine." Eboni tried getting out of his grasp.

He tightened his hold to let her know he hadn't finished talking to her yet. "It's two in the morning. You're going to wake everyone in your home. Can't you just call them in the morning?"

"No, I really should--"

"Don't make me tie you down to the bed." He nuzzled his face into her neck.

Eboni couldn't help but release a sigh. Even under her coat, goose-pimpled flesh covered her body.

Why the hell was she fighting this? She knew Gunnar would be leaving. What he did for a living didn't sit well with her. She couldn't imagine being outside the ring or the cage or whatever he fought in while she watched some man punching and kicking him.

"Don't do this. I have to go." She managed to get out of his grip. "This is not a part of our deal." She turned around to face him. "Flings don't spend the night."

"Remember I told you I wouldn't treat you like a fling. Why are you running from me?"

Before she could lie and say that running from him had been the last thing on her mind, Gunnar trapped her against the door. He put a hand on the door over her shoulder and faced her as she pressed her back against it.

"I get it. You want to take care of your family. No one understands that better than me. But it's early. You know the roads will be bad. If you really want to go, let me get dressed and I'll take you home."

"That's crazy. That means you'll have to come pick me up in the morning for me to come back and get my car."

"Or you just let me play chauffeur for you for the day. I'll come take you to work. When we get off, I'll bring you back here. Of course, Mom won't let you leave until you at least have dinner. Then, if it's a decent hour, you can go home." He placed his other hand over her other shoulder. "Unless there's something else you wanted to do."

Eboni kept her stare on his eyes. She couldn't break away from his hypnotic trance. When a tree branch buckled under the weight of snow and ice and crashed against the window, Eboni and Gunnar both broke from their gazes to look out the window.

"Stay." He kissed her forehead.

Eboni loved the feel of his warm lips against her skin. Although her body desired more, she had to be strong.

"I can't." She pushed against him to break free.

"What do you think will happen if you stay longer?" he posed.

Eboni didn't want to answer that. With each day that passed, she became too comfortable with him. She'd been in that space before. What she thought would be forever had ended. This time, she had to protect her heart.

"I'll see you at work." She gave him a quick kiss and managed to escape before he could convince her to stay. She ran down the stairs, burst through the garage door downstairs, and made sure to lock it behind her. Not that she thought it would keep Gunnar away from her.

Eboni jumped in her car and started it. She turned her heat up to full blast along with her defroster. The time would allow her to think. Why had she allowed Gunnar back into her life? She leaned her head against the steering wheel.

"You can't let him get to you again, girl. Be stronger than that," she told herself.

When she heard a scraping sound against her window, Eboni gasped as she lifted her head. She found Gunnar scraping the ice and new-fallen snow from her windshield. Looking to the side, she also saw his Hummer with headlights blazing in the driveway.

Eboni powered down her window. "What are you doing?"

"You won't let me take you home. So I'm going to follow you to make sure you make it." He finished off her windshield and stood by her door. "I'm your man. That's what I'm supposed to do."

Without confirming or refuting his claim, Eboni powered her window back up and sat silently in her car. Only once Gunnar had her windows cleared of all obstructions, did he allow her to leave. It didn't take her long to see his headlights in her rearview mirror.

As much as she didn't want to be impressed by his commitment to see her home safely, she did breathe a sigh of relief knowing if anything happened on her way home, Gunnar would protect her. That protection came at a price—her heart.

Eboni's heartbeat slowed as soon as she pulled up to her apartment building. She got out of her car and turned to see Gunnar had stopped in his truck and watched her as she walked up to her building. Before disappearing into her apartment, she did turn and wave at him.

Inside of her apartment, she pressed her back against the door. Through the door, she heard the rumbling of his massive vehicle motoring away. She had to smile at his obligation to her, to her safety.

She needed to do the same. She had to keep her heart safe. Unless Gunnar decided to keep himself home, she couldn't chance falling for him again.

* * * *

Gunnar sat in his vehicle behind the salon, shaking his head. "You should be home taking it easy."

His mother glared at him. "I'm not dead yet. I can come and see my folks for a little while. When I get tired, you can take me back home."

Gunnar shook his head. "Yes, ma'am."

He turned off his truck and got out so that he could open her door. He'd never thought any woman could be as stubborn as his mother. Then he'd met Eboni.

It still surprised him that she'd left his bed, hoping to get away from him without him knowing. Not a chance. If she'd thought he would let her go home without an escort, she really must have underestimated him. Gunnar would never forgive himself if she'd gotten into an accident or had been left stranded.

He helped his proud mother out of his incredibly tall vehicle and wrapped her arm around his as he walked her to the back door. Although he kept his attention on her, the fact that Eboni's car sat in the parking lot didn't escape his attention. It must have caught his mother's as well.

"I missed Eboni at breakfast." Ice crunched under his mother's steps.

"She wanted to be home to take care of her aunt." Gunnar crept to the door next to his mother.

"Please." Queen waved her hand in the air. "There's nothing wrong with that woman. She has lazy children who want to rob her of all of her money. Eboni is trying to make sure that doesn't happen."

Gunnar blinked at his mother's candor but didn't say a word. Eboni had mentioned that her cousin had tried sucking her aunt dry.

He opened the door. Chatter inside filled the place. Eboni's voice remained the only one he sought.

"I guess he's not going to show up for work," he heard Eboni saying.

"He's here." Queen Elizabeth pulled back the curtain and walked into the main salon.

The group, which included Tillman, Tisha, Monica, and Eboni, stood and applauded their leader. As her moniker suggested, his mother held up her hand and gave them a very royal wave. The Queen Mum had entered the building.

"Help me to a chair, dear." His mother patted Gunnar's arm.

As instructed, he brought her to Eboni's chair. Gunnar kept his attention on his mother until she settled into the stylist chair. Then he looked at Eboni, who looked like she wanted to avoid his gaze.

"Welcome back, Queen." Tillman approached the woman first and gave her a kiss on her cheek. "We've missed you around here."

"Yes, we have," Tisha said above a whisper.

The group got quiet as they stared at her.

"What?" Tisha, now in jeans and a slightly more formfitting sweater, shrugged.

"Baby, that's the loudest I've ever heard you speak." Elizabeth put her hand to her chest.

Tisha kissed Queen's cheek. "Gunnar helped me find my voice."

"You got a good boy there." Monica, still sitting behind the receptionist desk, nodded toward Gunnar.

"Sounds like you've done a good job in my spot." His mother patted his hand. She turned to Eboni. "See. I told you it would be good for Gunnar to be here."

Eboni smiled and patted Queen Elizabeth on her shoulder. "Would you like some coffee?" She strolled by Gunnar to the coffee station.

"Sure, dear. Plenty of cream and sugar."

Gunnar cleared his throat. He knew his mother had to watch her diet.

Elizabeth screwed up her lips. "Fine. Decaf. No cream. A packet of that fake sugar if you have it."

"Sugar substitute, Mom. It's not bad." He kissed her forehead.

"Don't stand here. We have a business to run. Open the door." She pointed to the front door.

"Yes, ma'am." Gunnar headed to the door and then stopped. "Wait. Where's Shay?"

The group remained quiet.

"Has she called? Has anyone called her?" Gunnar scanned the group for an answer. When they remained quiet, he pressed on. "Anyone have anything to say?" He stared at Eboni, who walked toward his mother with a white Styrofoam cup filled with coffee, decaffeinated he hoped. "Eboni? Have you heard anything?"

She shook her head.

Before Gunnar could argue with his mother about getting rid of the temperamental diva, the back door slammed.

Shay, still in shades, stomped over to her station. She kept her back to the group as she stripped off her coat and purse. When she turned around she glanced at each of them.

"What?" she asked.

"You're late." Gunnar glanced at his watch.

"Honey, let it go and open the door." His mother pointed to the door, which held back about four waiting customers.

"No, Ma. She needs to learn respect. You pay her to be here on time."

"Please. Open the door and let me work." Shay got her station ready while keeping her back to the group. "I promise to be a good girl and eat my vegetables and behave all day."

Gunnar looked to his mother. She gave him a simple nod, which let him know he needed to drop this subject now and open the door.

Gunnar blew out an exasperated breath. "Whatever." He unlocked the door and ushered in a string of customers. "Welcome to Press 'N Curl."

Each customer went to their stylist, avoiding the front desk. Gunnar started to go toward Shay to continue their conversation, but stopped when he heard his mother's voice.

"Gunnar, will you help me into the office?" Elizabeth stood and headed to her office.

By the time Gunnar reached her to assist her inside she'd already made it. He watched her glance around the space, probably looking for where he'd made changes. Wisely, as Eboni had suggested, he'd returned everything to its rightful place.

Queen Elizabeth took up residence behind the desk. In her gold suit, she looked more regal than an entrepreneur.

"Close the door and have a seat." His mother pointed to the door and then the chair in front of her desk.

Gunnar did as instructed. As soon as his backside hit the seat, his mother spoke.

"Did you take my advice and try to get to know these people?" She took a sip of her coffee in a method that didn't ruin her perfectly painted red lips.

"Yes. I took Tillman to breakfast so that we could talk."

Queen raised her eyebrows. "He must have *really* liked that."

Gunnar stared at his mother suspiciously. "You knew? You could have said something to me."

After placing her cup down, a frown settled into her features. "Tell you what? I don't define my employees by their sexuality in the same way I don't define our relationship on race. I taught you that. You don't go around saying you have a black mama just like I don't say I have white sons. Tillman is a really good employee."

Gunnar nodded, feeling stupid with the way he had previously thought about Tillman. "Yes, he is. The best. Very solid. He wants to do what you do. He wants his own shop."

His mother smiled. "Good to see he has ambition. And Tisha?"

"She's an excellent stylist. Quiet but so, so good. I've registered for the Atlanta hair show. I want her to present there."

This time, his mother blinked. "Are you serious? What did she think?"

"She said she loved the idea. She's coming out of her shell." Gunnar relaxed back in his chair.

"I'm proud of you, son. You did so well with those two. I need you to do the same with Shay."

Gunnar snickered and shook his head. "I've tried. Unless she's asking me out for drinks and, uh, more, she doesn't want anything to do with me. She didn't want me here. She undermines me every chance she gets. She's unpredictable."

His mother smiled.

"Care to let me in on the joke?"

"She sounds a lot like a young man I used to know. I would tell him to be home at a certain time, and he would stay out later. I'd tell him to clean his room, and he'd purposely trash it. He hated everything I cooked."

"Are you talking about your ex?" Gunnar spoke the words faster than he thought about how they may hurt his mother.

Her stoic expression let him know his dig hit its intended target, her heart.

"I apologize. You didn't deserve that. But if you're trying to say that Shay is anything like I was, you're mistaken. She's nothing like me." He sat up and braced his elbows on his knees.

"How do you know?" Elizabeth put her hands on top of her desk, which showed off her red nails.

"Because I was hurting when I acted out. I had a biological mother who'd abused me. I had been moved from foster home to foster home. I didn't think anyone loved me." He stared at his mother. "Until I got to your home."

"If you haven't talked to Shay, how do you know she's not hurting in the same way? It may not be foster care, but something else." His mother took another delicate sip from her coffee.

"Do you know what it is?" Gunnar asked.

"What I know I had to find out from her. If you want to gain her trust, I suggest you do the same thing. What do I always tell you?"

"I don't know. You say a lot of things." He smiled.

"You catch more flies with honey." She finished off her coffee. "Speaking of honey, how are you and Eboni?"

Gunnar stood. "I think I'm needed out in the salon."

"Excuse me. I didn't say you could leave." She motioned for him to take his seat again. "What's going on with you and Eboni?"

Gunnar slumped down into his chair again. "Nothing." He shrugged. "We're friends. That's it."

"No more?"

He shook his head.

"But you want more."

Gunnar could never lie to his mother. He paused thoughtfully before answering. "What I want and what's going to happen are two different things. We're living in two separate worlds. You're the only thing holding us together. Once you're better, I'll go back to my home and my job in Nevada." If he still had a job, he wanted to add. "She'll stay here. Her aunt, this salon, and the community center keeps her here."

Queen Elizabeth took a deep breath. "If you want to make it work, you can. Don't deny your heart, baby. I think you've done that for far too long."

Gunnar considered his mother's words carefully. "She doesn't want me solving her problems."

"So don't. But be there for her. And tell her how you really feel before it's too late."

Gunnar started to stand again but stopped. "May I be excused now?"

His mother smiled. "Yes. Go do what you normally do when I'm not here."

"I'm the shampoo boy." He held his hands up and wiggled his fingers.

"You're not styling?" Elizabeth cocked her head. "You do such great hair."

"I style if there's an empty chair. I'm a little rusty."

"You think you would have had enough practice with your own hair. When are you going to cut that stuff off?"

On instinct, Gunnar ran his hand over his head. "It's my look. I think the ladies like it."

He wouldn't tell her the real reason to keep his scalp covered. His mother had enough of her own issues. Gunnar didn't need to test her heart with revealing this bit of news.

She shook her head. "Kids. Thank you for the help, sweetie. I'm going to look around my office and see how you've improved it."

With that, he walked out without a word. He hoped he'd put everything back in its original spot. Knowing Queen Elizabeth, she would find something out of place.

Gunnar scanned the salon. Everyone had someone in their chairs and a couple of customers sat in the waiting area. He decided to address his easier targets before getting with his more difficult ones. He asked Tillman and Tisha if either of them needed help. When they both said no, Gunnar moved over to Eboni.

Eboni wouldn't be a pushover.

"You need help? I'm free. I can help shampoo or something." To illustrate his point, he pushed up the sleeves of his knit shirt.

"No. I'm okay." She flashed him a smile. "Thank you."

Gunnar started to walk away.

"It's great having Queen Elizabeth back here. I've missed her in the salon."

Unable to look at her expression, he moved over to Shay. "You need help?"

Still in her large, bug-eyed sunglasses, she turned to him. "You can buy a sistagirl a meal once in a while since it looks like drinking is off the table."

Gunnar crossed his arms over his chest. "Fine. You free for lunch?"

Shay's mouth hung open as she pumped up the chair holding her client. When she didn't answer, Gunnar turned to Monica.

"Monica, does Shay have any bookings for lunch?" he asked.

Monica scanned the computer screen. "Nope."

"Good. We'll go at noon." He smiled.

Shay didn't share in his happiness. She turned from him. In that motion, Gunnar thought he caught something. He hoped he didn't see what appeared to be a swollen bruise around her eye.

An immediate feeling of anger surged through his body. Gunnar gritted his teeth hard enough for a sharp pain to stab his head. He turned away and caught his mother standing in her office doorway.

To act as though he hadn't seen it, Gunnar smiled and continued to the back area. He braced his hands on the dryer and took a couple of deep breaths. If what he suspected had occurred, no way could he stand by and do nothing.

* * * *

Eboni kept her attention split between her clients and Gunnar's whereabouts. When he'd asked Shay out to lunch, she couldn't deny that a pang of jealousy had riddled her thoughts. Had he asked Shay out because she'd left him at two in the morning?

When she'd gotten home, as she'd suspected, everyone had been in bed sleeping. That didn't mean she needed to get too comfortable. Doing that in the past had gotten her hurt. Now that she knew the score, she wouldn't be blindsided.

Eboni put her client under a hairdryer. "I'll leave you for about thirty minutes."

Her client nodded. When Eboni turned around to clean up her station, she saw Queen Elizabeth standing in her office doorway.

"Darling, will you come here, please?" Elizabeth motioned to her office.

Eboni nodded and walked into the room.

"Close the door, please." Elizabeth sat behind her desk.

Eboni closed the office door and sat down. "What's going on?"

"I was going to ask you the same thing."

Eboni swallowed, unable and unwilling to talk about Gunnar to his mother. "What do you mean?"

"Your hair."

Eboni quickly put her hand to her head, although a small part of her had been relieved that Queen didn't want to talk about Gunnar. "What are you talking about?"

"I must admit. When you first had me put the weave in, I thought it was something you wanted to try. I didn't know you were going to keep getting it redone. I like your hair. Don't you?" Elizabeth looked at her with such warmth and concern in her eyes.

"I thought it looked nice. Is this your way of telling me I need a touchup?" Eboni smiled to lighten the mood in the office.

"It's my way of telling you I know you're hiding something." Queen chuckled. "I swear you and Gunnar are so alike. Both of you are just fighting it though."

"When you're all better, he's going to be gone. Where does that leave me?" Eboni felt her throat getting scratchy, but she refused to cry in front of this man's mother.

"Are you sure that he really wants to go back to fighting?" Elizabeth asked. "And are you sure you want to stay here doing hair, taking care of a relative who doesn't need caring and a place you're giving your full devotion to while cutting yourself out of the equation?"

"Queen, I--"

Elizabeth held up her hand. "No. Hear me out. I've sat back and watched you and I've seen you try so hard to cling to something after Gunnar left. Trust me. I didn't like that he left, especially with what was going on with you. But you two are adults. I thought by now you would have figured it out." She clasped her hands together and rested them on her stomach. "I'm kind of glad to have had this health scare if it's brought you and Gunnar together to figure out how to do it right. I will get better or die."

"Queen!"

"Stop. I can't live forever. Life is short. You remember that. Do you want to live that life authentically or with fake hair and lying to yourself that if that man walks out of your life again you'll be okay?"

This time, Eboni couldn't hide her feelings. She sniffed and wiped her eyes.

"I don't mean to hurt you. But someone has to be honest with you and Gunnar. Don't think he got away easy either. I love both of you. It hurts me to see you two so content to see the other go. You two belong together. Don't you see that?"

See it? Eboni saw it, felt it, dreamed it, and wanted it. Wishing for a relationship didn't mean she would get it.

Eboni stood. "I have to get back to my client."

"It hasn't been thirty minutes."

Ignoring Elizabeth's astute assessment, Eboni continued. "Thanks for the talk. Glad you're here."

By the time she walked out, she spied Gunnar walking out the back door with Shay. Could this day get any worse?

* * * *

Gunnar had made the mistake of asking Shay where she wanted to go for lunch. Little had he known she would ask him to take her to a restaurant in Hampton.

"We couldn't have gone to a barbecue place in Virginia Beach?" Gunnar asked as he held out Shay's chair.

"I love this place." Shay sat down and scanned the customers around them. She pushed her glasses up her nose. "Besides, you have to realize that when you roll with me I only want the best."

Gunnar nodded but said nothing. He would wait to see if Shay would say something first about her tardiness, her absences, and her need to wear sunglasses all the time.

"For as far as I drove on icy roads, this place had better be better than-
-"

"Sex?" Shay winked.

"I was going to say the barbeque place off Princess Anne Road. You like going to the sex angle a lot, don't you?" Gunnar kept his stare on Shay as she crossed her legs and returned his look with a more seductive one.

"It works for me." She ran her tongue over her lips.

"It doesn't work for me, so you can drop it. I'm taking you to lunch as a friend. I want to get to know you."

"Oh, honey, there are other ways you can get to know me." Shay put her hand on his thigh and crept it up to his crotch.

Fed up with her antics, Gunnar grabbed her hand, placed it on top of the table, and left his hand on top of hers to keep it still. "I'm not sure what kind of game you're playing, but I don't want any part of it. I think I've made myself pretty clear. If you keep this up, I'll stop this lunch right now, understand?"

The smile dripped from Shay's face. She snatched her hand from under his. When the waiter came with their menus, she grabbed it out of his hand. Gunnar showed a bit more tact and thanked the young man. They gave him their drink orders. With the distraction gone, the silence that hung between them felt eerie.

Deciding to break the ice, Gunnar asked, "How did you get started doing hair?"

Shay glared at him over her menu and dropped her gaze back to it without answering him.

"Okay, do you have any children?"

He heard Shay smacking her lips behind the menu wall she had erected between them. He put a finger at the top of her menu and pulled it down so that he could see her face.

"I'm assuming you're not married. Are you seeing someone?" he asked, desperate to open up any conversation.

"You don't care. You're only here because Queen Elizabeth made you." Shay slammed her menu closed and left it on the table.

The waiter returned and took their orders, although for a moment, Gunnar thought Shay would give up the lunch and demand to be taken back to the salon.

"I do care. I wouldn't ask if I didn't. I would think working with me you would know that. So can we start over?" When Shay didn't speak, Gunnar continued. "How did you get started doing hair?"

Shay let out a long sigh. "I hated school."

"That's something we have in common." Gunnar smiled to let her know he meant that sincerely. He wanted to show her he could be on her side if she would allow him to get close to her.

"I didn't want to do the college thing when I graduated. Except for working in a bank, it seemed like you had to have a college degree to get a high-paying job. So I first went to school for nursing."

Gunnar felt his eyes go wide at that bit of news. "Really? You hated school and you went directly into nursing school?"

Shay chuckled. "Yeah. Not one of my best decisions. I dropped out after a month. But I didn't learn my lesson, because I immediately enrolled in school for physical therapy. I figured out quick that I didn't like helping sick people."

"What clued you in to that?"

"I threw up on a patient when I saw his burn scars."

Gunnar tried holding back his laughter, but he couldn't stop himself.

Even Shay had to laugh at it. "I know. I felt so stupid. A friend of mine told me that I could do hair and makeup really well. I had a YouTube channel for a while when I was transitioning from relaxed to natural."

Gunnar nodded, knowing that she meant she'd transitioned from getting her hair chemically relaxed on a regular basis to her hair's natural, curly state. If asked, he preferred women with their real hair. He enjoyed the texture, the softness, the curls.

"So I went to cosmetology school. As soon as I got that certificate, I went door to door looking for a job. Queen hired me on the spot. She said she liked my vibe and energy. I told her I liked getting paid. It was match made in heaven." Shay cackled and took a drink of her sweetened iced tea.

Gunnar wanted to tell Shay that getting paid meant she needed to come to work and when she came to work, to be there on time. As he thought it, he could almost feel his mother kicking him under the table to behave himself.

Lunch came fairly quickly. Although Gunnar had hated the drive, he did enjoy the North Carolina-style barbeque sandwich and coleslaw he ordered. It still didn't justify traveling so far for this one meal.

"So any kids?" Gunnar asked as he downed the rest of his crinkle-cut fries.

Chuck would have hated to see him ingest a meal like this. For that reason, he dipped his next fry in a vat of homemade ketchup before popping it into his mouth.

Shay shook her head. "Nah."

"You want any?"

She cut her gaze up at him. "Are you offering?" Before Gunnar could call her on her heavy-handed flirting, she laughed and put her hand on top of his. "I'm kidding. Had to get one more in. Yeah. Someday I'd like to be a mom to some little babies. I don't think now would be a good time."

"Why not?"

Shay kept her gaze down and shrugged her shoulders.

"Shay?"

She waited a beat before she looked up.

"You got a boyfriend?" Gunnar swallowed hard as he waited for her answer.

He knew what she would say. He had to hear it from her.

Shay released a fake laugh. "I thought you weren't interested in me."

Gunnar reached across the table and held her hand.

"I need to go to the bathroom, and then I'm ready to go back to the salon." She slipped her hand out of his and ran to a side hallway.

Gunnar had gotten close to her, but she'd retreated when he'd started to open a painful wound. The one good thing about her picking a lunch spot so far away was he could talk to her on the long car ride back about her choices.

Gunnar paid for lunch and then helped Shay on with her coat. He walked her to his truck, helping her inside first before he got behind the steering wheel.

"That Eboni, she sure is a lucky woman." Shay shook her head.

"What do you mean?" Gunnar blasted the heat as much as he could before driving away.

"I prayed for a good man to come into my life, one who would love me and treat me right. You come in out of nowhere and she has you. You open doors for women, pull out chairs, pay for meals." She looked his way. "You're a nice guy."

"Thank you, but Eboni and I are just friends." Gunnar managed to cut his gaze away before he finished his statement.

"Liar." Shay laughed. "It is so obvious you two are hitting it. I see the way you look at each other."

Gunnar pulled out of the spot and got on to the interstate quick. What he thought would be a good thing as far as the time to get back to the salon now look like it may be an issue if Shay continued to ask probing questions.

"So you don't have a man?" Gunnar asked.

"I have someone. I don't know if I would call him a man."

Gunnar felt that familiar ripple going up the back of his neck. When he glanced at Shay, for a split second, he suddenly saw his mother. She, too, had sported the same large sunglasses to hide black eyes and bruises. He gripped the steering wheel to channel his anger.

"You know when I first got with Queen Elizabeth, I didn't treat her right." Gunnar heard Shay gasp.

"Are you kidding? Everyone loves her. How could you not love the woman who took you in?" She gave him a playful slap on his arm.

"It wasn't her fault. It was mine. Well, not exactly mine. I had some issues before she took me in. I had been abused." He glanced at Shay, who quickly turned to look at the road ahead. He continued. "My biological mother didn't want kids. She would beat me and Gideon all the time. By the time I had gotten to Queen, I thought all mothers were like that. I didn't know any better because I hadn't seen a good example of a kind mother. Then she showed me she loved me." He wouldn't go into the incident with the boys he thought had been his friends. "After that, I learned that not all mothers were like my biological one. If the man you're with isn't treating you right, you need to find one who will."

Shay chuckled. "Easy for you to say. You got lucky in your situation. You got with Queen."

"Yeah, but that was after years of being abused and bounced around. I was a child. I didn't have a voice. You're an adult. You have options. Hey." He waited until she turned around and looked at him. "You have friends."

A tear rolled down from under her sunglasses. She wiped it away while keeping her glasses covering her face. She did wince when she wiped under her eye.

"My mom had to be both mother and father to me. When it came time to talk to me about the birds and the bees, she didn't hold back. She gave it to me straight. She said, 'Gunnar, don't you ever hit a woman. Women are all queens. Treat them that way.' So I do. I hit punching bags and I hit opponents in the ring. That's it."

"So you don't spank in the bedroom?" A smile cocked at the corner of her mouth.

"There you go again."

Shay laughed. "For as much crap as I gave you when you first got there, I'm glad you filled in for Queen. I felt, I don't know, safer with you around."

"Shay, if you want to tell me anything, you can. I won't say anything to my mother or Eboni."

"It's not them that I'm worried about." She rubbed her forehead. "I'm fine. I'm a fighter. I'll be fine."

"Some things you shouldn't have to fight for. You fight for family. You fight for life. You fight for love."

"So what round are you in with Eboni?"

Gunnar wondered the same thing himself. "You're not alone."

"I'm glad it's Friday. One more day of work and then I can relax for a couple of days."

"Oh, speaking of which. Mom wants you all to come over to the house Sunday for a party. We're watching my brother play in his first Super Bowl ever. You're going to be there, right?"

"I don't know. I have to check. I might have a thing at my place." She turned her gaze away to look at the water they crossed over to get on the south side of the tunnel.

"Invitation is open."

She nodded but didn't turn back to him. Even when they got back to the salon and Gunnar helped her out of the truck, she kept her gaze away from him.

"Wow. That was a long lunch," Tillman said as soon as they strolled through the back door.

"Sorry. The diva here insisted we go to some place in Hampton." Gunnar removed his jacket.

In unison, the staff and some of the patrons in the salon all said, "Hampton?"

Then they looked at Shay.

"What? There's a really good barbeque place over there." She hung up her coat and called for her next client to come to her chair. "I can't help it if I know what I like. Ain't that right, Guns?" She blew him a kiss.

Now that he understood her bravado masked her pain, he played along with her. "Sure, Shay. Whatever you say."

"Glad you enjoyed your lunch." Eboni pushed past him to get to the back area.

"Maybe you should have brought something back for her." Tisha pointed to Eboni.

No, hunger didn't fuel Eboni's attitude. Knowing a strain of jealousy slithered its way through her had Gunnar tickled. That meant she cared.

At the end of the day, Gunnar swept up the hair on the floors while everyone else cleaned off the counters and the coffee area.

"Darling, can we stop off at a burger joint so I can get a nice, big, juicy burger and a pile of greasy fries and a milkshake?" Queen Elizabeth came out of her office and slipped on her coat.

"Very funny, Mom. How about a salad, grilled chicken, and steamed veggies?" Gunnar dumped the hair and dirt into a nearby trash bin and put the cleaning supplies away.

"Eh, you're no fun." She waved her had at him.

A blaring car horn sounded from behind the salon.

"What's that? Who's laying on their horn like that?" Gunnar started toward the door when Shay stopped him.

"I got it. It's for me. I got dropped off this morning, which is why I was late. My ride is here."

Shay opened the door to the sound of someone screaming, "Get over here now!"

Gunnar started to go out the door when Shay put her hand to his chest.

"I'm fine. I'll see you all tomorrow, okay?" She nodded and smiled.

"If you're so fine, why are you still wearing shades at night?" he asked her.

"Because I'm a diva, remember?" She patted her curly Afro and sauntered to the car. She got inside the passenger side.

Gunnar wished he could have seen the action inside. With the tinted windows and the driver now blaring rap music, he couldn't see or hear anything. The car made a U-turn in the parking lot and sped off into the street.

"See you all tomorrow." Monica waddled past Gunnar to her car.

"Did Queen tell you about the Super Bowl party at her house?" he called after her.

"Yeah. I'll be there. I'm bringing my nacho dip." Monica waved as she continued on her trek to her car.

Gunnar stepped back inside. After Tillman and Tisha left, he stood there with two women who had his heart, although one looked like she wanted to crush his in her hand.

"Joining us for dinner?" Elizabeth asked Eboni.

"No. I'm going home." Eboni put on her coat and grabbed her purse.

"Something wrong?" Gunnar asked.

"Nope. I realized I haven't been home a lot with my own family this week and I'd like to do that." She started to head out the door when Gunnar held her arm.

"Stop. Can we talk?"

"No, take Queen home. I'll see you tomorrow."

"If you go home, I'll come there after I take Mom home."

Eboni looked conflicted before she finally gave up. "Fine. Quick dinner and that's it."

"So I won't have to wear my headphones tonight again?" Queen Elizabeth asked.

"Mom!"

"I'll wait for you in your truck."

Chapter 15

Eboni didn't want to go to Gunnar's for dinner. She'd proven to herself that she had no self-control around him. After dinner, and with Queen Elizabeth in her bedroom, Eboni found herself in an awkward spot.

After she helped wash and put away the dishes with Gunnar, she headed to the living room to retrieve her coat and purse. "Thank you for dinner again. I'm going to go home."

"Will you come to my apartment?" he asked behind her.

Eboni turned and released an audible sigh.

In a look of surrender, Gunnar raised his sizable hands in the air. Eboni couldn't help but stare at them for a moment and remember the pure pleasure she'd received from them many times over since he'd come home. She shook her head and focused on him.

"I promise. I want to talk. I don't want you thinking that every time you come over I want one thing, although…" He trailed off with a mischievous smile.

"I'm going." She turned to leave.

Gunnar held her hand. "Wait. Please. I really do want us to talk."

Eboni made the mistake of looking into his eyes. His sincerity and the strength in his stare bowled her over. How could she say no to him?

"For a short while, then I really have to go."

Gunnar smiled. "Good." With him still holding her hand, he led her outside and across the yard to the garage.

At the top of the stairs, he opened the door for her. "Would you like some coffee or hot chocolate? I went out and got one of those single-serve coffeemakers. The woman at the store said everyone has one of these things." He smiled as he placed his hand on top of the machine.

"Coffee would be nice." Eboni wanted to remain alert and sober for whatever Gunnar wanted to talk about in the seclusion of his space.

After rattling off a bevy of choices, Eboni chose a caramel-vanilla blend. It didn't take long for the apartment to be filled with the soothing and sweet aroma. She took a deep breath as she closed her eyes. The dripping sound became a bit of white noise for her until it finished its cycle.

Gunnar carried a white mug to the living room area where she sat and handed it to her.

"Thank you." Eboni took a sip and let the creamy and sweet liquid coat her tongue and slide down her throat like hot ice cream. "So good." She glanced at him. "You're not having any?"

Gunnar shook his head. "I got it for guests."

Eboni stared at him suspiciously. "That seems like something you buy when you plan on being here for a while." She blew her breath over the liquid to cool it. "Are you?" As she awaited his answer, her heart pounded. She set her mug on the coffee table so he couldn't catch the slight tremble affecting her hands now.

"I've been thinking about it more and more." He sat next to her. "When Chuck showed up, it let me know that he sees me as a commodity, his meal ticket, not a person. And I keep thinking, what if I had a wife?" He stared at her. "What if I had kids?"

Eboni swallowed hard and scooted back on the couch to create more space in between their bodies.

"If I got hurt in the ring, how would they be taken care of?" he continued.

"You don't think between your mom and brothers that whoever you had in your life would be watched over?" Eboni knew how Queen ran a household. No way would she let any of her family members falter.

"I'm sure they would, but my wife and kids should be my responsibility." He put his hand to his chest. "I don't want to keep fighting."

Eboni had started to reach for her mug before Gunnar dropped that bombshell. She knew she couldn't hide the shock from her face. Gunnar suddenly wanted to abandon the one thing that had separated them.

"What are you talking about? Once Queen gets better, what are you going to do?" she asked.

"I don't know. I can't put my body through this anymore." He stared at her pointedly. "I'm tired. Being with you has made me realize that I have wasted a lot of time."

She blinked. "I didn't want you to give up your career."

He smiled. "If I hadn't thought about chasing the all mighty dollar, maybe we could have had a chance. I think about that all the time." He shook his head. "I never told you this, but I caught you and your family dumpster diving one time."

Eboni remained still. She didn't confirm or lie and deny what Gunnar had said. She remembered quite vividly what her family had had to do to survive, including going into grocery store dumpsters after hours to find food for the next day.

"So?" Staying defiant, Eboni jutted out her chin to show him her past had made her stronger.

"I never said anything to you, but after that, I vowed I would earn enough money to give you the best of everything. The best house, the best cars, the best clothes. Everything. You deserved it."

When he said that line this time, Eboni knew what he meant. "Oh, so you pitied me? Was that it?"

He shook his head. "Never. I wanted the best for you." Gunnar stared at her pointedly. "God, I messed up so badly with you."

Before Eboni knew it, Gunnar interlaced his fingers with hers. "Stay the night."

As Eboni opened her mouth to object, he continued.

"No sex. I want to hold you. Let me hold you." He brushed his thumb over the back of her hand.

Unable to verbally respond, Eboni nodded. He'd bared his soul to her and revealed something so mind-blowing that she doubted he had even told his mother.

Eboni should have taken that moment to tell him the truth about her, about them. She placed her free hand on her stomach. Before letting it rest there too long, she reached for her coffee again and took a sip.

"Will you tell me about your aunt? What's her medical condition?" he asked.

Eboni shrugged. "The stroke affected her right side. Going through physical therapy helped. She's gotten a lot stronger. But she needs help getting around."

"You ever think about life outside of Virginia? Would you ever move away?"

She felt her eyebrows knit together. "Why would I move? I have so much keeping me here."

"I know." To punctuate his statement, he gave her a knowing look. "I'm not saying you need to turn your back on your family, friends, and obligations...like I did."

It didn't help that he made the statement wearing a sheepish expression. She actually felt for him. Her heart thrummed as he spoke.

"You don't seem happy. You of all people deserve happiness."

Hearing that from Gunnar, Eboni suddenly felt overwhelmed and exhausted. She'd let so much get to her. Her aunt, her work, the community center, hell, even her hair.

"I'd like to lie down." She stood.

Gunnar stood with her and led her to his bedroom. After slipping off her shoes, Eboni slipped under his comforter wearing all of her clothes. Gunnar removed his boots and slipped in behind her. True to his word, he wrapped his arm around her waist and pulled her body close to his.

His heartbeat drummed a steady beat against her back. The sound, the feeling, lulled her to sleep.

* * * *

Eboni woke up with a start. She looked at the digital clock next to Gunnar's bed. Damn, what was it about two o'clock in the morning with her?

Gunnar still had his arm draped around her. Like the other morning, she lifted his arm and slipped from under him. This time, she didn't have the need to run home like before. Gunnar's words had hit home.

She'd spent so much time being angry, hating herself for waiting for him and forgetting about herself. Eboni padded to the bathroom. After relieving herself, she caught her reflection in the mirror over the sink. She couldn't help but gaze up at her hair.

Eboni touched it, feeling the tracks running around her head. She opened Gunnar's cabinet over the sink. When she couldn't find what she needed there, she checked the drawer under the sink and found a pair of scissors. She picked them up and closed the drawer.

When she caught her reflection again, the tears she'd been holding back came flooding down her face. She sniffed as she lifted a section of her expensive sewn-in hair and attempted to chop it off her head.

"Baby, what are you doing?" Gunnar stood in the doorway.

Eboni hadn't even heard him walking toward her.

"I need them out." She wiped her face with the back of her hand. "I don't want this weave anymore." She turned to him. "I hate it."

With a careful touch, Gunnar removed the scissors from her hands. "Sit down." He pointed to the toilet.

After she lowered the lid, she sat. Gunnar sectioned her hair and held it in place with a clip that he got from the same drawer.

"Are you sure you want to do this?" he asked before making any cuts.

Eboni nodded. "I want them all gone."

"Okay. It's been a while since I've removed weave from someone's hair. I'll be sure to be careful."

Gunnar used a delicate hand to snip out lines of added hair from her head. When he removed the first row of tracks, he asked her if she wanted it. Eboni took the hair and threw it in the trash can.

With each section removed, Eboni felt lighter and lighter, like years of burden had been lifted. After the last section of hair had been removed, Gunnar carefully undid her cornrows.

Doing that loosened the tightness in her head. Through her tears, she released a long sigh.

Gunnar ran his large fingers through her hair. "You want me to even that out?"

Eboni stood and looked at herself in the mirror. She shook her head. "I want it all gone."

"Babe? The big chop? Are you sure?"

Instead of answering him, Eboni removed every stitch of clothes she wore. Gunnar didn't stop her although he stared at her like she'd lost her mind. She started his shower and got inside. She picked up a shampoo bottle he had in the stall and shampooed her now shorter hair. With it rinsed from her head. She opened the curtain and found Gunnar still standing in the bathroom waiting for her.

Eboni wrapped a towel around her body and assumed her position seated on the toilet again. "Chop off the straight ends for me."

Gunnar didn't question her. Like he'd done with her tracks, he took time and care in cutting the relaxed ends out of her hair. Eboni watched section after section of straight, long hair falling down around her.

"Let me shape it up for you." Gunnar took a step back and looked at her.

Then he went to work like a pro. He snipped here and there to give her an even shape.

The decision to cut her hair had been impulsive but long overdue. If anyone had to help her, other than Queen, Eboni only trusted Gunnar.

As he continued cutting her hair, Eboni felt the need to reveal more of herself. "Right after you left, people kept coming to me and asking me about you. How could I let you go? Why didn't I go with you? Why wasn't I good enough for you?" She felt him stop moving at that bit of news. "I wanted to disappear. I wanted to be someone else. I added the hair." She snickered. "For a short while, I even rocked green eye contacts. After a year of that, I got rid of them. But I kept the hair."

"So why now? Why get rid of it now?" Gunnar asked as he continued working.

"When you mentioned how tired you were with fighting, I could relate. I shouldn't have had to hide myself." Eboni wiped her eyes. "I was tired of people seeing me as poor and worthless. I wanted to be different, to look different."

"Done. You want to see?"

Eboni stood and looked at herself in the mirror. She thought seeing herself with such short hair would make her cry even harder. Instead, she felt liberated. She touched her hair and felt its natural softness.

"I love it." She turned to Gunnar.

"Let me do something." He walked out of the room.

Eboni heard what she thought sounded like the refrigerator door opening and closing. He returned with a jar in his hand.

"I made this the other day." He smiled. "It's a deep conditioner."

"Experimenting again?" Eboni asked as she watched him scoop some in his hand.

"Oh, man. Do you mind? Do you want to try it? I guess I should have asked first."

Eboni touched his hand. "I let you cut my hair. I trust you."

He slathered the thick concoction on her hair, covering it completely. He covered her hair with a plastic shower cap. "Sit like that for about five minutes."

While she did, still with a towel around her nude body, he removed her clothes from the floor and took them to the washer downstairs. When he returned, he cleaned the hair from the bathroom floor. By the time he finished, he asked her to get in the shower to rinse it out.

"Join me." She stood and removed her towel.

Without question, Gunnar removed his clothes and jumped into the shower with her. He helped rinse out the conditioner that smelled like vanilla and rosemary.

While in the shower, she turned to him.

"You are so beautiful." He put his hand against her cheek.

For the compliment, Eboni eased her hand to the back of his head and brought him down to kiss her. Her body tingled as his lips vibrated against hers when he moaned.

"I need you." Gunnar broke from the kiss long enough to make the proclamation.

She nodded. He turned off the water. Without drying their bodies, he pulled her to his bedroom. Gunnar directed her to get into bed as he went to his drawer for his condom stash.

After freeing herself from the shackles of her hair prison, Eboni almost wanted Gunnar to make love to her without a condom. She realized that for as much as they had revealed to each other, they still needed to protect themselves in other aspects of their lives.

Gunnar got in bed with her. Eboni never felt so loved and desired. He pressed his lips against hers, kissing her so hungrily she thought he would consume her. Gunnar kissed down her body, licking her nipples and suckling them before he headed to the apex between her thighs.

The first swipe of his tongue over her pussy had her body shaking. She didn't move while he laved her. When he flicked his tongue over her clitoris, Eboni jackknifed her body straight up. She held the back of his head to keep him in his spot.

Gunnar gripped her thighs, keeping her legs apart as he continued to extract her essence. When she screamed, Gunnar held his mouth over her until her body settled.

When Eboni relaxed against his bed, Gunnar sat up on his knees and opened a condom package. He rolled it down the length of him.

For as passionately as he'd pulled her to bed, he became very gentle when he entered her. Fully seated, he held himself there, staring into her eyes and making that connection that broke her.

His long, slow strokes gave her time to enjoy him, enjoy his body. Eboni held on to his shoulder with one hand and gripped his firm ass cheek in the other. When he kissed her, she even liked the taste of herself on his lips. The briny flavor reminded her of what he'd done for her.

Eboni tried to get the big man to roll over. When he didn't budge, she said, "I want you on your back."

Gunnar rolled without argument and positioned her on top of him. He'd done so much for her. She wanted to give him pleasure.

Eboni's body undulated as she braced her hands on his chest. He held her hips. She ran her hands up her body to her newly shorn hair. It felt even softer after Gunnar's treatment.

She continued riding him, increasing her speed. Her thighs burned, but she couldn't stop.

"So good." She nodded her head. "Beautiful. Sexy."

Gunnar cupped her breasts and massaged them in his hands.

"Yes! Yes!" She gripped his wrists.

Eboni's body stiffened as she came. Before she had time to relax, Gunnar sat up, wrapped his arms around her waist and pulled her down. He lifted his ass from the mattress and drove himself in her.

This time, she felt him shaking. "Give it to me."

Gunnar growled and stopped for a moment as he climaxed. He gave her a couple of thrusts before settling back on the bed. "I swore to myself that I wouldn't have sex with you tonight."

Eboni laughed. "I'm glad you did. I wondered as you were taking out my tracks if you or any man would find me attractive without my hair."

"Oh honey. If you had a bald head, you would still be the sexiest thing on two legs." To prove his point, he kissed her hard enough that she knew her lips would be swollen.

She didn't care. Eboni started to like herself more. Once she unburdened herself from all things holding her back, she would know freedom.

* * * *

The morning came earlier than Eboni thought. She awakened when she heard a buzzing sound. Out of instinct, she reached over to the clock next to the bed. When she discovered that it hadn't been set, she sat up. Glancing around, she immediately noticed Gunnar had left the bed.

She crept out of the bed and slipped on one of his oversized T-shirts. As she approached the bathroom, the buzzing sound became louder and louder.

She pushed the door open and found Gunnar at the mirror shaving his head. Piles of his long, blond locks littered the floor around his massive feet.

Eboni covered her mouth with her hand. "Gunny, you didn't have to shave your head because of me."

"This is has been long overdue." He rubbed his hand over his head. "But not for the reason you think."

Even without his long hair, he looked sexy. "What do you mean?"

"I did something when I was younger that I'm not proud of." Before Gunnar could explain, he turned and showed a greenish tattoo etched in the back of his head.

Eboni didn't need to get close to him to see the familiar symbol of an equal sign with a slash through it. She'd seen lots of those around the community center, tagged by a local gang.

Chapter 16

Gunnar had been bound and determined never to let a soul look at the shame his hair covered. If Eboni had been brave enough to cut her hair and expose herself, he could do the same. When he caught her horrified look, he questioned his decision.

"What the hell?" Eboni pointed to him and backed out of the bathroom. "You were a No Equal? I knew you hung around some bad people back in the day, but I didn't know you were part of a gang."

Gunnar ran his hand over his head. "I was hanging out with a bad group of kids a few years after I first moved in with my mom. They accepted me, warts and all, or so I thought. So to show my allegiance, I got the tattoo. Aside from leaving you, this was the worst mistake I've ever made. I didn't want to come home and be reminded of all the mistakes I had made. I kept my hair long to cover it. But I can't keep hiding."

"So what are you going to do?"

"I want it gone. I know the removal process is painful, but I want it off my head." He rubbed his head. When Eboni remained quiet, Gunnar felt compelled to fill the void. "I don't feel anything for what this disgusting symbol means. I wish I had never gotten it."

"You got it when you were younger. How did you hide this from your mother?"

"I was clever back then. At least I thought I was. I would leave the house early for school. I would always face my mother. Kept my collar up high. As soon as I left the house, I wore hats. My brothers knew. They hated it. Deep down, I think my mom knew. She never said anything to me, although I did notice that we went to church a whole lot more."

Gunnar couldn't look at himself in the mirror. Even though he'd started the process of correcting his past mistakes, he still couldn't shake the disappointment he felt. He rubbed his head and kept his hand over the back of it, covering the tattoo.

"We were together. I don't remember it." Eboni studied him.

He snickered. "For what we used to do, you never got the chance to see the back of my head, except for when I left to train. By then, I had already started growing my hair out and it was covered."

"You're not going to work with that showing, are you?"

"Not during the day today." He shook his head. "I'll have to wear hats, which my mother will hate. But I'm tired of covering it up. When the shop closes, I'll get everyone together to talk about it. I will have to tell my mother first." He glanced at Eboni. "Second."

Eboni offered a small smile, which lightened the mood.

Gunnar knew more than anyone the magnitude of what he'd done to himself. The fact that Eboni hadn't run when she'd seen the horrific symbol encouraged him.

"Will you do me a favor?" He stayed in his spot. He didn't want to crowd her space.

Eboni approached him. She placed a hand to the side of his face. "Anything."

Gunnar turned his head and kissed her palm. "Will you take Queen with you to the salon? I'm going to see if I can see someone today about getting this removed."

Standing on her tiptoes, Eboni gave him the sweetest kiss on his lips. "Of course."

Gunnar held her around her waist. If he could stay in the apartment with her all day, he would be happy.

"Now will you do me a favor?" Eboni asked as she placed her hand on his chest.

"Anything." He smiled.

"Help me do something with my hair."

Gunnar scooped her into his arms. "I knew eventually you would admit that I'm a better stylist than you."

She gave him a playful punch to his arm. "Never."

Gunnar took another joint shower with Eboni. As he rubbed soap down her body, he decided he never wanted to leave that space. With them both exposed, he felt closer to her than even before. With her, he had nothing to hide. In front of his mother, that would be a different story.

Gunnar had no idea what Queen Elizabeth would think of his old but new-to-her head art. He kind of hoped that she already knew about it and wanted him to show her and explain. He would, but he wanted to see a doctor first.

With them both showered, dressed, and newly coifed, Gunnar walked Eboni over to the main house. As soon as his mother spied them, her eyes became wide.

"What in the world? You two look so different." Queen first touched Eboni's hair, which Gunnar had added some pomade and hair gel to give it a glistening, curly look. Then she headed to her son.

Gunnar made sure to face her. She reached up and brushed her hand against his stubble.

"Happy now, Mom?" He smiled.

"I didn't think you would go this drastic, but I like it. Let me see it all the way around." She twirled her red fingernail in the air.

Gunnar threw a baseball cap on his head. "I would model for you right now, but I have to go. After my appointment, I'll need to discuss something with you." He kissed her on her cheek. "Eboni will take you to work." He leaned over to Eboni and gave her a long kiss to let her know how much he cared for her. "Thanks for staying with me last night." He meant that.

The beginning of the night, when he'd held her until they both slept had been the best sleep he'd had in a long time. He could see his life with Eboni in it. Did she see that though?

"I'll see you both later." He walked toward the back door.

"Where are you going?" his mother asked.

"I have to see someone this morning. But I'll be in the salon later. Love you." Thankfully, Gunnar managed to escape without a lot of questions.

He scraped off his vehicle and then did Eboni's before he went to a doctor's office he'd found online that specialized in tattoo removal. He hoped the doctor would be able to fit him in and even do something today. Gunnar wanted to start his life fresh. This would do it.

* * * *

"What the hell?" Monica exclaimed as soon as Eboni and Queen Elizabeth strolled through the back door. "You cut off all of your hair."

Eboni hadn't felt self-conscious about her decision until that point. She reached up and touched her hair. Gunnar had done a great job of styling it for her.

"I think it looks great." Tisha smiled.

"Yeah, it makes you look, I don't know, younger, prettier. You can see your face." Tillman waved his hand in front of his own face to illustrate his point.

"Thanks, guys. I was ready for something new. Going natural would do it. Got rid of the weave and had Gunnar cut off my relaxed ends." She headed toward the office to put away her coat and purse.

"Did anything else get relaxed in the end?" Monica cackled at her own lewd joke.

"Let's just get the salon open and go on with the day." Eboni glanced over at Shay's station. "Anyone seen or heard from Shay?"

They each shook their heads.

Eboni turned to Queen. "Maybe Gunnar is right. Maybe we do need to talk about letting her go. If she can't come in on time to work, then--"

"No." Elizabeth shook her head. "You let me worry about Shay. If I need to work a station, I will."

"Oh, no, you won't," Eboni, Tisha, and Tillman all said in unison.

"You're probably not even supposed to be here." Tisha shook her head.

"Where's Gunnar?" Tillman asked.

"He had an appointment this morning," Eboni quickly supplied. "He'll be in later."

Eboni had to stop fighting her feelings. She found she couldn't wait to see him all the time. Hearing his name mentioned had her heart fluttering.

When he'd mentioned to her about leaving the state, giving up her job, her family, and the center, her heart had stopped. Could she turn her back on everything for him?

By lunchtime, Gunnar showed up, still with his hat on his head but with a scowl on his face.

"Hey, Guns!" Tillman waved to the big man as he strolled through the salon.

"Do you have time to do my baby's hair?" Marc asked as he held his squiggly child on his lap.

Gunnar waved to the two of them on his way to the office, where Eboni knew he would give his mother kiss on her cheek. Eboni's aunt had always said if Eboni wanted to know if a man would treat her right, she had to see him with his mother. Gunnar would treat her like a queen judging by the way he treated Queen Elizabeth.

After getting her client under a heated bonnet, Eboni headed to the office when Gunnar didn't reemerge.

"Did everything go okay?" Eboni asked him.

From the tension floating between him and Queen, Eboni felt like she'd stepped into a lion's den.

"No. But it will be." Gunnar gave Eboni a quick peck.

"Son, just tell me where you were so I don't worry. That's all I'm asking." Queen remained seated behind her desk but didn't break her stare from Gunnar.

"Not now. I'll tell you later."

"And take off that hat. You're in a building."

Ignoring her request, he headed out to the main salon.

Queen shook her head. "I don't like when Gunnar keeps secrets from me. It reminds me of when he was younger. That was not a good time. I can't go through that again."

Eboni knew what plagued him, but she couldn't betray his trust and tell his mother. "I'll see if I can get him to talk."

After scanning the main salon, she ducked behind the curtain to the back. She found Gunnar in the bathroom. He'd left the door open and braced his hands on the sink.

"It didn't go well today?" Eboni leaned against the doorframe.

Gunnar turned to her. "I went to three different places. They all looked at it. The good news is that because it's a homemade tattoo, it won't take as long to remove. But I have to do it in sessions."

Eboni nodded, trying to see this as a positive thing. "Okay, it sounds like it's at least possible."

"Yeah, but I have to wait between four to six weeks in between sessions." He shook his head. "I don't have that kind of time."

"You didn't know that before you went to the appointment?"

He shook his head. "I knew the removal would take a few sessions. I didn't know I would have to wait that long between sessions. You're talking to a man who was fine with having long hair."

"You blame me for you cutting your hair?" She took a step back from him.

He furrowed his eyebrows before answering. "God, of course not. I'm kicking myself for being stupid so many years ago. Now I'll have to find a place in Vegas that can do the work just in case."

Eboni swallowed. "I thought you wanted to give up fighting."

He turned to her. "I do. But I have to defend my title first before I can walk away. I know I have to have one fight before I can completely end it."

That one fight had Eboni more nervous than his entire career. She had no desire to see Gunnar fighting.

Eboni peered up. "I can cover that with makeup if you want."

Gunnar reached in his pocket and pulled out a black cloth. Until he took off his cap and covered his head, she hadn't realized he'd had gotten a do-rag. "Got that covered. Hopefully, my mom won't have a problem with this. I won't be able to keep why I keep covering my head from her for too long. I need the focus not to be on me before my brother's game. It should be about my mom and Gideon."

Eboni nodded. She reached up and straightened out his head covering. When their stares connected, she noticed he started to lower his head like he wanted to kiss her. Her heart started pounding hard behind her rib cage as she awaited this needed kiss.

A ruckus in the salon stopped him.

"Excuse me." Gunnar moved by Eboni and headed into the salon.

Eboni followed him and saw who'd created the noise and commotion. T-Lite, the young man who'd come into the place before had returned. He held up a duffel bag.

"Ladies and gentlemen, I'm still trying to get my band to camp. Y'all interested in buying some candy?" T-Lite reached into the bag. "I'm also selling some, uh, special brownies."

"Get out." Gunnar stood in front of the young man.

"Oh, look. It's Guns again. Hey, shouldn't you take off that rag off in here. It's disrespectful, right? That's what you told me." T-Lite laughed.

"I didn't stutter. Take the candy and those brownies and get out of this establishment." He pointed to the door.

"Or what? What are you going to do, old man?"

Oh, no. Did this boy think he could square off against Gunnar? As Gunnar approached him, the slamming of the back door stopped him.

Shay stormed into the salon and went directly to her station. Her large sunglasses still covered her face. When she sat her large saddlebag-sized purse on the counter, it fell over onto the floor, spilling and scattering the contents.

"Shit!" Shay bent over to collect the items.

"*Oh.* She cursed. Are you going to kick her out too?" The young man covered his mouth with a balled-up fist and laughed.

Before Gunnar could address him, the front door slammed open. A man about as tall as the teenage boy in front of Gunnar stormed inside, moved past Gunnar and Eboni, and went directly to Shay.

"Hey, who are you?" Gunnar dropped his attention from the boy and went to this man.

Before any of them realize what would happen, the man grabbed Shay's arm and pulled her back.

Eboni ran toward them but couldn't get there before Gunnar had gotten to the duo.

"Excuse me. You need to get you hand off her." He pointed to Shay.

The man scowled as he looked up at him. "Who the fuck are you? Don't get in my personal business."

"Shay is my business. She works for me here."

The man's eyebrows shot up. "Oh, so you're the dude who took my woman out, huh?" He yanked on her again. This time Shay's sunglasses fell off her face, revealing bruises around her swollen left eye.

A gasp sounded throughout the salon. Eboni could tell the man might as well have waved a red flag in front of this charging bull.

"Shay is my woman. She can't disrespect me by stepping out on me. She needs to learn that." He glowered at Shay. "You thought you were being slick by going to Hampton, didn't you?"

Shay kept her gaze down to the floor.

"Bitch, I got eyes everywhere."

Gunnar rolled up his sleeves. "Are you responsible for her black eye? Is that how you like to teach? I like that method." Gunnar stepped up to the man. "Hit me. Come on. Teach me not to take my friend out to lunch. Touch me. Put one hand on me." Without touching Shay's boyfriend, Gunnar managed to get him hemmed up in a corner.

"Gunnar, please." Shay tried pulling Gunnar back.

Gunnar kept charging. "Come on. Man to man, you teach me something. Put your hands on me. Come on." He turned his head. "I'll let you have the first swing. Right here." He patted his cheek. "Do it. Hit a man. Hit me." He ripped off the doo-rag and threw it to the floor.

A second wave of gasps sounded throughout the salon, but Gunnar didn't acknowledge it.

"Gunnar, stop it!" Elizabeth stood in the doorway of her office, holding herself up by gripping the frame.

"You're fucking crazy." Shay's boyfriend stumbled back against Shay's workstation, knocking down her styling tools in the process.

"You're right. I don't respect or respond to so-called men who put their hands on women like they have a right to. You're not a man if you need to do that. You're a punk and a coward." Gunnar continued pressing up against him. "If you're man enough to hit a woman, then knocking me out shouldn't be a problem, right? So do it. Knock me on my ass."

"Don't think I won't," her boyfriend challenged.

"Then do it! Knock me out. But if you don't, oh, partner, if you don't, no one will be able to get me off you."

"Gunnar!" his mother shouted.

"Tillman, do something," Shay said in between her tears.

Gunnar kept his laser-like focus directly on Shay's boyfriend. Eboni knew if someone didn't get in between these two, no one would be able to stop Gunnar.

Eboni ran to the men and put her hands on their chests in an attempt to push them back from each other. Shay's boyfriend definitely wanted to get away, but Gunnar felt like an immovable statue.

"Gunnar, stop fighting. Please." Eboni stared into his face until he finally broke his gaze from Shay's man to acknowledge her.

A look of realization crossed Gunnar's face. He turned back to the boyfriend. "If Shay comes back in here with even a split end, I will come find you. Are we clear? You will never, ever touch her again." He took one step back and stood there, expecting Shay's boyfriend to squirm his way around him and leave.

"You're crazy. All of you are crazy." He pointed to Shay. "You keep your ass here. Don't come home."

Gunnar turned and charged toward him, a motion that got Shay's man to sprint out of the salon.

* * * *

Gunnar had been oblivious to everything that happened around him until the man left. Like when he fought in the ring, he'd had that tunnel-like vision where this jerk had remained in his focus. Had he touched Gunnar, Gunnar would have choked him out.

When he turned and faced the people in the salon, he saw what his hotheaded nature had done. Eboni held Shay, who couldn't stop sobbing. When he panned his gaze over to the office, he saw his mother standing there breathing heavily like she'd been holding her breath for hours.

Alicia's crying caught his attention. Gunnar peered down to his side and saw the child clutching her father and crying into his neck.

"Gun-Gun scared me. Don't like it."

Gunnar started to kneel down to her but Marc shook his head as he rocked his child.

"Damn, that was amazing," T-Lite said as he held up his camera-phone to capture the intense moment. "I didn't know you're a No Equal." He held up his fist and turned it around so that Gunnar could see a similar tattoo on the back of his hand.

Gunnar's biggest fear confronted him. His past had caught up with him. He couldn't escape. He would always be that thug, fixing problems with his fists.

"Get out now." Gunnar did the same thing he'd done to Shay's boyfriend. He approached T-Lite and forced him to back up to the door and leave without uttering a word.

"But we're the same. We're supposed to look out for each other."

"I'm nothing like you." Gunnar pulled the door closed once T-Lite had stumbled outside.

With the two toxic forces out of the salon, Gunnar turned to the employees and customers. "I apologize for my actions." He looked at his mother. "Excuse me." He snatched his doo-rag from the floor by Shay's station and walked out of the back door.

He needed to clear his head. It had been a long time since he'd felt the need to fight anyone outside of the ring. He wished he hadn't lost his temper. When he'd seen Shay's black eye, it had reminded him of his mother when she had been with that asshole who thought putting his hands on her had been his right.

Gunnar had done a lot of things in life. Hitting a woman in anger had never been one of them and never would be. Queen had taught him and his brothers that. He'd used that lesson at fifteen years old to try and protect his mother against her abusive ex-husband. The fight hadn't gone over well for Gunnar, but that hadn't stopped him from doing the right thing.

After an hour of walking around, Gunnar, with tail firmly tucked between his legs, went back to the salon. After today, he wouldn't return to it.

He crept through the back door, making sure not to slam it behind him to alert anyone. Not that it mattered. He would have to cross the salon to get to the office to get his jacket. As soon as he pulled the curtain back, a barrage of applause and whistles hit him.

Gunnar blinked as he looked around. Clients all stood on their feet and clapped for him. It felt surreal, like he had been transported to one of his matches.

He turned to Shay. She glared at him as she approached him. Standing a foot away from him, she stared at him for a beat before she wrapped her arms around his neck and cried against his chest.

Gunnar held her as he looked for Eboni for a response. She kept her arms around her body as she nodded.

"Thank you. Thank you." Shay gripped his shoulders.

"It's okay. I wished you had said something earlier. We could have helped you." Gunnar patted her back.

Crystal B. Bright

When she pulled back from him, she gave him a kiss on his cheek before going back to her station. Without her sunglasses, even with her swollen eye, she looked stronger than ever. She looked like a survivor.

Gunnar faced the people in the salon. "I need to apologize. I should have handled that differently." He looked at Marc, who held his child's little hand as she sat in Eboni's chair. "I didn't mean to frighten Alicia."

Marc stood and used his hands to cover his child's ears. "When I saw what he'd done to Shay, I wanted to punch him myself." He smiled. "I'm glad you're here. We already all said that if that asshole tries to have you arrested, we'll testify against him. You can't mess with one of Queen's employees and think it'll fly."

"Yeah. We feel safer with you here, Gunnar." Tisha smiled.

"I shouldn't have met violence with violence." He turned to the office where he saw his mother standing. "My mom taught me better than that."

"That's nice and all, but some jerks need their bell rung. He was one of them." Monica gave Gunnar a thumbs-up sign.

Gunnar patted his head. "And as far as what you saw on the back of my head. I had that put on a long time ago when I was young and dumb. I'm not affiliated with them at all. Now that I know that T-Lite is one of them, he definitely will not be allowed back in here. You all do not need that type of energy in here."

At the time Gunnar had joined the No Equals, he'd thought it made him a big man. The gang had claimed that no one could equal them in anything--looks, power, and danger. It hadn't taken Gunnar long to see that he had aligned himself with a group of cowards and had broken free from them, another great reason he hadn't wanted to come back home. He had to face his fears.

"I can't go home now." Shay shook her head. "All of my stuff is at his place."

"You can stay in my apartment." Gunnar offered.

"Excuse me?" Eboni immediately asked.

Gunnar shook his head. "I'll sleep on the couch in the main house." He faced Shay. "Maybe if you're with my mom, you'll come to work on time."

A ripple of laughter sounded through the salon.

"Oh, you got jokes." Shay cocked a smile at the corner of her mouth.

"Let's go now to get your stuff." Gunnar turned to Tillman. "You got my back?"

Tillman grabbed his coat. "Let's bounce."

Monica stood from the desk. "Then I guess I'll be shampoo girl for a day. Go on and do your thing."

Gunnar went to the office. Before he crossed into it, he gave his mother a knowing look. She said nothing. She nodded and let him go by. Before leaving the salon, he had to do one last thing.

Gunnar wrapped his arm around Eboni's waist and pulled her in close. He kissed her gently at first, merely brushing his lips against hers until he pressed his full mouth on hers until she moaned.

When Gunnar broke from the kiss, he said, "I'm crazy about this woman." He smiled as he pulled back from her. "I don't care who knows."

Eboni smiled. "I'll get you for that later."

Gunnar gave her another quick kiss before leaving with Shay and Tillman. Today had been the first day he felt respected and needed at the salon. He felt like these people had become his friends.

Now that he'd brought his and Eboni's relationship out in the open, he knew they could go to the next level. If he could get his career in line and fix his mother's health, everything would be perfect.

Chapter 17

Eboni had skipped going to Gunnar's for dinner last night. She found it hard to reconcile the whole situation in her head after what had happened at the salon. Eboni felt anger on behalf of her coworker, but she never wanted to see that violent side of Gunnar. Although she hated to admit it to herself, seeing that violent side of Gunnar had frightened her.

Eboni knew his reaction had come from a desire to protect Shay. That didn't take away the fact that Gunnar could snap at any moment. At least she could be assured that he would never hit her. She believed every word he'd said when he said men should respect all women.

With it being Super Bowl Sunday, she couldn't avoid him anymore. He and Queen Elizabeth expected her to be at Queen's house for the party. She'd already told Elizabeth she would help her with the food and getting her house ready.

"You're leaving?" Craig asked from the couch.

"Going to a party." Eboni slipped on her coat.

"Have a good time."

Eboni headed to the door.

"Be sure to tell your baby's daddy hi."

She turned to him. "What are you talking about? I don't have any children." Eboni swallowed hard, knowing that her cousin had found out her secret.

"I know. Not now. Now how do I spin that? Did you lose Guns's love child, or did you abort it? Which story will get me more pay from that tabloid website?"

Eboni approached her cousin on the couch and slapped his face. "You're fucking selfish, you know that?"

Craig rubbed his cheek. "And you're a fucking whore and a liar."

"Get out. I want you out of this apartment. If you don't leave, that'll be fine. My lease is up at the end of this month. I'll move, and I'll take your mother with me."

"Bitch! By the time I sell the story, I'll have enough to buy a fucking mansion!"

Tired of Craig's venomous words, Eboni bolted from her home. Although she didn't want to reveal to Gunnar today of all days about her losing his baby shortly after he left to train, it looked like her lazy cousin had forced her hand. She hoped he could forgive her for withholding the information for all these years.

* * * *

"No, move the couch more that way." Queen Elizabeth pointed to where the couch had been before.

Gunnar tried hard not to roll his eyes, but it happened...and his mother caught him.

"Don't you roll your eyes at me. I want the room set up properly. There has to be a feng shui element to it." She scanned the space and put her finger to her chin in a thoughtful manner.

"Your feng shui is killing my back." Gunnar stood up straight and stretched.

"Oh, stop it. You're young. I'm sure you've lifted heavier things in the ring." His mother plopped down on the couch, which relieved Gunnar.

He saw it as a sign that she liked the placement. His back loved the gesture.

"Come sit with me, darling. We can talk before anyone shows up." She patted an area on the couch next to her.

"Ma, I have to still move the cars out of the way." Gunnar jutted his thumb over his shoulder.

"Humor an old lady." She smiled.

Gunnar sat down next to her. "Yes, ma'am."

"The doctor's office called me. My surgery is set for Tuesday." She maintained her smile.

"This Tuesday? Not a lot of time." He ran his hand over his head, still covered under a do-rag.

"No, but then again, for what they want to do, do you really think they should wait?" She laughed a little but Gunnar could sense her fear.

"Have you told Gid and Thane yet?"

"I'll tell Gideon after his game. I don't want him distracted. I talked to Thane."

Gunnar nodded. At least he knew Thane would answer the phone for his mother. As though she'd cued it, the phone rang.

"How much you want to bet it's Gideon." Gunnar stood and answered the cordless phone. "Hey, bro. Everything good?"

"Hey, yeah. Getting my mind right. I know you know what I mean," Gideon said.

"For sure. Good luck today. You won't need it though. You're the best quarterback in the league."

"That's what I keep telling my bosses whenever they think about cutting me." Gideon laughed. "Hey, put Mom on."

"You got it. Love ya, man." When Gideon expressed the same sentiment, Gunnar handed the phone to his mother.

A knock sounded on the front door. Gunnar answered it and found Tillman on the other side.

"Hey, man." Gunnar shook his hand as he pulled him into the house. "You're really early but that's cool. We're getting set up."

"I wanted to see if you had been online recently." Tillman removed his coat and hung it on the coat rack in the corner.

Gunnar shook his head. "No. I've been helping set up for the party. Did I miss something?"

"Not yet. Some gossip site has hinted about having some info."

"Info about what?" Gunnar headed to the kitchen.

"About you, man."

Gunnar turned to Tillman, who looked ultraserious.

"My life is an open book. Folks know I'm adopted and who my mother is. They know all the problems I had as a teen and that I was in and out of juvy. I don't know what they could reveal."

"I don't know either. But with your brother's big game, I'm sure it'll be something that'll take away his thunder. If there's something you know, you had better try to nip that in the bud. Don't you have a manager or someone to take care of those things for you?"

Gunnar did, but since he'd sent Chuck hightailing it back to Vegas, he doubted the man would do anything to help him.

"I'm not going to worry about anything until there's something to worry about." Gunnar put his hand on Tillman's shoulder. "Don't sweat it."

"Gunnar. Can you move this couch back about two feet?" his mother requested from the other room.

"Great timing. Now you can help me." Gunnar put his arm around his friend and led him back to the living room.

During the trek, he wondered what this news could be. He also wondered why Eboni hadn't arrived yet. Why hadn't she wanted to come over for dinner? Why hadn't she answered his calls? She would have a lot to explain. Once she did, he had a surprise for her.

When Gunnar bent over to move the couch, the ring box he had his front pocket dug into his thigh. Enough with the games. He had to tell her how he felt. In the short time he'd come back, she'd captured his heart again. Gunnar had fallen in love with Eboni again. He had to come clean.

* * * *

"Shit! Shit! Shit!" Eboni sat in her car about a block away from Queen Elizabeth's house. She'd been checking all gossip sites on her phone for the last hour to see if anything had popped up on Gunnar. She hoped that because of him being an MMA fighter that he wouldn't be considered newsworthy.

She chewed on her lower lip and flicked her thumb over the wide screen. Nothing so far, but a teaser about something coming out about him flashed across one site's page.

If her news came out and Gunnar heard it from someone else besides her, he would be so upset.

Damn Craig and his big mouth. No, more like damn her and her Aunt Bettie and their mouths. She should have known that Craig wasn't asleep on the couch when her aunt had blurted the news about her and Gunnar.

No time like the present. Eboni drove to Queen's house and parked out front. She wouldn't dare park in the driveway and take the chance of getting trapped if someone parked behind her and Gunnar asked her to leave once he heard the news.

By the time she got to the house, cars filled the entire driveway. Since Gunnar had parked the Hummer in the street, Eboni assumed he wanted to allow people more room to park in the driveway.

After a couple of deep breaths, Eboni went up to the house. She could hear the cheers and chatter inside. She knocked on the door, feeling silly doing so considering she had keys to the place. When no one answered, she walked inside.

Monica and her husband sat next to each other on the couch along with Elizabeth facing the large-screen wall-mounted TV. Tillman and Tisha made their place on a loveseat that lined the opposite wall. Shay stood by the kitchen talking to Gunnar. When Shay saw Eboni, she raised her hands in surrender.

Eboni noticed Gunnar looking confused until he turned and saw Eboni.

"I was just talking to your man, nothing else." Shay moved away from him.

"I know, Shay." Eboni hugged her. "How are you doing?"

Shay nodded. "Better. Happy to be here for a bit until I can get my stuff together." She gave Gunnar a playful punch on his arm. "He's been like a great older brother." She strolled by Eboni and leaned down next to her ear. "I can see why you like him."

Eboni felt her cheeks getting warm. She imagined she must be blushing so brightly by now. Gunnar wrapped his arm around her waist and pulled her close to him.

"Glad you're here." He kissed her. "I missed you last night. I got used to you being here."

Eboni tried to smile. "Hey, I need to tell you something, but I was trying to wait until after the game."

Gunnar's eyebrows drew together. "What is it?"

"Is there somewhere more private where we can--"

Gunnar flinched and reached into his pants pocket. "Excuse me." He grumbled and sounded like he cursed under his breath. "They got an alarm at the salon."

"And we're all set for the kickoff, folks. This is going to be an exciting game between the Virginia Beach Wolves and the Maui Sharks. With this being breakout quarterback Gideon Wells's first big game, I'm sure the former all-star will be pulling out all the stops," the announcer said.

"I have to go. We can talk when I get back." Gunnar kissed her forehead. He walked in front of the screen, which got the crowd to groan their displeasure.

"Son, where are you going? We have enough food and drinks." Queen tried summoning Gunnar back.

"I got an alert that the alarm is going off at the salon. I'll be two seconds. I know you're recording it so I won't miss a thing." Gunnar started to open the door.

"Come give me a kiss before you go." She raised her arms in the air.

Like a good son, he kissed his mother's cheek. Eboni knew he would have made a great father.

"I'll be back. No betting while I'm gone unless you're betting my brother comes out on top." Gunnar walked out of the house.

At least this break would give Eboni time to think and come up with a way to tell Gunnar about the pregnancy.

Shay sauntered back over to Eboni. In a low voice, she said, "I know what's going on."

Eboni wanted to ignore Shay but with the lithe woman blocking her view of the game, she had to give Shay her full attention. "What are you talking about?"

Shay pulled Eboni into the kitchen. "News going around that Gunnar had a lovechild."

Eboni tried not to gasp but it came out anyway.

"Did you know about the child?" Shay asked. When Eboni didn't answer, Shay filled in her own blanks. "You're pregnant."

Eboni didn't confirm or deny Shay's assessment.

"You *were*," Shay continued.

Eboni's gaze dropped.

"Shit, girl, you need to go after your man. He's going to the salon. You two will be alone. Tell him there."

Eboni grabbed her purse and coat. As Shay had suggested, Eboni would go after her man. She hoped he would understand her side.

* * * *

Gunnar expected to see police in the parking lot when he got to the salon. Instead, he found nothing. He went into the back door and disabled the alarm to the main salon so that he could walk around. He kept the alarm on for the front door until the police arrived. As he was about to walk into the main area, the sight of a gun muzzle through the curtain stopped him.

Gunnar raised his hands in the air. The curtain pulled back to reveal the person holding the gun.

"Don't do this," Gunnar said just as a flash erupted from the gun's barrel.

Gunnar fell back on the floor. Searing heat and pain ripped through his side. He heard footfalls stomping out of the front door and the store alarm sounding.

He struggled to his feet and stumbled to the office. He managed to get to the security camera. Like he'd done when he and Eboni had had their connection by the washing machine, Gunnar managed to erase the last hour recorded on the security camera.

"Gunnar?"

He heard Eboni's voice at the same time he heard sirens.

"Don't come in," he said weakly.

By the time he saw her, he fell to the floor. Eboni's scream rang through his head before he blacked out.

Chapter 18

Eboni sat in the hospital room with Gunnar's still body lying on the bed next to her. She wouldn't let his hand go until he woke up.

Doctors had said the shot went into his side. It had punctured his small intestines and gone through his body. She'd been told that Gunnar must have had a horseshoe and rabbit's foot in his pocket for his incredible luck. Eboni had almost laughed. Getting shot didn't seem like a lucky happenstance.

Who the hell would do that to him? Shay's ex-boyfriend came to mind first. If that fucking bastard had hurt Gunnar, there wouldn't be a place in this world where Eboni wouldn't go to find him to exact some revenge.

Eboni kissed the back of Gunnar's hand. "I know you're sleeping, but I need to talk to you." She rubbed her thumb over his knuckles. "I didn't want you here when you first arrived to fill in for Queen. I thought you would be a distraction." She laughed through tears coming down her cheeks. "You were a great distraction. You made me remember our time together. You made me get in touch with my feelings for you. You made me remember that I loved you." She squeezed his hand. "I still love you. I love you, Gunnar Wells."

Eboni put her forehead on the mattress and sobbed.

"You're not going to let me sleep, are you?"

She brought her gaze up and saw Gunnar smiling down at her. His eyelids hung halfway down over his eyes.

Eboni leapt from her chair and embraced him so hard she thought she would hurt him, but she didn't care. "I didn't think you would...I thought you were going to--"

"Stop. I'm alive. I'm here. Does Mom know?"

The hospital-room door opened. Elizabeth sauntered inside with a scowl that would scare the dead. When she got close enough to Gunnar, she picked up a pillow from a cart next to him and swatted him with it.

"Come on, Ma." Gunnar put his hand over his stomach.

"You scared me to death. Why did you go into the salon without the police? You're not Superman."

Eboni backed away from Gunnar long enough for Queen to embrace her son and kiss his cheek.

"I thought the alarm was a fluke." Gunnar squeezed Eboni's hand and then took his mother's in his other.

"The police asked us who we thought would do this." Elizabeth patted Gunnar's arm. "Shay is giving them every detail of her creepy ex-boyfriend."

Gunnar shook his head. "It wasn't him."

Eboni furrowed her eyebrows. "You know who did it? You have to tell the police. They've been waiting for you to wake up."

"I can't help them." Gunnar shook his head. "I know it wasn't that guy." As he smiled at his mother, he proclaimed, "You're closing that salon."

Queen's eyebrows furrowed. "No, I'm not."

"I wasn't asking. You need to close it. It's attracting a dangerous element there. It's not safe for you to keep it open."

"That's not for you to decide. It's my business. I'm keeping it open. People in that community need me, need my services. I can't turn my back on them."

"Gunnar, we can beef up security. And you're--" Eboni had almost said that he would be there, but with his look, she knew he still planned on leaving.

A nurse walked into the room, breaking up the tension. "Good morning, Mr. Wells." She dragged in behind her a machine on its own stand. "It's not often we get a celebrity in here. The guys in here are going crazy."

Gunnar offered a slight smile.

"And the women are just--" The nurse cut off her statement when she saw Eboni's expression. "Let's just say you've definitely made an impression."

"When can I get out of here? I have things to do." Gunnar rubbed his hand over his eyes.

"That will be up to the doctor." The nurse wrapped a cuff around his arm and engaged the machine to get his blood pressure. "We have you on antibiotics now. We'll keep your bandages changed. If all goes well, maybe in a few days. But that's my guess."

"I've canceled my surgery."

Gunnar shook his head. "No. You need that surgery now."

"And what? Both of us will be laid out at the same time. No, I'm going to make sure you're all better before they cut me open." Elizabeth grabbed his hand again.

"That's crazy. I'll be fine. You need this surgery."

"I need my children all happy and healthy." She patted Gunnar's shoulder.

"Speaking of your children, did you see Gideon?" Gunnar smiled. "I can't believe he came here right after the game when he heard about me. He was tight-lipped about the Super Bowl results. Did he win?"

Elizabeth looked forlorn. Eboni tried hiding her laughter considering she knew the results.

"He lost?" Gunnar asked.

Queen Elizabeth beamed. "Just teasing. His team won."

Gunnar nodded. "Awesome. I'm telling you. You raised a family of champions."

The nurse removed the cuff and wrapped it around the monitor she'd pull into the room. "I know." She patted Gunnar on his shoulder. "You're an MMA champ. Now you have a Super Bowl champion in the family. And I hear congratulations are in order."

"Yeah, Gideon Wells is an awesome player." Eboni patted the back of Gunnar's hand.

"No, I saw online that you're going to be a dad."

Gunnar's eyebrows rutted together. "I'm not going to be a dad." He turned to Eboni. "Am I?"

Eboni didn't answer. She couldn't move. She hadn't expected the news to be blurted out by a nurse. Being in a hospital room with the TV turned off and Gunnar's phone away from him, she thought she would have time to break the news to him.

The nurse continued. "I saw the story online and the ring in your pocket, and I just assumed--"

"Ring?" Eboni had to sit down again.

"I'll leave you all alone. The doctor should be in shortly." The nurse backed out of the room.

"Eboni, even when I left, I've only thought of you. Every day, every moment, I wanted you. I thought you wouldn't want me again after I left, so I never tried to contact you again." Gunnar hit a control on the inside of his bed to bring his head up. "When I saw you taking care of my mother when I came home, the old feelings came back. You have my heart completely. I don't want to spend another moment without you. I don't know where it is in the room, but I have a ring for you."

Both Eboni and Elizabeth gasped.

"Will you marry me? Please say yes, or I'll pull the guilt card and say that I almost died." Gunnar laughed and quickly held his side.

"Gunnar, before I answer anything, I need to tell you something." Eboni's stomach flipped. She wanted to hold Queen's hand in case Gunnar got out of bed and walked home. "What the nurse said."

"About me having a kid? Not true. I wasn't lying when I said I hadn't slept with anyone else since moving away to train."

"You're partially right. You don't have a child. You would have." Eboni maintained eye contact with Gunnar until realization crossed his face.

"You were pregnant? When?"

"I found out after you left. I was depressed and getting sick. I thought it was because I was crying all the time." Eboni didn't mean to make Gunnar feel guilty. She needed to tell it all. "When I wasn't crying, I was eating everything in sight. My aunt told me she thought I might be pregnant. I took an at-home test. It came out positive." She averted her gaze. "I didn't want to believe it. I mean, we were both so careful. You wore condoms and I was on the Pill."

Gunnar adjusted himself in bed as he split his gaze between Eboni and his mother.

"I decided to get an official word. So I went to the doctor. He confirmed that I was about two months along."

Gunnar sat up taller. "So what happened? I haven't seen a child around you since I've been home. You haven't mentioned having a kid."

Eboni glanced up for a moment and then dropped her gaze again.

"You got an abortion?" Gunnar slipped his hand from hers.

"No. Of course not. Even if you had said you never wanted to see me again, I would never do that. I lost the baby. For the longest time, I blamed myself. I thought I had done something wrong. Then your mother explained that sometimes these things happen."

Gunnar turned to his mother. "You knew? All these years, all the phone calls we've had. Never once did you say, 'Guess what, son? You were going to be a father but Eboni had a miscarriage.' Never crossed your mind to tell me something like that?"

"It wasn't for me to tell you. This was Eboni's news and your business." Queen's voice came out low and slow.

"*My* business? Oh, no. Apparently, it's the world's business now. How did this get leaked to some gossip site? Is that why you didn't come by the other night?"

"Stop it, Gunnar. I wouldn't do that. My cousin overheard my aunt mentioning it. He blabbed the news. I was going to tell you last night before you left for the salon. Then I thought that if I had caught you at the salon we could talk there."

"I'm not mad that you miscarried. It happens to lots of women. I'm pissed that no one who claims to love me bothered to tell me. I would have come home to be with you had I known. Did you think I stopped caring about you? Or did you stop caring about me?"

"Gunny, that's not fair. I had no idea where we stood." Eboni wrapped her arms around her body.

"When you two went out to dinner and I asked you if you'd talked, I thought you talked about that then." She glanced at Eboni.

Eboni had already felt guilty for not telling him right after it happened. One look from Queen Elizabeth and Eboni felt like dirt. She returned her attention back to Gunnar, who looked like he wanted to melt her in her spot just from his glare.

"It didn't matter if I were in prison. A part of me was in you and it died and no one thought it was my business to know. I had a right to know. I had a right to be involved whether we were together or not."

Eboni swallowed. "You're right. I'm sorry."

"I am too. As soon as I get clearance to leave, I'm going back to Vegas." Gunnar turned to his mother. "Hopefully, Gideon will be here soon. He can take care of you."

"Gunnar--"

"I'm really tired. Could you turn off the lights when you two leave?"

Eboni's heart sank to the floor. She'd known Gunnar would be mad. She'd never thought he would turn his back on both her and his mother.

Queen Elizabeth approached her son. "I know you're angry. Get some sleep. Think about everything. Remember that we love you." Despite Gunnar turning his head, she managed to kiss his cheek. "I love you. I will always be there for you."

Queen stepped away from Gunnar to give Eboni a chance to kiss Gunnar good-bye as well.

Eboni couldn't muster the strength to approach Gunnar. Not initially. Then she realized that she did love Gunnar. She hadn't withheld the information to hurt him. She approached the side of the bed. He flipped his face to the other direction, away from her.

"I love you, Gunnar. I love you." She kissed his cheek, his temple, the side of his neck, anyplace she could reach. "If it means anything to you, I couldn't wait to have *our* child."

Gunnar remained quiet.

As he had requested, Queen turned off the lights when she and Eboni walked out of his hospital room. When Eboni heard his door click shut, she fell into Queen's arms and wept.

"I thought you would have told him by now. Why didn't you said anything?" Elizabeth stroked Eboni's back as she hugged her.

"I knew he had a dream with this fighting thing. I thought if I told him and he came all the way home, he would resent me." Eboni's breath caught during her explanation. "Now he hates me." This time, she sobbed. She felt like Gunnar had left her all over again. This time it hurt even more. This time he had asked her to marry him.

"Give him time. Gunnar is reasonable. He can't stay mad forever."

* * * *

As the nurse had mentioned before, Gunnar remained in the hospital for a few more days receiving antibiotics and having his bandages changed daily. Like clockwork, both his mother and Eboni showed up to his room every day.

Determined not to talk to either of them each time they visited, he sat in silence. Not these stubborn women. His mother could talk a blue streak anyway. With Gunnar offering no volleying conversation, his mother spoke about everything from how there were no good romantic comedies anymore to the reason she chose one red nail polish over a different red nail polish.

When Eboni visited, he felt conflicted. He wanted to be angry with her. Too bad every time he saw her, his heart melted.

"I know you're angry at me. I wish you would talk to me," she said as she sat in a chair next to him. "Fine. You don't want to talk? I'll do all the talking. When I found out I was pregnant, you were the first person I wanted to tell. I must have picked up the phone to call you about a hundred times. Each time, I stopped myself and I would run different scenarios in my head." She crossed her legs and leaned back in her chair. "In one scenario, you come rushing back home to be with me. I carry to term with you by my side the entire time, because Queen Elizabeth's boys would always do the right thing. Then a year or two down the road, you hate me for making you feel trapped."

That statement got Gunnar to glance at her. He almost opened his mouth to refute her claims but remained quiet. He would have dug ditches if it meant being a family. Didn't she know that?

"In the other scenario, you come running back home to me to be by my side. I lose the baby like I did for real. But since you gave up your training, they refuse to take you back. So, again, you're stuck at home with me. Third scenario, I tell you I'm pregnant and you tell me you don't care. You accuse me of trying to use the baby to get money from you."

Gunnar balled his hands into fists. No way did Eboni think he could treat her that cruelly. Then again, he had refused to talk to her since finding out her news. She had been partially right.

Eboni turned her head. "As you can see in every scenario, it doesn't end up great for me."

"You forgot one scenario."

Eboni wiped under her eyes and regarded him. She didn't speak. She waited for him to share his thoughts.

"You tell me as soon as you find out you're pregnant. I do come home to be with you and I beg you to marry me and come with me back to Vegas. I take care of you and our child. I treat you like a queen. We live happily ever after. You ever think of that one?"

Eboni wiped her nose. "No. You know why? It means I would leave my family. I would leave my home."

Gunnar nodded. "Fine. Stay here with these people." He lowered his bed and swung his legs over the side.

"What are you doing?" Eboni stood.

"I have to walk around." He unplugged his IV unit from the wall socket and slipped on another hospital gown to cover his exposed backside.

"I'll walk with you." She headed to the door to open it.

"I don't need help." Gunnar took careful steps toward the hospital hallway.

"And I wasn't asking." Eboni threw her shoulders back as she waited for him to walk by her.

Before he could take a step, his hospital room door opened. Gunnar stared at two official-looking men who didn't look like they worked in the hospital. Eboni moved back from Gunnar's bed.

"Mr. Wells, good to see you up." The first man, a tall, authoritative figure with a buzz cut and a wide jaw, approached him and put out his hand. "Detective Murphy, in case you don't remember." He turned to his partner, a shorter, stockier man. "This is Detective Stiller."

The other man shook Gunnar's hand.

"Good to see you again," Stiller said.

Gunnar nodded and regarded both men. "You said you've met me already?"

Murphy nodded. "We tried talking to you the first night you arrived to the hospital. Unfortunately, you were so drugged up that you didn't make much sense."

"You asked about Ms. Danielson a lot. You wanted to make sure she was okay," Stiller said and nodded toward Eboni.

Gunnar didn't remember asking about Eboni that night, but he couldn't imagine that he would want her placed in harm's way. Watching out for her well-being sounded like something he would have wanted. He still couldn't look at her though.

"How can I help you?" Gunnar asked.

Both men opened notepads and poised their pens over them.

"We need you to walk us through what happened that night," Stiller began. "The good news is that we know you weren't trying to commit suicide." He turned to Eboni. "And we've ruled out Ms. Danielson as the perpetrator."

Gunnar glanced at her. "What do you mean?"

"We tested her hands for gunshot residue, and we questioned her that night. You two were the only ones in a closed business. It's suspicious. We wanted to make sure she hadn't come after you or hired someone to harm you."

Gunnar's jaw flexed as he ground his teeth.

"Eboni wouldn't do anything like that. She's a good person." Gunnar connected his stare to hers for a millisecond before he looked away.

No matter what, Gunnar knew Eboni couldn't harm him. So why couldn't he look at her for more than a second? Why did his heart still hurt?

"Don't involve her or my mother in this investigation. My mother is about to have major heart surgery. I don't want her stressed." Gunnar put his hand to his side when the painful throbbing in his wound got to be too much.

On some levels, Gunnar felt he deserved the pain. He'd put his family and Eboni through a lot.

"We'll try." Murphy nodded. "So that night, run us through the chain of events, please."

Gunnar released a long breath. "My phone is set up to get the security alarms at the salon. Super Bowl night, right before kickoff, I got a message that there was an alarm at the salon. I went down to check it out."

"Alone?" Stiller asked.

Gunnar nodded. "I assumed it was nothing. My family was having a party at the house to watch the Wolves go against the Sharks."

"Congratulations on your brother's win." Murphy patted Gunnar on his shoulder.

Gunnar managed a slight smile before continuing with his story. "I came through the back door. I turned off the alarm in the main area of the salon so that I could walk around and not set anything off."

"But you kept it engaged for the front door and back door?"

Gunnar shook his head. "Just the front door." He put out his hand in front of him. "I pulled back the curtain that separates the back from the main salon. I saw the barrel of a gun. I would say it was a .22."

The two men started scribbling something in their notepads.

"I continued opening the curtain until I could see a person. Whoever it was wore a black hoodie over his or her head."

"You think it might be a woman?" Stiller asked.

"The shooter was about five-foot-four or so. Slight frame. It could be a short man or a woman. I didn't see a face. The person wore black baggy jeans. The sneakers were black. I told the shooter not to shoot. That's when the shot sounded and he ran. Or she."

Murphy crossed his arms over his chest. "Okay, this is where it gets interesting, Mr. Wells. You're saying you got shot in the back-room area, right?"

Gunnar nodded.

"So how did you end up in the office? I sincerely doubt Ms. Danielson is strong enough to drag you there. What did you do right after getting shot?"

Gunnar glared at the detective. "The shooter ran out the front door. I heard the alarm for it going off. I--I, uh, really don't remember much after that." He glanced at Eboni. "I remember hearing her screaming."

"So you don't remember stumbling to the office?" Stiller pressed.

Gunnar shook his head. "No."

"So you don't remember tampering with the security camera?" Stiller pulled out his phone, tapped his fingertip over the screen, and showed Gunnar an image. "We found your bloody fingerprints on the keyboard. Coincidentally we found about an hour's worth of video erased."

Gunnar regarded the shorter African-American man who shown him the picture of a computer keyboard covered in blood. "I'm sure I was trying to preserve the information. Why would I erase it?"

Gunnar wouldn't admit why he'd done what he did that night, not until he did his own investigation. He knew how the justice system worked. He'd been through it enough in his lifetime. When he got what he needed, he would involve the police. Not right now.

"That's what we wanted to know." Murphy moved in closer to Gunnar. "We checked out your past. The tattoo on the back of your head confirms a lot."

Gunnar didn't move. He felt like a powerless teenager again, getting labeled for how he looked.

"Are you back to your old habits, Mr. Wells?" Murphy asked.

"Getting the band back together?" Stiller seconded.

"I'm getting the tattoo removed. I can tell you the doctor I went to and show you that I've already gone through one session. That tattoo is a part of my past. I have done nothing but work in my mother's salon and looked after her since coming back to town." Gunnar tried to keep the level of frustration from his voice but couldn't mask it that well.

"You know, there hasn't been an incident of theft, vandalism, or assault with any kind of weapon in that area of the city until you showed up." Murphy stared at Gunnar.

Gunnar, a fighter, stared right back at him without blinking. The stance reminded him of how he would react in every fight, determined yet guarded. Neither one planned on surrendering.

"Hey, come on. Gunnar has helped as much as he can." Eboni, just like when Gunnar had squared off against Shay's boyfriend, tried intervening between Gunnar and this detective. "I'm sure if he knew anything he would tell you."

Gunnar did know something that he didn't want to reveal yet. He'd seen a revealing piece of evidence that would identify the shooter. He had a suspicion of who to go after first.

"If you remember anything"--Stiller reached into his coat pocket and pulled out a business card--"give us a call." He handed it to Gunnar. "We want to help catch the person who could have killed you."

Gunnar accepted the card and glared at both men as they exited his room. With both men gone, he threw the card on his meal tray and stood again. Gunnar wanted to walk now to clear his head. From the way Eboni stepped up next to him, he could tell she wouldn't let him do that alone.

If he was honest with himself, he would admit that he liked her company. Her soothing aroma lulled him into a peaceful state as he shuffled down the hall.

They walked in silence around the hospital hallways. A few of the guys who recognized Gunnar gave him a high five as they passed him. Some of the women smiled as they looked at him.

During their silent walk, Gunnar's hand brushed against Eboni's. He glanced at her and she stared at him. To rectify the situation, he moved the IV stand to the other side of himself to put a barrier between him and Eboni.

He had battled opponents in the ring that didn't make him feel as uncomfortable as being with Eboni.

"Who are you protecting this time?" Eboni asked.

Gunnar knew what she meant. He couldn't look at her or respond.

"You can hate me as much as you want, Gunny." Eboni's strong voice echoed down the hall. "I will always love you. Even after this we end up just being friends, I'll take that. You asked me to marry you. I know you care about me."

Gunnar couldn't say anything. If he opened his mouth, he would confess that he wanted her in his life. Even though both she and his mother had lied to him by keeping secrets.

By the time he got back to his room, he wanted to tell her his true feelings. He loved her. He wanted her in his life again. He needed some time to heal. Maybe going back home for a short while will help clear his head.

It shocked him to see Chuck next to Gunnar's doctor.

"Great. You're up and walking around. Awesome." Chuck clapped. "I think the doc here has some good news for you. Tell him, Doc."

"You're going to be discharged today. The nurse will be in soon with your discharge instructions, like no heavy lifting for six to eight weeks, watch your diet, and walk every day. Your bandages will need to be changed daily. We can arrange for a home health nurse to come do that."

"If properly trained, can a family member or loved one do it?" Eboni offered.

"Certainly. I can have a nurse come in and show you." The doctor typed some information on a computer in the room.

"That's not necessary. I'll be flying home to Vegas soon." Gunnar went to the closet and pulled out a white paper bag that contained his personal items.

"You shouldn't fly right now."

"I didn't hear the word *can't* in that statement," Chuck said, beaming.

Gunnar hated Chuck for loving this so much.

"Gunnar, don't do this." Eboni tried making eye contact with him, but he kept his gaze averted.

"Don't worry. I'll be sure to tell everyone good-bye."

Eboni shook her head and walked out of the room.

"That's the Gunnar Wells I remember. Get that fight back in you." Chuck slapped Gunnar on his back.

Yes, as soon as he could get away from the East Coast, things would start to make sense for him. Maybe he could learn to push Eboni out of his thoughts again.

"I'll be sure to prescribe you some pain meds to take when you're home," the doctor said while keeping his gaze on the computer screen.

"No, I'll deal with the pain." Concentrating on something other than Eboni may help him deal with the heartache.

Chapter 19

Eboni sat at her kitchen table determined not to cry again. She'd cried herself to sleep every night since the night of Gunnar's shooting. Occupying her time at the center every day did little to help her forget the pain she'd caused Gunnar. It made her wonder if when he'd first left to go to Vegas, had he felt this guilt-ridden, this torn, this hollow?

She barely heard her aunt coming into the room until she sat at the table across from her.

"Hey, Aunt Bettie. You ready for lunch?" Eboni sprang to her feet.

"Sit down, baby. We need to talk." Her aunt patted her hand on the table.

"Okay. What is it?"

"I know your lease is up at the end of the month."

Eboni nodded. "Yes, I've been checking out nice two-bedroom apartments closer to your doctor offices. I think I found one that's reasonable."

Her aunt shook her head. "Don't look for a place with me in mind."

"What? Of course I am. You're my family." Eboni reached across the table and held her hand.

She'd already lost Gunnar. She couldn't take losing another family member.

"Baby, I appreciate everything you've done for me. But it's time you let me go." Her aunt smiled as she delivered this news.

"No. You helped raised me. You're important to me."

"And I get that. You are my world. I love you like my own. But I'm not that ill, not so incapacitated that you need to take care of me. I haven't been for quite some time. For that reason, I've been checking out some places on my own." She reached in her robe pocket and pulled out a brochure. "I've secured a condo space in this independent-living facility. They have a shuttle that can take me to my doctor's appointments. Plus,

I'll be around other people. When you go to work, it's just Craig and whatever stupid girl he brings here. He doesn't talk to me. He's interested in eating, watching TV, and doing things young men do with women with loose morals."

Eboni smiled. "I like taking care of you."

"I know you do. But you need to start taking care of yourself. You're using me to keep from spreading your wings. I'm telling you it's okay for you to go. I'll be fine. You'll always have my number and you can visit me, but just call me first. I might be entertaining." Her aunt gave her a saucy wink.

Eboni laughed.

"Yep, as soon as I get settled, I'll be going on a cruise. I can't wait."

As soon as her aunt shared that news, Eboni realized that not only had she held herself back, she had restricted her aunt as well. She'd never figured that her aunt would want to go out and meet other people her age.

"What about Craig?" Eboni asked.

"He needs to grow up and get him a job and take care of himself." Aunt Bettie stood. "But you take care of yourself. You'll find that things will work out on their own."

Eboni stood and kissed her aunt on her cheek. "Thank you."

"No. Thank you. You treated me better than my own kids. I'll always be grateful for that."

Eboni glanced at her watch. "I need to go to the center. I'll see you later."

With permission from her aunt to live her life, Eboni felt a burden lifted from her shoulders. If she could be assured that the center would be okay, she would happy. No, she would be happy if she had Gunnar back in her life.

Since the doctor discharged him two days ago, she hadn't seen or heard from him. Each day, Eboni walked around with a void in her heart. It only beat out of necessity. If it stopped, she would be okay. Who needed a heart when the love of her life had walked away from her? She had put herself out there for him. The next step had to be his.

＊ ＊ ＊ ＊

Gunnar had wanted to get on a plane the day he got discharged from the hospital. A couple of things kept him from doing that. He needed to pack up his belongings, and he really didn't want to leave town without resolving issues between him and his mother, and with Eboni. Especially with Eboni.

Gunnar rubbed his pocket and felt the ring box again.

"Are you decent?"

Gunnar turned around and saw Gideon standing in the doorway of the sewing room that used to be Gideon's old room. With Shay still in the apartment over the garage, Gunnar had to find another spot to sleep. Since his mother had a futon in her sewing room, she thought Gunnar would be more comfortable in there than sleeping on the living-room couch.

Gunnar could barely fit on the futon. His feet hung off the edge unless he slept at an angle. He at least had privacy. He could close the door when his mother refused to leave him alone.

Queen Elizabeth had even recruited help. Shay had no problems arguing on behalf of his mother. Gunnar suspected that Gideon had been sent to him to do the same thing.

"What's up?" Gunnar continued packing...slowly.

The stitches in his side had him moving at a rate that snails could pass him. As long as he kept moving, it meant progress.

"I came up to see how you were doing." Gideon sat on the futon. "Can't believe you let Mom see that."

Gunnar turned to see what Gideon meant. When his brother motioned to the back of his head, he understood.

"I thought it was time. I went to get it removed. I had one session but the guy says I need about two, maybe three more before it's all gone." Gunnar rubbed the back of his head.

"You don't have to leave town. I have that huge house down at the Oceanfront. Come stay with me. I could use some company." Gideon braced his elbows on his knees.

"Thanks for the offer. I think I need to split." This trip had Gunnar's head spinning.

"Why don't you sit down and talk to me? We haven't really talked since I got into town."

As he scanned his brother, Gunnar remembered what Gideon had looked like growing up, not the grown man in front of him. He kept his dirty-blond hair almost as long as Gunnar's hair had been before he'd shaved his head. His blue eyes always looked crystal clear, like the man had nothing to hide. Bruises covered his neck and arms, showing the results of his recent victory.

"You're not here to tell me what an asshole I am because I'm not talking to Mom, are you?" Gunnar eased down in a chair across from his brother.

"No. I'm going to tell you what a model son you've been and how forgiveness has always been your strength."

"Fuck you."

"Oh, and your eloquent way with words." Gideon laughed. "You know what your problem is? You've had this issue since we were kids."

"Please, enlighten me."

"You've always wanted to be treated older than your age, but essentially you want to be a kid. Mom told me why you're pissed at her."

"Wow. So she can tell my brother that my former girlfriend miscarried as soon as you walk in the door, but she couldn't open her mouth to say a thing to me."

Gideon's face froze. "Eboni was pregnant? She didn't tell me that. She said that you and someone were going through a situation that she knew a little bit about and had expected two grown folks to handle their own business."

Gunnar snorted. "Whatever. She's my mother. She should have been looking out for me."

"She did. She raised you to think on your own and to be a man about your business. Do you think ignoring her or Eboni is going to fix anything? Is that being a man?"

Gunnar remained quiet. He held his side that had now started throbbing in pain. His brother's verbal jab hurt him deep.

Gideon continued when Gunnar remained quiet. "Mom loves you. It's killing her that you've shut her out. Before she goes under the knife, which will be soon, make it right, man." He stood and held his hand out to Gunnar so he could help him to his feet.

Gunnar accepted the offer. "You're younger than me. How did you get so wise?"

"What can I say? I'm the middle kid. I've been made a mediator all my life." Gideon put his hand on Gunnar's shoulder as he led him to the door. "By the way, I saw Eboni again. When did she chop off all her hair?"

"About a week or so ago, same time I did mine." The reminder had Gunnar turning back in his room to grab his hat. He couldn't see his mother with that symbol on the back of his head.

"Sounds like she's been a good influence on you."

"She lied, man."

"No, she didn't. She spared you some misery. Sounds like she cares about you."

Gunnar stopped at the top of the stairs. He looked at his brother. "I would have been a good dad, right?"

Gideon smiled. "The best. You're a nerd. You're always sticking your nose in other people's business. And your pants are already starting to creep up to your chest."

Gunnar jabbed his elbow into Gideon's stomach. "Remind me again why I missed you."

"I'm the only brother who will talk to you."

Gunnar looked up the stairs. "Low blow."

He strolled into the living room, where he found his mother sitting on the couch doing some knitting. Gunnar didn't know how to approach the woman who had done more for him than any mother or any woman he'd been with, with the exception of Eboni.

Gunnar stood behind the couch, trying to come up with a way to break the ice.

"Will you pour me some tea, darling?" his mother asked without turning around.

"Yes, ma'am." Gunnar went to the kitchen and found a kettle already hot on the stove.

He poured the hot water over a tea bag in his mother's favorite mug. Even though she hadn't asked for any, he placed some of her own chocolate chip cookies on a saucer and brought the duo into the living room. He placed them on a table by the couch next to her. Then he continued to stand.

"Ma, uh, Mom?"

She broke her stare from the TV to regard him.

"I'm sorry for what I said."

"No, you're not."

Gunnar's stomach dropped to the floor. His mother didn't want to forgive him.

"You apologize. But there's absolutely nothing sorry about you. I'm sorry."

Gunnar shook his head. "You're not--"

"No, this time, son, I really mean what I said. I'm sorry. I'm a sorry mother who should have told the news that would have affected your life. Even if Eboni had told you, I should have said something to make sure you were okay. I should have known something was wrong. Good or bad, you tell me everything. Had Eboni said something to you, you would have talked to me, right?"

Gunnar knew his mother had him pegged. If he hadn't come home after hearing about Eboni's pregnancy, he would have called Queen to talk about it.

Queen Elizabeth continued talking. "I would be worried about you if you heard Eboni was pregnant, lost the baby, and you were relieved because you wouldn't have any responsibilities. But you weren't. You're very passionate about family. You love truth and honesty. I love that about you. For that, I owe you an apology."

Gunnar sat next to his mother.

"You're right. Even though you and Eboni are adults, sometimes even adults need guidance. I should have said something to you as your mother. I don't want you to ever feel like you can't tell me anything or that you can't trust me." She held Gunnar's hand. "I hated that you wouldn't talk to me. That was a bad punishment for me."

"I was feeling a bit raw."

Queen nodded. "I get it. I promise you that I will never keep anything from you. So some truth time. I've been dating a man for a while. His name is Fred and he's a lovely man I met when I took that Cruise to Nowhere out of Norfolk."

Gunnar felt heat traveling up his body. The last man his mother had been with had hurt her. "I want to meet this guy."

She patted his hand. "Calm down, Gunnar. He's a good man. You'll meet him soon. I promise. They have rescheduled my surgery for next Monday. When are you leaving out for Las Vegas?"

Gunnar regretted making arrangements to leave now. "I was supposed to go tomorrow. But I'll cancel. I can't leave you."

Elizabeth squeezed his hand. "I'm so glad to have my boys around me. But there is something you need to do."

"Name it."

"Call Eboni. Better yet, go see her. She's been so down since you stopped talking to her. I truly believe her when she said she didn't tell you because she cared about you. Think about it. When you first got back in town, she could have told you the news then, when she didn't really like you. But she didn't. She loves you. You know this."

Yes, Gunnar knew it. He knew he loved her, too.

"You wouldn't have bought her a ring if you didn't love her."

On reflex, Gunnar touched the ring box in his pocket.

"If you still want this woman in your life, go after her."

Gunnar stood and started to walk out the room. He stopped, turned back to his mother and kissed her cheek. "May I be excused?"

She swatted his backside. "Go. I want to see that ring when it's on her finger."

"Yes, ma'am." Gunnar hoped he still had a chance with her.

Would Eboni want to be with a pigheaded man? He could only hope.

Gunnar first went to Eboni's apartment. He tried keeping a straight face when her cousin answered the door. Not interested in having any trouble with him, Gunnar tried to talk to him like a reasonable adult.

"Hey, Craig. Is Eboni home? I'd like to talk to her." Gunnar even completed his query with a smile.

"I'm sure you would like to do a lot of things with my cousin. You can knock her up again. This family could use some of that championship money of yours." Craig laughed as he leaned on the open door.

"Don't talk about your cousin that way." Gunnar balled his hands into fists and hoped Craig didn't notice.

"Or what?"

Gunnar almost went into a tirade about what he could do to him but stopped. He didn't want to be a man that solved all of his problems with violence. "I didn't see her car outside, so I'll assume she's not here. I'll just find her on my own."

"You do that, loser."

At that insult, Gunnar turned and faced Eboni's cousin. "I love Eboni. Had I known she was pregnant, I would have been right back here for her. I'm a man. I don't depend on a woman to provide me my living. I don't lay up on someone's couch and make judgments. I work. I'm going to work hard to get Eboni to forgive me. I suggest you do the same thing."

He turned on his heel and headed back to his vehicle. With it being Monday, he knew the salon would be closed. He went to the community center, Eboni's other home away from home.

Gunnar walked into the front of the building. As soon as he spotted Drew, he went directly to the man.

"Oh, hey, Gunnar. I saw on the news about you getting shot around here. That's crazy." Drew shook his head.

"I'm okay. I'm looking for Eboni. Is she here today?"

"Yeah. Last I saw her, she was in the activity room." Drew pointed in the direction of the room.

Who Gunnar saw at the opposite end of the room almost had him dropping to his knees. "Excuse me, Drew."

Gunnar headed toward the basketball-court area, then ducked into the locker room. He walked down the aisle scanning both sides to look for the person he caught. At the last aisle sitting on a bench sat T-Lite. With his head down, he didn't look like the braggart he had presented himself as in the salon.

"Hey!" Gunnar approached him.

The young man's eyes widened as he stood and tried to run. Luckily, Gunnar managed to grab the back of the boy's shirt and coat and drag him to a wall. Stabbing pains filled his side, but Gunnar wouldn't let it stop him.

"Oh, no. You're not running anywhere. You're going to tell me why you shot me."

T-Lite swallowed hard. It looked like tears crested his lower lids. The longer he stared at him, the more the boy reminded him of himself. Damn. Had he really been that lost? The symbol on the back of his head should be enough proof.

"Dude, I heard you were shot." T-Lite fidgeted in his spot.

"Don't give me that. You may have been wearing a hood, but I saw your face." Gunnar lifted T-Lite's hand. "I also recognize this crappy homemade tattoo on your hand."

T-Lite snatched his hand away. "What? Plenty of guys have this symbol on the exact same spot on their hands. I ain't the only one. Hell, you have it on your head. You're one of us."

"I told you before, I'm nothing like you or any of the hoodlums you hang out with." Not falling for T-Lite's excuses, he continued asking questions. "Did you do it as some sort of gang initiation? Was that it?"

"I don't know what you're talking about, man."

Gunnar pounded his fist into the wall next to T-Lite's head. The boy jumped and got quiet quickly. "Don't play with me. You could have killed me, or is that what you were trying to do?"

"I wasn't trying to."

Gunnar stood up straighter when T-Lite started telling the truth. The throbbing on his side started to subside.

"The guy paid me to mess up the salon. He gave me a gun in case someone showed up to stop me. But I didn't know you were going to be there. I held up the gun to scare you. Then it went off."

"Who paid you?"

"I don't know his real name. He saw the video I uploaded of you yelling at that guy in the salon from a couple of weeks ago. He contacted me and said that he had a job for me. So I met him at a McDonald's. He gave me five thousand dollars and the gun."

Gunnar racked his brain to try and figure out who would want to ruin the salon or hurt him. "What did the guy look like? Was it the guy I was yelling at?"

T-Lite shook his head. "I've never seen him before. He had a shaved head, kind of a crooked smile and a little taller than me."

Shit. Chuck. Gunnar knew his manager wanted him back to work. He hadn't known what lengths Chuck would go to achieve that.

Gunnar stared into T-Lite's eyes. "You are going down a bad path. If someone else had come into the salon instead of me, that person could have shot and killed you. If the police had been there, they could have shot you. You are going to have to change."

"Easy for you to say. You're rich."

Gunnar shook his head. "I started out just like you." To punctuate his claim, he pointed to the back of his head. "I made a lot of bad mistakes. Having great role models around me helped steer me on the right path. That's what you need. I'd be willing to mentor you."

T-Lite looked at him suspiciously. "Serious, man? For real?"

Gunnar nodded. "Boxing classes would give you confidence and discipline. I could teach you."

T-Lite smiled. "All right!"

"That is after I turn you over to the police."

The young man jerked like he wanted to run. Gunnar pulled him back and pressed him against the wall harder.

"You would rat me out?" T-Lite asked.

"Yes. You vandalized my mother's business. You had an illegal firearm. And you shot at me. You can't be rewarded for that. However, I will speak on your behalf. I'm sure as long as you testify against the guy who gave you the money and gun, the judge will go light on you."

The young man snickered. "Great. I'll tell them I have no idea who the guy is or where I can find him."

"But if you saw him again, you could identify him, right?"

T-Lite nodded.

"Good. That's all I need to know. Now let's find Drew and get you to the office."

"Damn."

"Watch your language."

Gunnar led the boy to the Drew, who quickly ushered them both to the office. After hearing what had happened, Drew wasted no time contacting the police.

The next call Gunnar made went to his manager. "Hey, Chuck. Are you still in town or did you already go back to Vegas?"

"Of course I'm in town. I plan to fly back on the same flight with you tomorrow."

Relief and anger washed over Gunnar. "Good. I'm here with the police and they need to question you about possible suspects. Can I meet you in your hotel lobby or something?"

"Uh, yeah. Sure." Chuck gave Gunnar the name of his hotel.

Gunnar gave that information to the police. The police managed to keep T-Lite, or Terry, as his parents had named him, hidden until Chuck came out to meet Gunnar.

"How are you feeling, champ?" Chuck asked him.

"Sore, but hopefully better soon." Gunnar peered over at the front desk where they had Terry hidden. He saw the boy nodding his head emphatically. "Yeah, I'm going to be feeling great in a minute."

Two uniformed officers approached Chuck.

"Hey, gentlemen. I understand you wanted to question me."

"More like get a confession. You're under arrest for conspiracy to commit murder for hire." One of the officers pulled Chuck's arm behind his back to put the handcuffs on him.

"I can't believe the lengths you went to just to get me back into the ring," Gunnar said to his former manager. "That child you gave a loaded gun to could have killed me."

"You don't understand what your little sabbatical is doing to the business. Every day you're out of the ring is costing me money. I had to do something."

If the officers hadn't been there, Gunnar would have decked Chuck.

"I'll be happy to give you all a statement and testify when it comes time." Gunnar shook the detectives' hands and watched them take away a part of his life he wanted to forget.

One part of his life remained broken. He had to find Eboni.

Chapter 20

"Drew, are you pulling my leg?" Eboni had to lean against the counter at the salon as she pressed the phone to her ear. She could barely hear Drew over the sounds of construction happening around him.

"Nope. We received enough money to fix the pool, redo the basketball courts, and even update the tennis courts. They're starting the work now. Can you hear it?" The glee couldn't be mistaken in Drew's voice. It didn't take him long to get the work started at the center.

"That's amazing. Who made the donations? Was it one business or several?" As soon as Eboni asked the question, she looked up and saw Gunnar walking through the front door of the salon.

Sounds around Eboni drowned out as she watched him stroll toward her. Her mouth went dry, but only her mouth. Her armpits, her palms, and the apex of her thighs all became moist as soon as she caught Gunnar in her sights. She dragged her tongue over her lips in the hopes of being able to say something witty or even intelligible.

Several of the clients gasped. News about Gunnar's shooting had kept some of the business away. Their die-hard customers had remained loyal.

Summoning some strength, Eboni finally spoke. "Uh, Drew, I'm going to have to call you back."

"Hey, Eboni, you know the guy who made the donation. He's that guy you brought here. Gu--"

Eboni disconnected the call and kept her stare on Gunnar, who carried a shopping bag in his hand. She hadn't talked to him since he'd been discharged. She had heard from her cousin that he'd stopped off at the apartment. She'd hoped to see him at the community center, but she'd remained in the activity room helping the smaller kids paint.

"Good to see you up and around, boss," Monica said and winked at him.

"Hey, Monica." Gunnar kept his stare on Eboni.

"Welcome back," Tisha and Tillman said at the same time.

"There's Superman. Faster than a speeding bullet. Almost." Shay laughed.

Eboni found nothing funny about the joke. Gunnar could have been killed.

When Gunnar stood in front of her, she opened her mouth to get out all her feelings. "You still want to sell this place?" Eboni planted her fist on her hip.

Gunnar didn't speak.

Eboni filled the still air. "This place offers these people a job." She scanned the clients seated in the stylists' chairs. "These customers depend on us being here. You can't think you can come in here and decide what's best for them." She halted her speech when she realized how much it reflected back to her.

Gunnar still said nothing. He stared at her. From his stoic expression, Eboni didn't even know if he still harbored some anger toward her or if he'd made the trip to tell her good-bye.

Unable to wait any longer, Eboni crossed her arms over her chest. "Well?"

Gunnar surprised her by kissing her first. He cupped her cheek in his large hand and lowered his head to connect his lips to hers.

Magic. Although she should have been happy, tears ran down Eboni's cheeks. She'd missed the kisses. She missed him.

When Gunnar pulled back, Eboni said, "Oh, my God, I missed you. I should have told you."

Gunnar shook his head. "Let me start and then you can say what you have to say, okay?" He wiped her tears away with his thumb. "You asked me why I never came home after I left. Besides you and my family, there were too many bad memories for me here. I wanted a clean slate, but I didn't want to lose you. You were so set on staying here, I knew I couldn't get you to leave. I didn't want to hear you turn me down. So like a coward, I never asked you to join me. I wanted to." He gripped her shirt and pulled her close to him. "I wish to God I had. Good or bad, I would have known. I could have given you the option. Maybe then we could have talked about what had happened with you." He brushed his finger over her stomach.

Eboni held his hand and kept her stare on his eyes. She started to open her mouth, but he stopped her.

"Please. I'm not finished." He cleared his throat and looked up at the people in the salon. "You should all feel safe to come here. The shooting that happened here was my fault."

Eboni gasped and moved in closer to him.

"My former manager paid a young man to vandalize the salon. I walked in on him and he shot me."

Mouths of everyone in the salon hung open.

"I was able to identify the shooter from a tattoo on the back of his hand. I found T-Lite, or Terry, at the Oceanfront Community Center. He confessed everything and we arranged a sting to get my former manager arrested." Gunnar brought his gaze down to Eboni. "He tried to trap me into doing what he wanted. You've never done that. Thank you."

Eboni smiled. Her insides felt warm the more he spoke.

"I apologize for bringing that kind of element in here. This salon is a good place." He nodded. "Virginia Beach is not a bad place to be. I shouldn't have stayed away so long."

"I don't know about that," Monica began. "I could live in Vegas."

Slight laughter filled the salon that had become deathly quiet when Gunnar had started talking.

"You told me how important the center is to you. I didn't want to help because that place held bad memories for me." He placed the bag he carried on a table next to Eboni. "After I confronted T-Lite, I realized how right you are about wayward kids needing a place off the streets. So"-- Gunnar reached into the bag and pulled out a couple of containers--"I decided to take your advice, and I made some of my own hair products." He handed one to her. "That's the deep conditioner I used on you after you did your big chop. This one's a moisturizer." He tapped the bag. "I have shampoos and conditioners in here. I've talked to a product distributor. She wants me to try out the products here in the salon to see how people like it before it's released to the public. Once it is, I've already arranged to have a portion of the proceeds to go to the center. I won't earn a dime from it."

Eboni smiled and wrapped her arms around Gunnar's neck. "Thank you." She pulled back from him. When she glanced at the jars, she gasped. "You're calling the products Eboni's Essence?"

He nodded. "You're the inspiration. What else could I call it? Gunnar's Hair Goop?" He laughed.

"Wow. What a man," Shay said. "He started a product line and named it after you." She fanned her face. "Oh, my God. If he was single…"

Eboni thanked her lucky stars Gunnar wanted her and only her.

"Needless to say, that means I'll be around town a whole lot longer. Hope you're okay with that."

Unable to speak, Eboni nodded her head.

"I'm also not going to fight anymore, and not because of the injury. My heart isn't in it anymore. I'm tired. It's time for me to do something else. As champion, I will have to defend my title at least one more time. Win or lose, at the end of the match, I'll turn over my belt."

"Guns, you're giving up the MMA game?" Tillman asked.

Gunnar nodded. "Ten years is enough. Time for me to do something else. I like the idea of training. Plus, I'll have product line and the salon, well, that's if my mom allows me to be a stylist."

"I'm sure she will." Tisha beamed.

"Thanks, Tisha." Gunnar directed his attention back to Eboni. His expression became somber. "I apologize for hurting you. I was upset and I didn't trust you. Thank you for not giving up on me."

She shook her head. "Never. I love you too much."

Gunnar breathed a sigh of relief. "Good. Because I believe you still owe me an answer." He reached into his pocket and pulled out a black ring box.

"Oh my word!" Monica sprang from her chair.

When Gunnar lowered himself on to one knee in front of her, the patrons and employees rushed to the duo and created a semicircle around them.

"Eboni, I have loved you ever since I first met you. I was a fool to leave to train for my career. You're right. I should have asked you to marry me. So I'm fixing past wrongs. Will you marry me?"

Eboni heart wanted to scream *yes*. She had to make some demands first. "Before I answer, I have a few questions for you."

The crowd around them groaned.

Eboni didn't care. With Gunnar at her feet, she needed answers. "Do you trust me now?"

Gunnar nodded. "With my life."

"Did you give a donation to the community center recently?"

Gunnar paused before he answered, but he eventually nodded. "You weren't supposed to know. I wanted it to be a surprise. I wanted to help."

She smiled.

"Is that it? No more questions?" he asked.

"Only one. You don't want us to get married in Vegas, do you?"

Gunnar beamed. "We'll marry wherever you want."

"Then, yes, Gunnar Wells, I'll marry you."

Gunnar slipped the ring on Eboni's finger and stood as quickly as he could. If he'd had the strength to pick her up and swing her around, he would have. For now, she would have to settle for a kiss.

"Hot damn. We get to go to a wedding." Shay clapped her hands.

"I'm just glad our girl found her man." Tillman laughed.

Eboni had waited a long time to get Gunnar. Now that she had him, she would never let him go.

"We don't have to stay in Virginia if you don't want to." Eboni patted his chest.

Gunnar blinked. "You would move? What about your family?"

"I'm moving out of my apartment, and my aunt has secured herself an assisted-living condo. My cousin can fend for himself. For what he did to you, he should live under a rock. With your recent donation and this potential business, we don't have to stay here if you don't want to."

Gunnar held her around her waist. "Baby, me wanting to leave this place had nothing to do with me being bored or wanting something different and exciting. I had issues here. I don't anymore. Now I have you. Anywhere you are, that's where I'll be."

Gunnar had given Eboni the answer she'd been wanting to hear for over ten years.

"I love you, Eboni. I've always loved you. I always will." He kissed her.

"I love you too. I'm never letting you go."

"You'd better not. If you do, I'll be there quick to snatch him up!" Shay sashayed back to her station.

"Hey, easy. He has two other brothers. Go after them." Eboni laughed as she held on to her man.

Her man. She liked the sound of that.

* * * *

Gunnar paced in the room. He kept his gaze down to the carpeted floor. When he got to the end and glanced up, he noticed bathrooms at the end of the hall. He turned and paced the other way toward the large window that overlooked a fountain and the hospital parking lot.

A twinge of pain hit his side. The doctor had told him walking would be good for him. He ignored the pain and continued his march. No way he could relax now.

Gunnar swung his arms around him to loosen up his tightening muscles. His mind swam with possible outcomes. One outcome he didn't want.

"Baby? Come sit down. You're making me nervous."

Gunnar turned to Eboni, who sat so poised in the hospital waiting room. He sat in between her and Gideon. Both Gunnar's and his brother's knees bounced as they waited to get an update on their mother's surgery.

"Are you sure Thane knows about the surgery?" Gunnar asked his brother.

"Mom said she called him last night." Gideon wrung his hands together. He glanced at his watch. "It's been two hours. Shouldn't we have gotten an update by now?"

Eboni held Gunnar's hand. She squeezed it as though reassuring him, or maybe she wanted to remind him of her presence.

"She'll be okay." Gunnar leaned back in the chair. "I keep telling myself that."

"Family for Elizabeth Sommerville," the information desk person bellowed.

Even with his injury, Gunnar managed to get up first and get to the desk. "Yes?"

"The surgical nurse is on the phone for you."

Gunnar picked it up. "Hello?"

"Hi, your mother is doing fine. Her heart is strong, which is helping. We'll be another hour and a half or so and we'll let you know when the surgery is over."

Gunnar breathed a sigh of relief. "Thanks so much for the update." He turned to his family, his brother and his future wife. He liked thinking of her in that way.

"The nurse said Mom is doing fine so far. Her heart is strong. She's got another ninety minutes or more in surgery." Gunnar sat down next to Eboni.

"Good. I'm starving. Anyone else hungry?" Gideon stood.

"No, I'm too wound up to eat." Gunnar shook his head.

"I'm fine." Eboni waved her hand at him.

"Okay. I'm going to find the cafeteria. I'll be back."

Eboni interlaced her fingers with Gunnar's. "Did you ever think we would be back together?"

Gunnar turned her hand over to look at her engagement ring. "Deep in my heart, I had hope we would."

"I can't wait to start my life with you."

Gunnar couldn't wait either. "We could elope. I don't want to miss a second not being your husband."

Eboni started to look like she wanted to agree, then she stopped. "Your mother will kill us if we don't have a big wedding."

Gunnar laughed. "You're right about that." He put his hand to her stomach. "I can't wait."

"I know. Trying again should be fun." She placed her hand on his leg.

Gunnar arrested her hand to stop her. "Keep it up and we'll be finding an empty room."

Eboni laughed. "I love you, Gunnar."

"I love you too. I have to warn you. You're marrying in to a crazy family."

Eboni smiled. "Ditto."

Gunnar laughed. If he had to spend eternity with a wacky family, Eboni would be the only person he could do that with. She fit in his life perfectly.

Meet the Author

Crystal Bright graduated with a B.A. from Old Dominion University with a major in Creative Writing, a minor in Communications, and an emphasis on Public Relations. She earned her M.A. from Seton Hill University in Writing Popular Fiction. She is a member of Romance Writers of America and Chesapeake Romance Writers. For more information about Crystal and her writing, please visit her website at www.CrystalBrightWriter.com. You can also find her on Facebook at https://www.facebook.com/crystal.bright.397, or follow her on twitter: https://twitter.com/CrystalBBright